LIES THAT BIND

LIES THAT BIND
By Valerie Davisson
Copyright © 2020 Valerie Davisson

LIES THAT BIND is a work of fiction. Names, characters, places, and incidents are the product of the author's imagination or are used fictitiously. Any resemblance to actual events, locales, businesses, or persons, living or dead, is coincidental.

Published by Vaughn House Publishing, Depoe Bay, OR
First Edition

Print ISBN - 978-1-7340119-5-1
Ebook ISBN - 978-1-7340119-6-8

Cover and Interior Design by Kimberly Peticolas, www.kimpeticolas.com

Library of Congress Control Number: 2020917232

10 9 8 7 6 5 4 3 2 1

LIES THAT BIND

A Logan McKenna Novel

VALERIE DAVISSON

This book is dedicated to my fierce and fiery sister.
She is missed every day.

Michelle Claudia Montclaire
1950 – 2020

PROLOGUE

Charlie flipped on the light, threw her towel on a chair, and kicked off her shoes. She had the place to herself. The cavernous room stretched before her. Warm, steamy air tinged with the familiar acrid smell of chlorine enveloped her. The white, tiled floor was slick and wet. Walking with practiced care to the deep end, she stood at the edge of the pool for a minute, rolling her shoulders, shaking her arms out, loosening up.

She really needed this.

This week had been a real ball buster. First, the unending arguments with her grandmother. Why was she so against her and Wade getting married? Saturday night, when she told the indomitable Charlotte Collins in no uncertain terms that she and Wade were going ahead with the wedding, with or without her permission, the woman just about had a stroke.

And the hotel. They'd never agreed about that. Why couldn't her grandmother understand that she didn't want to run a hotel—*any* hotel? The Collins may be Grandmother Charlotte's whole life, but it wasn't hers. She thought she'd made that clear four years ago, when she'd majored in anthropology, not hospitality. But Charlotte Collins wasn't one to give up easily.

She knew her grandmother saw this trip as one last chance to change her mind, but she wasn't going to budge. She was so tired of talking about it that, like a coward, she'd been avoiding her since their big blowup Sunday morning.

Sunday, she'd waited until she heard Grandmother's Mercedes crunch down the gravel driveway before calling Wade to let him know the coast was clear. At least for a few days. They were looking forward to the break. They'd worked it all out over breakfast.

Grandmother would be away at her gardening conference up in Portland for most of the week. They were going to sit her down and talk about this rationally when she returned. Grandma would just have to accept that Charlie had a life of her own to lead, and it didn't include running The Collins.

All she and Wade wanted to do was live their own lives. In just a few weeks, they were going to a small, rural village in India, putting their education and skills to good use. Clean water for villagers was a lot more important than clean sheets for wealthy hotel guests. Wade was a genius. His water filtration system not only cleaned water, but had a desalinization component. They had a real chance at helping people, making the world a better place—saving lives! Why couldn't Grandmother get that through her thick skull?

It was sad, the way things had turned out. Growing up, they

had always been close. Grandmother Charlotte had practically raised her. Her mom shipped her out to Oregon the day after her sixteenth birthday, after an unfortunate incident involving a fifth of Scotch and a cute senior named Jared. There were other reasons her mother had sent her to live with her grandmother. But Charlie chose not to focus on those. Sometimes the memories were so distant and hazy, she wasn't sure they'd actually happened.

Besides, Charlie loved living with Grandmother Charlotte here on the coast. She and grandmother even looked alike. The first time she'd seen the family portrait over the fireplace, she did a double take. People always said the woman in the picture looked like her, but that portrait had been taken back in the forties. She was the baby in great-grandmother's arms, not the southern beauty standing in back, next to her husband—Charlie's grandfather—Emerson. Same dark hair, though. Blue eyes and ivory skin. Both strong willed. Even that seemed to come out in the portrait.

But that's where the resemblance ended. Grandmother Charlotte, a true southern belle steeped in good manners and appearances, knew exactly how a lady should behave and expected her namesake to conform.

Charlie, on the other hand, was a tomboy of the first degree, preferring fishing off the rocks or exploring the vast tracts of forest that stretched for miles behind the town. She built her first tree house when she was nine from scraps of lumber she hauled from a construction project behind city hall. Grandmother had not been pleased, but Charlie was still her favorite. Her older sister, Amanda, had lighter coloring and took after their mother.

Adjusting her swim goggles, Charlie looked out over the smooth surface of the water. Anticipating that delicious first plunge, she took a deep breath, then dove smoothly into the pool. She went deep, stretching her hands in front of her in perfect form, then scooped up just before she reached the bottom, allowing the momentum to propel her to the surface, pretending to be a dolphin or a mermaid, like when she was little. She knew it was silly, but it never failed to make her smile.

She loved the feel of water pushing against her face and along the sides of her body. Breaking the surface, she kicked off, reaching into her strokes, finding a relaxing rhythm. She'd do her twenty laps, shower off, then go back upstairs to the room. To Wade—to her future. Grandmother would come around.

For the next twenty minutes, Charlie's muscles gradually released the tension she'd been holding all week. Flip-turning gracefully, pushing off the end after each length, she was halfway across the pool after lap eighteen when it hit. A fierce cramp like nothing she'd ever felt before, forcing her body to contract into the fetal position. It felt like someone stabbing her in the stomach. Before she could make it to the side to pull herself out, a wave of nausea gripped her and she cramped again.

What was happening?

She'd had a mild case of the flu a few days ago, but this felt much worse than before. She'd never have gone swimming if she'd thought she was still sick. Unable to reach the edge, she tried to turn herself over and float—force herself to relax until the cramp passed—but her arms and legs wouldn't work right. Within seconds, the severe cramping began again, followed by a hose of vomit. Her bowels emptied violently. She hadn't eaten much all day, so it was mostly liquid.

They'll have to drain the pool.

She realized how odd the thought was even as she had it. As if that were her main concern.

She had to get out.

She struggled to get her body to obey her commands. She had to get to the side of the pool. It wasn't that far . . . She knew she couldn't swim in this condition, and was too cramped up to even pull herself out, but maybe she could hand-walk her way along the edge until she reached the shallow end. By using the handrail, she could crawl her way up the steps and lie there until she could move or someone came to find her.

If she could just get herself out of the water.

After what seemed like forever, but was probably only a few seconds, she felt the tips of her toes dragging along the bottom of the pool.

Thank God!

Facing the wrong direction, she couldn't see it, but at least she now knew she was at the shallow end.

Just then, a whooshing sound announced someone's arrival as the door opened into the pool room. Relief flooded through her. Probably Wade coming to join her or see what was taking her so long. Sometimes when she was in the zone, she lost track of time.

For some reason, she couldn't call out. All she could make was a gurgling sound. But surely, he'd see her.

Another spasm hit and she vomited again, unable to keep her body from folding forward, throwing her face into the water. She tried to hold her breath, but with every cell in her body desperately screaming for oxygen, she found herself inhaling deeply, searching for air, but only water filled her nostrils and rushed into her lungs.

Where was Wade?

Just before she passed out, she thought she heard splashing behind her. With every second she clung to consciousness, she expected Wade to pull her to safety, but the next human touch

Charlie felt was a strong hand clamped onto the top of her head, pushing her completely under and holding her there. She couldn't put up much of a fight. Whatever signals her brain was sending weren't reaching the rest of her body.

Seventeen seconds later, the lights went out and the door to the pool area clicked shut, plunging the room into utter darkness.

Only the distant thrum of the water pump and a slight lapping of the water against the sides of the pool could be heard. Soon, even that became perfectly still.

The body at the bottom of the pool wasn't making any waves.

1

SUNDAY

FEBRUARY 7, 1932, 12:03 A.M.

WHALE COVE

CENTRAL OREGON COAST

The two men crouched low, hunched against the wind on the precipice of a sheer cliff. Sixty feet below, gentle waves lapped on a narrow crescent of sandy beach, but beyond these sheltered waters, the angry ocean roared, throwing itself repeatedly against the black rocks guarding the narrow entrance to the cove.

"They're not coming."

"Don't worry—they'll be here. This is the night. You just can't see them—They're waiting for the right wave—better a full boat, late, than splinters and dead men floating in on time, right?" Frankie said, slapping Jacob on the back.

Jacob said nothing, but simply stared harder into the inky dark, straining for the reassuring shape of the boat. This was his fifth trip, and if all went well, his last.

In spite of—and maybe because of—the moonless night, the frothy wave caps glowed brilliant white against the smooth licorice-colored waves as they pushed into the cove, skimming over a massive chunk of basalt lurking just below the surface, equidistant between the steep sides of the narrow opening, waiting to rip into the bottom of any boat that dared enter. Even if you knew it was there and it was broad daylight, it was almost impossible to get around.

Frankie stomped his feet and headed back to the truck to get warm.

"They always make it, don't they?" he said, slamming the door shut. "You worry too much."

Jacob looked back. Frankie's freckled face and bright red hair flashed into view as he struck a match and lit a cigarette. He was probably right. Frankie never worried about anything and he seemed to be doing okay.

Jacob turned his attention back to the sea, listening hard for the sounds of an engine. There was a reason no one but rumrunners used this place. But because no one did, it was perfect. No houses, no lights, no nothing. Stretching only a third of a mile across at its widest point, Whale Cove wasn't on any mariner's map as a safe harbor on the central Oregon coast. If any boat managed to make it in, the water was calm. Steep, rocky cliffs kept the cove hidden from view from the sea.

For the smugglers, it was perfect. Their vessel, the Sea Island, a sleek powerboat out of Victoria, BC, was only thirty-six-feet from stem to stern, but could carry over three thousand gallons of whiskey and rum.

Frankie kept telling him it was easy, and Jacob had to admit, so far, it had been. The Canadians worked out the system long before he and Frankie were enlisted to accept the product and help with the deliveries. The distribution routes, established years before to accommodate the opium trade from China, meant everything went as smooth as silk.

On each run, once the Sea Island was in safely, it was a simple matter of offloading the cases of liquor, hauling them up the cliff with rope and steel cables, then loading them onto the truck. Whale Cove was only a half mile from Depoe Bay and ten from Newport, but the roads were mostly deserted after dark.

Under cover of night, and after only a few hours of driving, pharmacies, back porches, and speakeasies from here to Florence restocked their hidden stashes with no one the wiser, except those patrolmen paid to look the other way. As long as he and Frankie didn't partake of any of the merchandise, the drive back was easy and perfectly safe. If stopped, they were just two men going to work after visiting family, or looking for work, or whatever.

By tomorrow, Jacob would be driving home with enough money in his pocket to finally get out from under his father-in-law's thumb. Or at least be closer to that goal. The man was nice enough, but he and Irene had their eye on getting their own place, a boarded-up trading post in Depoe Bay, right next to the harbor with plenty of room for little Aaron to play. With a little fixing, it'd make a great rooming house. Irene could cook and he could build or fix anything. It was a humble start, but they had big plans.

There just wasn't enough room at her parents' house for their little family. In the new place there would even be room for his mother. She was getting too old to do laundry anymore. And she could help Irene with the Aaron. She'd like that.

Just a few more runs.

2

If the Sea Island made it tonight, Jacob promised himself he'd look for other work. This just didn't sit right with him, but he needed the money. He'd made the down payment, but Woodrow said he had to come up with the rest of the cash by Wednesday or lose what he'd given him already. It was a gamble, but worth the risk. Rum money was pretty much a sure thing. Nothing had ever gone wrong before. The Sea Island had never been late and definitely never been caught.

He looked at Frankie in the truck, leaning back now, his feet up on the dash. Frankie wouldn't quit. He loved it—all of it. The danger, the rush, the money. Getting something for nothing. Not having to work a real job. According to him, Frankie Collins had never worked a day in his life. And he was proud of it.

Jacob, on the other hand, had done nothing but work since the day he was born. At least that's how it felt. His father, James Ellis, a large, burly man, died in a logging accident when Jacob was six years old. Until that time, they'd enjoyed a fairly comfortable life. He had a change of clothes, new shoes, and rarely went hungry. They even had a few books and education was highly valued.

After his father died, his mom managed by taking in laundry and sewing, but it wasn't enough to keep him and his sister fed and clothed. The large, drafty house they were forced to move into had been unwisely built out on a rocky spit of land. Buffeted by merciless winds, it had known better days. The formerly grand residence had long ago been subdivided into smaller, shabbier units. A management company sent a check to the one surviving inheritor in Ohio. Jacob's mother was able to secure two rooms in the back on the second floor and a shared bathroom. The only luxury they enjoyed was a spectacular, unobstructed view of the ocean.

A quiet boy with his mother's short stature and his father's black hair, fair skin, and blue eyes, Jacob had no way to articulate his grief or fear, but opening the window to stiff blasts of freezing, salt air seemed to help. He didn't know why. Although he was usually a very obedient child, he nonetheless risked his mother's wrath and the extra wood to heat the room for this luxury whenever he could. But he kept an ear open.

When he heard his mother coming up the stairs, he pulled and latched the window shut as quietly and quickly as possible, wiping away the moisture on his cheeks with his sleeve, scuttling off the ledge to busy himself with some chore, usually a book he was supposed to be reading, although they didn't have many.

His mother talked often of where he would go to college and of his becoming a doctor or lawyer—fulfilling the dreams she and his father had for him. But soon, they both gave up the pretense and accepted the realities before them. Jacob Ellis was the man of the house now. And the man of the house needed to work.

The summer he turned nine, Jacob got his first job delivering his mother's laundry to the Finns in town. As he grew up, he did whatever odd jobs came his way, from cleaning fish guts up at the Kernville cannery—work even the Chinese wouldn't do—to delivering supplies and running errands for the guests at one of the new hotels up in Taft. Sunup to sundown, Jacob was working.

It was Abrams, the man who ran the rooming house in town with his wife, that showed him the future. Abrams converted the front half of his home into a general store, then rented out the rooms in the back. He was in the process of building several cottages on the property for 'clamdiggers' from Portland. He and his family started out living over the store, but were now building an expansive, gracious home on the hill.

"Picks and shovels, young man!" old man Abrams told him. "Picks and shovels, that's where you'll make your fortune. I learned that up in the Klondike. Leave the gold digging to the dreamers. Dreams don't put food on the table. And logging will get you killed."

Jacob knew that only too well.

Just then, he felt a shove against his shoulder. It was Frankie, pointing down into the cove with a big grin on his face.

"See! I told you they'd make it!"

3

Jacob let out a breath he didn't realize he'd been holding and peered into the dark. Sure enough, Frankie was right. The boat was late, but the Canadians had arrived. He could make out the ghostly, white shape of the Sea Island through the gathering mist, coming around the north end of the cove. But something was wrong. He could hear the engine sputtering and it was going way too slow. Then things got worse.

A violent crack ripped into the night, followed by a quick series of small popping, snapping sounds.

Damn! They hit the rock.

With the help of the cables and rope they'd lowered over the side of the cliff in anticipation of hauling up the cargo, he and Frankie began scrambling down the rocks.

Knowing it would be suicidal to jump in and try to swim out to the foundering boat—they'd freeze before they were halfway there and probably get their heads bashed in by debris for their trouble—the two men stayed put, ready to pull any survivors to safety. For now, all they could do was watch and wait.

Miraculously, the Sea Island hung together, although it was obvious the crew was not in control of their boat. Eventually, the wounded craft drifted in and was carried by the incoming tide to gently rest on the beach. Jacob splashed in, caught the line, and passed the end back to Frankie. The crew rolled into the water and between the five of them, they dragged the Sea Island up to shore.

"Let's get her unloaded, then," the captain said, as if nothing untoward had happened.

Patrick was not an official captain, but he was definitely in charge of Billie and Arthur, his two-man crew. Tall, slim, and broad-chested with even features and close-cropped, sandy hair, he worked with an economy of movement. Steady, gray eyes looked out through wire-rim glasses. Somehow, this didn't take away from the menace of the man. You knew.

His crew would have been surprised to learn he had originally studied to become a Jesuit priest, not a gangster. When his parents were killed, he'd reluctantly allowed himself to be recruited by the local crime syndicate to keep his brothers in school and off the streets. If he ever regretted the choices he made, he didn't say. The circumstances of his new life jaded him considerably. He now quoted Nietzsche more often than the man from Nazareth. Heaven was a long way away.

Even though Jacob assumed Patrick was a criminal because he wanted to be—after all, he was very good at it—as he watched him work, he couldn't help but admire the man. Patrick was at least ten years older than the rest of them, and as cold and wet, but bent his back to the job at hand, silently and efficiently offloading cases and barrels as quickly as the younger men.

Jacob looked back up the cliff to the highway. It was still quiet, but the sky would lighten soon. He could just make out the top of the truck. He wondered what the plan was now. Usually, by this time, the boat was unloaded, cargo transferred, and he and Frankie were halfway through their deliveries.

With a nod from Patrick, the two crew members retrieved several shovels from on board what was left of the Sea Island.

"Now we dig," he said.

This wasn't entirely unfamiliar territory. They'd buried cargo before, when circumstances required it, and come back to pick it up later. But not in broad daylight. And not with a storm brewing on the horizon.

Racing the clock, they dug like hounds after a bone and within an hour and a half, they'd safely stashed the lot. Jacob hoped this didn't mean they wouldn't get paid. After all, they had been there—on time—and helped rescue the men and the cargo. It wasn't their fault the boat was late and then cracked open on the rock like a bottle of whiskey.

But Patrick had a plan. Speaking to Jacob, he told them he'd pay them each their $50 now and said there'd be an extra $100 in it if he and Frankie could get him and the two crew members safely to the border.

Frankie was pissed. He felt he should be the man Patrick addressed. He was, after all, the senior guy in the outfit. He'd noticed Patrick had taken a shine to Jacob, taking him under his wing, which bugged him, but there wasn't time to argue. If they were going to earn their bonus, they needed to get on the road. As it was, they'd be driving into the teeth of the storm.

Jacob thought about it. The Canadian border was over four hundred miles away. Irene would wonder why he was late, but with the extra money he hoped she wouldn't hold that against him. With this unexpected windfall, they could not only buy the property they'd been looking at, but could begin to fix up the building, and even furnish it the way Irene wanted to and put money aside for their child's education. If he could pick up some more jobs in town, they'd be ready to open by spring.

Quickly doing the math, he made up his mind and told Patrick he was in. Frankie was already in. Always up for an adventure—he was already halfway to the truck. If Frankie was worried about the storm, he didn't show it.

As always, Frankie drove . . . and talked. He could talk the ears off a rabbit and proceeded to showcase his storytelling skills to anyone and everyone who would listen. Patrick and Jacob rode in the bed of the truck so they didn't have to. Billie and Arthur weren't so lucky. Still, it was cold and would soon be wet, but there was a tarp in the back. They would just pull that over themselves if need be.

To fill the time as much as anything, Jacob found himself opening up to Patrick. He shared his and Irene's plan of establishing and running a motor lodge in Depoe Bay. He saw the future and it was filled with people vacationing at the coast. He talked about Aaron and the future children they planned to add to their little family. Irene wanted at least three. He was surprised, but Patrick actually seemed interested.

When Patrick drifted into a pensive quiet, Jacob decided he was talking too much and shut up. Hopefully, he hadn't been too annoying. Maybe Patrick was just worried about getting to the border without being caught. He'd been stupid for rambling on about clamdiggers and rooms to rent. Patrick had much bigger things to worry about.

In the meantime, the other two crew members didn't mind being squished into the front seat. They enjoyed being regaled by Frankie's stories and it didn't hurt that Frankie had snuck a few bottles out of the last crate to make the ride bearable. They were also celebrating making it in. The storm had only brushed her wings over them as she passed by, having spent her fury at sea.

Thirty-five miles and two bottles of good, Canadian whiskey later, as they were nearing Hebo, an overly confident and definitely inebriated Frankie swerved to avoid a downed alder and promptly rolled the car.

4

Logan McKenna leaned forward and squinted into a gaping, black hole, following the man's flashlight beam. Covering her nose with as much of her jacket as she could push against her face, she recoiled and tried not to gag. The smell was horrific!

"Raccoons, probably, or squirrels. Mice maybe . . . or rats," the man said, "My bet's raccoons. They take up residence when a house has been vacant for a while."

Switching off the flashlight, Clay, the handyman they'd hired to check out the place, escorted Logan back outside, onto the side porch. Following as close as possible, she breathed deeply, inhaling multiple lungfuls of cold, clean air as soon as she cleared the threshold in a vain attempt to scour her nasal passages.

"What was that *smell?*" Logan asked. "Did a raccoon die in there?"

"Probably . . . but I expect it was mostly urine . . . ," Clay said, ". . . mostly."

Clay Sorens, a tough, stringy man somewhere between seventy and dead scratched his chin and waited for his potential client to recover. Not only from the smell, but from the news that the house she and her husband—or boyfriend, he didn't know the details—picked out online, needed a lot more than just a slap of paint and some carpet. Some of the critters had eaten through a whole nest of wires in the back bedroom. And he hadn't even told her about the plumbing yet.

A local resident all his life, Clay knew the history of most of the sprinkling of houses and shops along this mile-and-a-half stretch of Highway 101 that comprised the town of Depoe Bay, Oregon, from the Shell station on the south end of town to the pot shop on the right as you drove north toward Lincoln City. With a population of only about fifteen hundred people, that wasn't exactly hard to do.

The three-bedroom-plus-parlor house wasn't a showpiece, but a solid, plain home that had been built to last. It had weathered more winters than he'd been alive, that was for sure. He knew the house had already dropped out of escrow twice. He hoped for Wade's sake this woman had more backbone than the other potential buyers. He was itching to work on it. And he was pretty sure Mrs. Ellis's kids needed the money.

It's not that Clay needed the work. His needs were simple. He was more comfortable financially than he appeared, but he liked bringing homes back to life. Back to being snug and dry in the winter, open and welcoming in the summer—wood gleaming, fireplaces functioning, chimneys scrubbed—places families gathered. Children's laughter floating out the windows to greet you as you walked up the drive.

LIES THAT BIND

Tucked up and away as it was, up against the forest, off a dog leg at the end of Baird Street, you couldn't see the house from below. But once you made it up the steep gravel road to the property and looked out, you had a grand view of the ocean, and you could still hear the roar of the waves, if a bit dimmed, even this far away.

This was the old Ellis place, but not many knew the family. The Ellises kept mostly to themselves. Mrs. Ellis's husband, Archer, had been in and out of mental hospitals for years and was now out in that home in Salem. She had done the best she could, but other than having her son, Wade, paint and patch leaks when he was in town, the property had only been minimally maintained. She couldn't afford to hire anyone and would not allow Clay to work for free, even though he'd offered multiple times when he was in between projects. The Ellises didn't accept charity.

Two years ago, when the old woman died, the kids put the house up for sale. Wade found some work in Eugene and had only been back to town every once in a while. His sister, Suzi, had married and moved to Wyoming years ago. 354 Barber Road had sat vacant ever since. Wade kept the heat on, so at least there wasn't any mold. As far as he'd been able to tell so far, anyway. Sad family. He'd heard the rumors, but who knew if they were true. Wade was a good kid, anyway.

Dragging his mind back to the present, Clay waited for the woman to speak. The next few minutes would tell. He wondered if a woman from California—*Southern* California at that—would be willing to put some elbow grease and money into this place, or if she would give up and find easier pickings.

Maybe.

She didn't look like a typical Californian. He approved of the boots. And she wasn't all tarted up. She wore no makeup at all—certainly not those spider web eyelashes women glued on these days—what was that about? And her hair, this woman's hair was pulled loosely back from her face, anchored with a baseball cap. Least it didn't have any purple or pink stripes like he saw all the time now. What were those women thinking?

Unaware she was being appraised, Logan took another gulp of clean air, leveled her gaze at him, piercing his brown eyes with her green ones.

"This can be fixed, right? I mean, how much needs to be torn out and replaced versus just cleaned to get rid of that smell?"

Clay smiled. A woman after his own heart.

For the next hour, he took Logan through the house, pointing out what needed to be done now, and what could wait, with a rough estimate for each task. He wouldn't give her firm estimates on each job until he priced out parts and checked on the availability of a few guys he'd need. It being the start of winter, the roof would have to wait until spring. Luckily, it wasn't leaking, but once the rain started, all bets were off. During one of his good spells, old man Ellis had put in a beautiful, shake roof, but it was nearing the end of its life. There were a couple of spots that needed attention and the whole thing would need to be replaced soon. No one put in shake anymore. Too expensive and it was, he had to admit, a fire hazard.

When they finished the tour and the handyman had delivered all the bad news he had . . . for now . . . they walked up the outside stairs to the wrap-around deck. Out here Logan could smell the ocean and hear the winter waves boom against the rocks below. It was only a few blocks down the hill to Highway 101, where a sea wall ran along a narrow strip of rocky land. Just south, turbulent waves shot seawater up and out of a small sea cave, delighting tourists with drenching saltwater sprays. During big storms, Clay told Logan, it often reached all the way across the highway to the shops. From up here, she could only see bits of ocean in spots through the lacy tops of the trees.

Shaking hands with him at his truck, Logan told Clay she'd call him in the morning. The man didn't seem concerned about the deal falling through. Said he'd get started on those estimates. She liked Clay's unhurried, steady nature and knew Ben would too.

Starting up her own car, an older model Toyota Highlander Rita Wolfe had loaned her, she zigzagged over and down Barber, Baird, Williams, and Collins streets and turned onto Highway 101. Rita had said she could use the Toyota while she was staying at her place, a second home Rita owned at the south end of town.

Rita Wolfe was the director of the privately funded, progressive New School, an hour outside of Portland. She had been trying to hire Logan full time for several years. A couple of years ago, she finally succeeded in luring her north a few times a year by finding funding for Logan's innovative Music/Math program, Fractals.

Pulling her attention back to the road, Logan turned left at the bottom of the hill and pointed her car to Rita's place.

5

Five minutes later, Logan pulled off the highway at a low-slung sign announcing the entrance to Little Whale Cove (LWC). Technically still in Depoe Bay, LWC was a unique community of about two hundred and forty homes located just over the bridge and half a mile south of the tourist shops and whale-watching center in town. Logan had been here several times before, but the community had lost none of its charm. It still felt like entering a fairytale forest. October was one of the most beautiful times of the year there. Golden light slanted in, painting some of the alder leaves bright yellow, while deeper into the thickets on either side, lacy boughs of western hemlock and cedar, soaked in innumerable shades of green, soothed the eye. Logan's blood pressure always dropped several points by the time she reached the clubhouse at Eagle Lane.

Created in the seventies, LWC's most salient feature was the stated desire to keep things natural. With few exceptions, there were no lawns, no fences, and no street lights. As much as possible, the forest in which these homes were nestled was kept intact. Several miles of wooden boardwalks and walking paths wound through the woods and along a spectacular, open stretch along the ocean, atop a rocky bluff.

The ocean path was only a five-minute walk from Rita's place. And it was Logan's destination—as soon as she found something to eat and called Ben. She parked the Toyota and walked in. No one locked their doors around here. Digging her cell phone out of her purse, she shrugged off her coat and hung it on the back of a chair on her way to the kitchen. Dialing Ben, she opened the fridge to see if food had miraculously appeared while she was gone.

Her call went to voice mail as she half expected, since he was probably still at work. She left a message and surveyed the contents of the fridge. Half a bottle of white wine and some Mexican takeout she'd picked up her first night. She opened the lid on the container. Only rice, beans, and a soggy tortilla were left—she'd eaten the good stuff already. She leaned in and sniffed.

Maybe not.

Rita's compact cottage, surrounded on three sides by mixed conifer forest, was always stocked with the basics, which Logan appreciated. She'd already worked her way through the fresh groceries she picked up at the store on her way in last week. Digging around in the cupboards, she found a can of chili with a pull top, put it in a bowl, sliced up a hot dog, and zapped both in the microwave. At the last minute she added a slice of Tillamook cheddar cheese and zapped it again to melt it. She hadn't realized how hungry she was. Sticking a spoon into the steaming combo, she carried it to the back deck and set it down on a blue-tiled cafe table Rita had added since the last time she was here. Since the air carried a definite chill, she went back for her jacket while her lunch cooled from lava to scalding. On her way back, she slid her laptop off the counter and tucked it under her arm.

Pulling a chair around so she was facing the forest, she put her laptop next to her lunch so she could check her email while she ate.

A slender Douglas squirrel, its caramel tummy flashing bits of orange against the gray-brown bark of a nearby cedar, ran up, down, and around the trunk, chattering at her in an almost human voice.

"Oh, sorry, Dougie," Logan said. She held up a finger, "I forgot. Wait right there!"

Dougie did as instructed, eyes alert, holding his body perfectly still. Only the top of his tail twitched, ready to skitter away if necessary. Logan returned with some saltine crackers. Crumbling them up, she laid them on the two-by-six railing a few feet away from the cafe table. Then, knowing the routine, she went back to her seat and ignored him. When he was satisfied her attention was elsewhere, he nimbly jumped onto the railing and made short work of his snack—keeping an eye on his benefactor just in case.

Scrolling through her inbox, skimming and deleting emails from every company she'd ever ordered anything from—and falsely friendly emails from both political parties asking for donations, Logan kept the two real ones—one from Amy and one from Bonnie. She really needed to unsubscribe from all the junk mail. Of course, she'd made that resolution before and rarely got around to it. And even when she did, they kept popping back in. Satan must have invented spam.

She clicked on Amy's email first. Logan never had found a use for Facebook or Twitter or any of the other social media sites, so her daughter had finally given in and gone old school email. Sometimes she even picked up the phone and called. Miracle of miracles. Amy was also on Instagram which was all pictures as far as Logan could tell. How do you communicate with just pictures?

Today's email opened with a short video and several stills of Logan's grandson Ian and his latest accomplishment. In the video, great globs of glowing, viscous liquid dripped down the toddler's face and arms as he studiously sucked all the amber goo off the knuckles of his left hand. Early Sunday morning, he'd gotten into the cupboard, opened the honey jar all by himself and was slowly savoring the delicious sticky treasure. Definitely print worthy! When she got home, this one was going up on the family photo wall.

In the second email, after asking how the house hunting was going, Bonnie shared the latest gossip. Apparently the principal at her school, a woman Logan knew only well enough to say hello to, had been caught by the custodian in the multi-purpose room after hours, behind the stage, with one of the fourth grade teachers—a very married man at least twenty years her junior. Logan just shook her head.

To each her own.

Next, Bonnie provided a rapturous review of a 'fabulous' new Cuban restaurant she and Mike had discovered, then moved on to updates about her kids, particularly Haley, her eighteen-year-old, who just started her freshman year at UC Irvine, Logan's alma mater. A couple of years ago, no one thought the rebellious teenager would graduate from high school. Haley'd given her parents a run for their money, but after witnessing the effects of domestic violence on a little girl she babysat, in her junior year she decided she wanted to work with abused children and turned her life around. She'd even gone to summer school, graduating with several college credits toward a child psychology degree. Logan was glad to hear she was doing well.

Haley's looks, like her mother's, often caused people to underestimate her intelligence.

Bonnie's bubbly personality, big boobs, rosy cheeks, and

head of bouncing, blonde curls were in total contrast to Logan's Scotch-Irish lean, athletic build, freckled cheeks, and long, auburn waves. Bonnie had a rambling, noisy house full of children with her husband, Mike, a local fireman. Bonnie was baby showers, sorority sisters, and throw pillows. Her shoe rack held at least twenty pairs of very high heels.

Logan kept things simpler. Other than spending time with Ben, her family, her music, and her rescue cat, Dimebox, Logan enjoyed her solitude. She wasn't a lady who lunched. And if she needed high heels—which was next to never—she borrowed them from Bonnie. Playing Bella, her violin, enjoying the ocean view from her rooftop deck, and beach runs were more her style. But their differences worked—the two women had been best friends since forever.

As she was finishing Bonnie's email, which included a hilarious recitation of Mike's attempt to get their youngest to try okra—Mike had a huge vegetable garden and was always trying something new—another email came in at the top of her inbox. Madison, from Hale & Patterson Law Offices. Taking it for more junk mail, she was just about to delete it when something about the name snagged her attention. Madison . . . who did she know with that name? Hale & Patterson didn't ring a bell. Law offices . . . ?

Logan opened it and scanned to the signature at the bottom. Madison Olivia Landers.

Well, whaddya know.

6

Logan read the signature again.

Madison Olivia Landers.

Olivia.

Logan had been expecting some contact, but it had been over a year since her mother, Sofia, showed up on her doorstep with the bombshell that she had a thirty-three-year-old half-sister living in New York.

When she didn't hear from her, Logan figured Olivia had been as surprised as she was to find out she had a half-sister almost three thousand miles away. She probably had no interest in complicating her life with an unexpected addition to her family tree. It was okay with Logan. No harm, no foul.

Good old Mom left Logan and her brother high and dry when Logan was thirteen and Rick was nine. No note. No letter. Just gone. They hadn't heard from her all those years. But once she'd listened to her mother's side of the story, Logan realized it may not have been entirely Sofia's fault. Her mother's version of events didn't exactly match their father's. As much as a clearly delineated, black and white world appealed to Logan's sense of right and wrong, as she grew older, she realized the world consisted of a lot more shades of gray. She'd probably never know the whole truth.

Olivia's email was short and to the point. Her signature showed she was an attorney with Hale & Patterson, NYC.

Logan opened up another tab and googled it. Small firm. Looked like they did a bit of everything. She wondered what Olivia's specialty was, or if she had one.

Olivia didn't say why she'd waited so long to get in touch, but said she had a conference on the west coast, in Portland, OR at the end of January. She could catch a short flight down to Orange County if Logan was open to getting together. No need to pick her up, she'd rent a car at the airport. They could meet for lunch if Logan knew of a place near John Wayne.

Signed Olivia, followed by her home, cell, and office numbers.

Logan leaned back, staring at the screen, re-reading the invitation.

Was she open? She wasn't sure. At least she wasn't far way. She'd have to tell Olivia she was only a couple hours from Portland. She wouldn't have to fly down to So Cal.

Dougie scampered onto the railing again, looking for another snack. Logan tossed the remaining crackers in his direction. Most of them landed on the deck, but one of them managed to make it to the railing and was quickly grabbed by the enterprising squirrel.

Two points!

A maelstrom of emotions began to churn in Logan's gut. An attorney. She hated attorneys. At least she thought she did. She really didn't know any all that well. But their comparison to blood-sucking mosquitoes in popular culture had always seemed appropriate. Money. That was their focus, wasn't it? All those billable hours? Isn't that all they cared about? Logan wasn't against money per se, it just wasn't her *raison d'etre*. And law school was expensive.

And money was kind of a sore spot. Good old Mom hadn't sent a single cent toward either her or Rick's college educations. Logan had had to cobble together a combination of scholarships and part time jobs, working every summer. That's how she'd earned a double major in math and music at UC Irvine. Her dad helped, but one income in Southern California didn't go far. Sofia probably sent Olivia off to Europe every June.

The scarcity of funds hadn't affected Rick as much. He didn't much like school—quit after two years of community college, entered the police academy and became a police officer. For the last few years, he'd worked as a K-9 cop and loved it. Still . . .

Logan suddenly realized she was clenching her jaw, her heart was racing, and she was no longer paying attention to Dougie or the beauty of the forest around her.

Just a few unresolved issues . . .

It didn't take a psychologist to see exactly why she hadn't tried to get in touch with her half-sister. Olivia was the child her mother had raised from start to finish. Olivia had it all. A full-time mother and father. Support. Love. And no unanswered questions left dangling for years. Logan just didn't know if she could keep that ball of emotions stuffed down deep enough to meet the girl and be civil. The grown-up part of her knew Olivia was not responsible for their mother leaving . . . well, Sofia being pregnant with her was the reason she left, but Olivia wasn't even born yet. Not her fault. Logically, Logan knew it wasn't her fault. It was just all so complicated.

She turned her attention back to her screen. The ball was now in her court.

Logan made a face at her computer. This would definitely require a second glass of wine and a phone call to Bonnie or Ben, whoever picked up first.

Both Bonnie and Ben were still at work, so she left messages and decided to use the rest of her afternoon working on some songs she'd started back in Jasper. She missed Ben, but it had been great to have chunks of uninterrupted time to sit with her thoughts and allow the notes and musical phrases floating around in her head and heart to take shape. It was all in there, they just needed time and space to come together.

She pulled out her score, laid a pencil within reach and picked up Bella. For the next couple of hours Logan went to a place that had always given her great joy. She couldn't explain it, even to Ben, but she thought he knew. She saw it in the passionate way he spoke about his landscape projects and the set of his shoulders, the absolute peace emanating from him when he kneeled in the garden, happily digging in the dirt, placing new plants just so in the rich soil he had prepared for them, arranging, pruning, observing. Now and then, he'd stop and tilt his head, observing. She swore his plants were talking to him, telling him what they needed.

Logan had been doing a lot of composing lately. Since she'd increased Tilly's hours, having her take over much of the day-to-day running of Fractals, Logan's calendar had freed up considerably. She'd even been able to record some songs with Ned & Sally for their new album. They had a small, local following in Jasper and bluegrass festivals in the surrounding area. Ned, always a big supporter, had encouraged her to do an original solo on this one. That lit the fire under her and she'd been in composing mode ever since.

Setting bow to strings, she sent a long, plaintive strain out into the forest. A Swainson's thrush responded, adding deep, clear notes to the song. Logan stopped and wrote it down, then picked up her bow again and played the new phrase.

Perfect!

She wondered how you paid birds royalties. She didn't want to be sued for copyright infringement.

7

By some miracle, when the car veered into the ditch and rolled, no one was killed, just banged up to varying degrees. Undaunted, after they brushed themselves off, the Canadians decided to walk into town and catch a bus to Portland where they would then be able to hop a train back to Canada.

That left Frankie and Jacob to figure out a way to get themselves home. Frankie's cousin lived just outside Hebo. He was pretty sure he'd let them crash at his dairy farm for a while, then give them a ride back to Depoe Bay.

No delivery, no bonus. Or so he assumed.

Jacob was disappointed, but he hadn't counted on it anyway. At least they'd been paid their regular fee. He would still have enough. No sense being greedy. He had to admire Patrick's calm in spite of the setback. The Canadians would be lucky to make it all the way to the border without being stopped by the police.

They could have been spotted anywhere along the way. Someone could have seen the Sea Island's arrival or noticed them driving through one of the small towns on the way. You just never knew. Jacob found himself hoping Patrick, at least, got through. He knew he was a criminal, but he wasn't like the others.

None of them had luggage, of course, and nothing to carry away from the wreck, but Frankie went back with Billie and Arthur to the truck, ostensibly to see if he could find his hat, but really to see if the last bottle he'd slid under the seat had survived the rollover.

Waste not, want not.

Patrick stayed behind with Jacob, taking shelter from the rain that had turned into a soft, but steady curtain, behind a bank of blackberry vines that had grown up and around some boulders a few yards away from the wrecked truck. Neither man spoke. Finally, when he saw his crew was coming back to get him, Patrick reached into his inside coat pocket and removed a red, velvet pouch. Turning back with a smile, he looked at the little bag, weighed it in his hand a few times, then tossed it up one last time before catching it again. After only a second's hesitation, he threw it to Jacob, whose left hand reflexively shot out to catch it.

He was always picked for catcher.

Not waiting for him to open it, Patrick strode off, calling over his shoulder as he went, "No sense letting the County Mounties get it, eh, Jacob? Besides, I know you'll put it to good use. Maybe I'll come stay at your motor lodge someday."

He stopped mid-stride and turned to give Jacob a hard look. For a second, Jacob thought he was going to take it back, whatever it was, but Patrick simply had one more thing to say.

"This is for *you*, not Frankie. I don't want you coming out on any more jobs. You're not invited to the next party down here. You're done." He jerked his head back toward the three men coming their way. "Best put that away before those pallys see it. They'd just waste it."

For a second, Jacob stood there, holding the bag, watching Patrick walk away. Then, before the others arrived, he dropped it quickly into his pocket.

✿ ✿ ✿ ✿ ✿

Frankie shook his head to clear his vision.

What?!

What just happened? He'd been drinking, sure, but he saw what he saw. Patrick tossed a small, drawstring pouch to Jacob. Something valuable. Something obviously meant just for him. Frankie felt like he'd been slapped in the face with a cold fish. He checked to see if Billie and Arthur noticed, but they were too busy fighting over the last swallow in the bottle.

For now, he said nothing. He clamped his hat on his head, which had been in the truck, pulled his coat tight around his body and stuck his hands under his armpits to get warm.

When they joined him, Jacob had nothing in his hands. Must have slipped it into a pocket.

So that's the way you want to play it.

Frankie fumed. Jacob offered him his gloves, which—unlike Frankie—he had remembered to bring, but this kindness only made Frankie more furious. He didn't want Jacob's damned gloves, he wanted whatever was in his pocket. After all he'd done for him! He'd gotten him this job in the first place.

When the Canadians said their goodbyes and headed north into town, Frankie pointed east and he and Jacob began trudging over the muddy fields toward his cousin's place, about a mile away. He could have confronted him right then, but he kept waiting for Jacob to pull it out and show him, share whatever was in it with his best friend.

Maybe he didn't have it on him. Maybe he hid it. If he asked him now and he didn't have it on him, he may never get it. This was more than Frankie's tired brain could handle. By the time he'd just about decided to risk it and beat the shit out of Jacob if he didn't tell him where it was, they had arrived at his cousin's dairy farm. It was still dark out, but farmers started their days early.

Sal had already done the milking, and they'd just finished breakfast, but his wife, Beulah, stoked the fire and put a couple of plates of food together for them. Sal said yes, he'd drive them back to Depoe Bay the next morning. This being the Sabbath, though, Beulah said they'd be spending the day in church and then visiting shut-ins.

Frankie snuck a look at Sal, who just shrugged. Sal in *church*? He'd only been out of the hoosegow a few years. Sal was one of the blacker sheep in the family. Maybe his churchy wife had tamed him.

There was leftover stew from last night, fresh bread—she'd just baked—with lots of yellow butter and honey to slather on it. Jacob and Frankie tucked in and didn't stop until they'd each had several servings, wiping the large bowls clean with the thick, brown bread.

Jacob praised the cook and thanked them for taking them in at the last minute—said tomorrow was just fine for the ride back, but he'd like to call his wife if he could. They didn't have a phone, but their neighbor did, a widow woman named Leonore. In her eighties, Leonore wasn't an early riser, but when they got back from church, they'd take him over there. She was one of the shut-ins they visited every Sunday.

Beulah insisted they join them for church. Clad in muddy

work clothes and unbathed, they weren't exactly dressed for it, but she boiled up enough hot water for them to make themselves presentable and loaned them some of Sal's clothes. Nothing they could do about the shoes. Sal had a couple inches on both of them, so the pants covered those pretty well.

Later, when they got back from church, their hosts did as promised and took Jacob over to the widow's house, but she wasn't home.

"Probably at her daughter's place in Taft," Sal said.

Disappointed, Jacob tried not to show it. It wasn't these people's fault they didn't have a phone. Irene's father didn't either. He would have had to call the drug store in town and leave a message, which may or may not have been delivered, depending on whether or not the druggist could spare his delivery boy. He'd just have to hope Irene wasn't too worried.

8

No work was done on the Sabbath, another rule of Beulah's. She used her quiet time to study the Good Lord's word. They were each welcome to do as they wished as long as they didn't disturb her. Jacob listened to Sal's wife read aloud and nodded by the fire. He still hadn't slept, but he didn't want to be caught snoring. He managed to stay awake, but just barely. Frankie had no such qualms. They could hear his snorts through the bedroom door.

Sal and Beulah's grown son had just married, so she offered them his room. Jacob said Frankie could have the room—he'd be fine with a pallet and some covers next to the stove.

Other than the evening milking and the washing up after a simple dinner of salted ham and boiled potatoes, the rest of the day passed the way that sleepy Sundays of church-going people do. He had vague memories of going to church with his mother when he was younger, but it didn't stick. He wasn't against church, just never gave it much thought. They did have canned peaches for dessert, which Jacob thought were the best he had ever tasted. He told the cook so and she appreciated the recognition. If church involved peaches, he was all for it.

The sun was still a few inches above the horizon when their hosts retired—they had cows to milk in the morning. After everyone said their goodnights, he quickly arranged his bedding as close to the fire as he could get, placing his shoes carefully next to the stove before he got in. He lay awake thinking of the events of the last twenty-four hours.

The last rays of the setting sun slid behind the remaining jar of peaches on the kitchen counter, making them glow in the reflected light. It reminded him of what was in his pocket.

He didn't know what was wrong, but something was bugging Frankie. He had hardly spoken to him all day and when their hosts went to bed, Frankie had followed suit without even saying good night. He'd have to ask him about it tomorrow. Could he have seen Patrick giving him the bag? He didn't think so. Patrick's back was to his friends. Frankie couldn't have seen past him.

Besides, wouldn't Frankie have said something by now if he saw? It all happened so fast. Jacob wasn't sure how he felt about it. He knew Patrick was right. His friends were like Frankie. They would just blow it and Frankie probably would, too. It wasn't just that he would spend it on liquor and women. There was a dark side to Frankie. Jacob had never seen the fullness of it, but it was there. And Patrick had been clear that this gift was intended for Irene and Aaron as much as him. Patrick specifically said it was to go to his family. Maybe he should give Frankie part of the money. After he sold the gold nugget. But part of him knew Frankie wouldn't accept part.

He'd want it all.

Jacob was just too tired to think about it now. All he really wanted to do was get home to Aaron and Irene. Talking with Irene always settled him. She'd help him see things clear.

He let out a breath. It had been a hell of a night. Wrapping the thin, wool blanket Beulah had given him around him, scratching his whiskers against the rough weave, he touched the pouch in his coat pocket. Listening until he heard soft, snoring sounds coming from his hosts' bedroom, he quietly lifted it out.

◊ ◊ ◊ ◊ ◊

He still couldn't believe it. Gold! His fingers were touching a hunk of gold!

Roughly two inches wide and three inches long, it was the biggest nugget he had ever seen. Of course, he'd only seen one before. A much smaller one. Mr. Abrams had one and pulled it out to show him once. He was very proud of it. Said the miners used to pay him in gold up in the Yukon—when they had any, which was rarely.

Abrams used the gold they gave him to invest and buy property, while most of the miners spent the money they got and went out to dig for more, always hoping for a bigger, better score. There was always a deeper, richer vein . . . they just had to find it. Abrams kept the one nugget, he told him, to remind himself of those poor fools who spent their lives chasing the seductive, glowing metal, allowing it to drag them to their cold, shallow graves, far from family and friends.

Taking it out of the bag, Jacob placed it in his left hand, cupping his fingers around it, rubbing the smooth surface with his thumb. It was just a dull, misshapen lump until the light from the fire hit it. And then it glowed. Deep yellow, almost orange, reflecting the flames of the fire. Light danced and played over the surface, mesmerizing him. All he could think about was how he would never have to leave his son and Irene again, never be beholden to her father, and most of all—never have to do another rum run.

Tonight had been too close a call. Some of the cove could be seen from the road. If anyone had driven by while they were desperately digging in the sand, burying case after case of illegal alcohol, it could have been over. Not all of the police were bought off. All the police carried guns, and the federal ones weren't afraid to use them.

Lost in thought as he was, he didn't hear the footsteps behind him.

9

Frankie lay rigid, listening to Sal and Beulah settle in. They'd had beans with dinner and he could hear Sal fart. Or maybe it was Beulah. That old bible thumper was certainly full of enough hot air.

Frankie pulled both blankets up to his chin. The heat from the potbelly stove in the kitchen didn't make it this far. He was freezing.

Good ole Jacob made sure he was comfortable, though, didn't he? While making it look like he was giving up the comfortable bed, he made sure he got the spot in front of the fire, wrapped snug as a bug in a rug. Somehow Jacob always managed to win. And look like the good guy doing it. He'd already married the prettiest girl in town. It's not that Frankie wanted to marry Irene, but he wouldn't mind bedding her. And he would have if Jacob hadn't swooped in.

The air pressed cold against his face. He'd slept hard this afternoon and wasn't a bit sleepy now. He was all keyed up. Finally, it was quiet. He started reining in and sorting through his spinning thoughts.

For whatever reason, Patrick had given something to Jacob and not to him. In secret. Something obviously of value.

Patrick didn't seem like the kind of man to throw away cash. Was it cash? The pouch or bag or whatever it was, wasn't large enough to hold much actual money. Was it a watch or a ring or . . . ? And why hadn't Jacob showed it to him?

Somewhere in Frankie's gut, he knew why. There was something about Jacob that made people trust him, like him, love him, want to take care of him. Hell, he'd fallen for it. He and Jacob had been friends for years. He'd recommended him when Patrick said they could use another guy, and did he know of anyone who could be trusted?

Trusted. What a chump he'd been, falling for Jacob's innocent act. He'd taken what should have been his. If Jacob hadn't been there, Patrick would have given the pouch to him, he was sure of it!

Jacob had betrayed him. It was that simple. Once Frankie made up his mind about that, the solution to his problem was also simple.

Waiting until his cousin's farts turned to snores, Frankie pushed the blankets off his fully clothed body and placed his feet silently on the floor. He lifted his belt from the end of the bed. Holding the buckle end so it wouldn't jingle, he made his way to the bedroom door and listened. Nothing. He'd just have to take a chance. Hopefully, Sal kept the hinges oiled. Pulling it open an inch at a time until he could fit through, he exhaled as evenly as he could. So far, so good. He peered into the main room, to the dark form bundled on the floor in front of the stove.

Jacob lay on his side, curled toward the warmth of the banked fire, with his back to him. Frankie couldn't tell if he was asleep or awake. Slowly, he made his way across the floor in his stocking feet, placing each foot down carefully from the outside in—Indian tracker style—like his daddy taught him when they went hunting.

Jacob didn't stir, but he couldn't be sure he was asleep, either.

Quick as a snake, Frankie struck.

Both ends of his belt wrapped tightly in each hand, in one movement, he kneeled down and whipped it over Jacob's head, yanking back with as much force as he could, to prevent him from crying out.

A gold nugget rolled onto the floor. Seeing it only added to Frankie's fury.

Within seconds, Jacob's body went limp.

A rush of adrenaline surged through him. Problem solved! He couldn't believe it would be so easy. Unsure, he slowly released the belt. When Jacob's body remained still, Frankie reached over to retrieve the nugget and pushed it into his pocket.

"He's not dead yet."

Whipping around, Frankie saw Sal. He was standing directly behind him.

Had he seen?

"Grab the other end," Sal said, as he walked forward and reached calmly under Jacob's limp shoulders to get a good grip under his arm pits.

Stunned, Frankie looked toward the door to see if Beulah was joining them next, but the door to their bedroom was shut and he could hear her soft snores.

"Sleep of the righteous," Sal said. "Not something we'll ever know."

Frankie couldn't argue with that.

'Sides, she got kicked in the hip by one of the new cows three weeks ago last Saturday. Doc gave her some laudanum for it. She'll sleep."

Trying not to panic, Frankie did as instructed, grabbing his former friend's feet. The two men lifted Jacob's dead weight and carried him outside to a large shed on the other side of the barn, away from the house.

Adrenaline retreating, Frankie started to shake, dropping into a seated position, crouching on his heels. He held his head in his hands before he passed out. A storm of thoughts and emotions roared through him.

Had Sal seen the gold nugget? Had he killed Jacob? What if Sal was right and Jacob wasn't dead, but woke up? How could he fix this? What should he do now? How could he ever explain this? Had he really killed his best friend?

He didn't have time to contemplate his situation for long. Jacob started to make horrible gagging sounds and thrash his legs, unable to breathe even though there was no longer a belt around his neck. Frozen in place, Frankie watched as Sal calmly lifted a square shovel off its hook on the wall and brought it down onto Jacob's head. Smashed it like a pumpkin.

Checking it for blood first, Sal calmly hung the shovel back on its hook. He kicked the body.

"Need to get him outta here 'fore Beulah wakes up. She'll be out to the barn for the milking in a few hours."

Unable to find words, Frankie helped Sal roll the body—it was definitely a body now—into a tarp, then load it onto the back of Sal's truck. He'd heard about Sal's dark side, but hadn't seen it before. He'd been so calm. Sure, Frankie knew he started it, but he had a reason. Sal didn't. Sal just killed Jacob like he was swatting a fly. Scared the shit out of him. He'd never be able to look at the man the same way again at family picnics.

Tucking the tarp securely around the body, the two men returned to the shed. Under Sal's direction, they scrubbed off the shovel, replaced the blood-stained straw with fresh—the wet straw to be burned out back later, when it dried. Sal said he'd take care of it.

"We'll leave after breakfast," Sal said, walking back to the house.

Frankie was still in a state of shock.

"What'll we tell Beulah?" Frankie said, ". . . about . . . about where Jacob is?"

"You'll think of something," Sal said.

Really cold now, still shaking from what they'd just done, Frankie returned to bed, laying there for another few hours until he had a good story lined up. It felt like he'd just drifted off to sleep when the smell of bacon woke him up.

Beulah's breakfast was delicious. Frankie was surprised he had an appetite, but he dug in and had seconds on the fried potatoes. Potatoes made anyway were delicious, but browned to a crisp in bacon fat . . . well, there just weren't things much better than that in life. Except maybe getting away with murder.

Thanking his hosts profusely for their kindness—he could be as appreciative and gracious as Jacob, he thought—he and Sal gathered their things for the trip back to Depoe Bay. Frankie promised Beulah he'd make sure Jacob got his care package of biscuits and butter, with several strips of crispy bacon. He passed along his friend's thanks to Beulah. Jacob surely appreciated the hospitality, but he hadn't wanted his young wife to worry. When he saw headlights on the distant highway, he decided to walk back and hitch a ride home.

"True love!" Frankie said, waving goodbye.

10

"Thalia! . . . Large Americano . . ."

"Roberto! . . . Soy mocha, triple espresso . . ."

The early morning rush was over, but Pirate's was still buzzing. Scanning the room as she got in line, Logan spotted Sam, who had secured one of the few tables in back. She waved and pointed, indicating she was going to order first, then join her.

If it weren't for the hot pink, rhinestone-encrusted cat-eye glasses perched on her face, Logan may not have seen her. Samantha Badger, Sam to her friends, was only 5'5" and didn't weigh more than a hundred pounds soaking wet.

When her large coffee was called, Logan added a scone to her order, then threaded her way through the crush and sat down at Sam's table, careful not to spill.

"Those are awesome," Sam said, nodding at the scone, pushing a strand of shiny, black hair behind her ear. She had one of those short, sleek bobs that held its shape perfectly no matter what she did to it. Low maintenance hair was a must in her line of work.

"You were lucky," Sam said, pushing her backpack out of the way to make room. "They usually run out of the cranberry-orange ones before lunch."

Logan put down her food and took off her jacket—shaking off the water before hanging it on the back of her chair. She was still getting used to the rain. Sam said it was an unusually wet winter, but Logan had no comparison. She'd only visited the Oregon coast in the summer and when she was here in the fall with Ben, rainy season hadn't really kicked in yet.

"How's the house?" Sam asked. "Did you decide about the fireplace?"

"Good, it's all going well," Logan said. "I think I'm going to leave the hearth as is, maybe get one of those burlwood mantles, all glossy with the bark along the edge—leave that side natural, clean up the bricks, replace any broken ones."

"Sounds good—that place right next to the gas station has raw wood pieces. You can probably find something there. When can you move in?"

"Well, I'm kind of moved in now," Logan said, "He's got the downstairs bedroom and bathroom done. The one with the clawfoot tub, which I LOVE! Plumbing's all fixed. New hot water heater. I'm sort of camping out in those two rooms for now. The kitchen will be a while. We've got water, but he's waiting on something to get approved before he can install the appliances."

When she and Ben flew out during the holidays to work on the place, Clay had already accomplished a lot. The smell was gone, the raccoons had been given their walking papers, the flooring, woodwork, and windows had been repaired and refinished when possible, the rest replaced.

The only fight they'd had was about a very macho thing Ben wanted to do. Since the house was at the top of the hill, backed onto the forest, kind of isolated from neighboring homes, he wanted her to have a gun—just for emergencies. Wolves, bears, intruders off the highway, zombies . . . Ben's imagination tended to run wild when it came to protecting Logan. She'd absolutely refused to have one in the house. They'd left it at a standstill, but she knew they'd be having this discussion again. Ben was as stubborn as she was.

Since this was Logan's first official Oregon winter, she soon realized her Southern California wardrobe was woefully inadequate. Everyone said it was drier last year, but she didn't believe them. The weather's only saving grace was that it made everything green. And, she had to admit, when they had a sun break, which was often, it was dazzling. The white caps in the bay were blindingly bright against a jewel-toned ocean, and the air was fresh and cold.

Taking off her thick, navy beanie, Logan released her mop of damp hair, then gathered it into a loose braid that hung halfway down her back. She rubbed her arms to warm up. She almost reached for her coat, but decided she'd be too hot. Opting instead for a long pull of hot coffee, she placed the thick, ceramic mug carefully down on the table and began slathering her scone with butter. Just in time, she remembered her manners.

"You want some?" she said, her mouth already stuffed.

Samantha rejected the offer with palms out, "OH, Noooo! You go right ahead. I've become very attached to my fingers."

Logan rolled her eyes, but quickly polished off the rest of the humongous scone all by herself. These weren't Tava'e's cinnamon rolls, but they'd do. Tava'e and her husband Jean owned the coffee shop down the hill from Logan's place back in Jasper. Jean did the baking, while Tava'e mothered the whole town and held court daily as the reigning chess queen. Logan had become friends with the massive Samoan woman over the last few years. She and her husband Jean had even catered Amy's wedding.

"So," she said, licking the last of the crumbs off her lips. She nodded toward Sam's laptop.

"What are you working on?"

Sam was a reporter with the local weekly paper, the News Herald. The paper came out Wednesday mornings, so the rest of the day would be slow. She scrolled through her calendar.

"Nothing much. Cleaning up my inbox, returning calls, looking at next week. Got a meeting at city hall, then a quilt show, oh, and a piece on mushroom hunting . . . you know, the usual exciting stuff," Sam said.

A former big city investigative reporter, Samantha Badger knew exciting, but if she missed the action, she never said. Her voluntary exile from the halls of power in Olympia, where she had struck fear into the heart of many a corrupt politician and helped put a few criminals away, was the fault of a local fisherman named Tim Pullman.

Tim and Sam met when she chased a story to the Oregon coast a few years ago. She'd met him through his sister, the local Medical Examiner. They'd been together ever since. Logan didn't know him well, but he seemed like a nice guy and Sam still glowed when she talked about him.

Ahhh, young love.

Logan thought back to when she first met Sam. The year before, a local charter boat captain had been murdered on his own boat in Depoe Bay Harbor. Being the most experienced and only full-time reporter on staff, Sam got the story. And all of the attendant side stories, including the one where Logan was taken hostage by a Chinese national and barely escaped with her life.

Fun times!

It was during one of the follow-up interviews, when they met at a local restaurant, Saigon Noodle House, that Sam and Logan discovered a mutual love of *pho*, the fragrant and filling Vietnamese soup. And it didn't hurt that they were both rabid Pink Martini and Allison Kraus fans.

But Saigon Noodle House was in Newport and Sam lived in Depoe Bay, so Wednesdays at Pirate's Coffee was more convenient and had become something of a habit when Logan was in town.

While Sam checked her phone for messages, Logan warmed her hands on her mug. She still couldn't believe how quickly her life had changed in the last six months. A lot had happened. Not the least of which was finding and buying a house up here. With Ben.

That had been scary, on multiple levels, but the timing had been right and they'd decided to take the leap. So far, so good. To her relief, Ben seemed satisfied with the status of their relationship. He'd been so busy flying back and forth doing projects here and keeping his landscape customers happy back in California, he hadn't mentioned the M word in weeks. Which was fine by her. She liked things the way they were.

It's not like they were moving in together. They still each had their own home back in Jasper, CA. This was only a vacation home. Ben still had his landscaping business in Jasper and Logan ran Fractals mainly from her home next door. Besides, Amy, Liam, and Ian were there. They lived just down the road. She loved spending time with her grandson. Flying back and forth between Portland and Jasper for work made it easy to rationalize buying a vacation home on the Oregon coast.

At first, she didn't think she'd have much time to spend up here, but lately, Fractals practically ran itself. Even though Tilly was going through a divorce, she hadn't missed a beat. Everything ran so smoothly, Logan hardly needed to show up.

Her life was shifting, which brought on some feelings of unease if not outright panic, but for now, she decided to trust it was in the right direction.

Breaking into her thoughts, Sam put her phone down and asked, "When is your sister coming in?"

"Half-sister," Logan clarified.

Sam rolled her eyes, ignoring the half-sister clarification.

"Tomorrow," Logan said, "She's renting a car."

"What's her name again?" Sam said.

"Olivia," Logan said, "Madison Olivia Landers—she uses her middle name."

"Why?"

"Don't know," Logan said.

"What are you guys going to do while she's here? Is she staying long?" Sam asked. "Is she staying with you?"

Logan didn't know the answer to either of those questions. She'd racked her brains, but really had no idea what a thirty-three-year-old New Yorker would want to do in what to her would surely feel like the middle of nowhere. At least there were some good restaurants here. As for where she was staying, Logan had explained the state of her house and sent her a list of vacation rentals in the area. Olivia said she'd probably only come down for the one day, then drive back to Portland and catch a red-eye back to New York. Logan sent her a list of motels and day rentals that looked good anyway.

"Not really sure yet. Thought we'd go to Tidal Raves for

dinner. Or maybe Side Door Cafe. You want to come?" Logan said, hopefully. She needed a buffer. Besides, Sam was closer to Olivia's age.

"Let me consult my busy schedule . . . ," Sam said, pronouncing the word 'schedule' like someone from the royal family. Picking up her phone, she pretended to check, then almost dropped it when it rang for real. Seeing who it was, she tapped the screen, suddenly all business.

"Jerry," she answered, all attention to the caller on the other end of the line.

Jerry was her news editor.

"Be there in five!" she said, practically bolting from her seat as she disconnected the call and dropped her phone in her bag. Next, she began patting her pockets, but didn't find what she was looking for.

"Shit!" She turned to Logan, "Can I get a ride? Tim's car is in the shop. He borrowed mine and dropped me off while he ran some errands in Lincoln City."

"Sure," Logan said, grabbing her coat, following her out.

They were halfway out the door before she thought to ask where they were going.

"To see a dead body," Sam said.

Well, this day just got a lot more interesting!

◊ ◊ ◊ ◊ ◊

They buckled in and Sam gave Logan directions.

"Who died?" Logan asked, turning right onto Highway 101.

"Collins," Sam said, "Charlotte Collins Schmitt."

The name Collins rang a bell. Logan tried to remember where she'd heard it before. "Didn't you just run a story about The Collins Hotel?" she asked.

"Yep," Sam said, "That's the one."

According to the feature spread, The Collins Hotel, a local institution, had been owned by the same family for several generations. Logan had never been to the hotel, just driven past it on her way to and from her new house in Depoe Bay and Rita's home in Little Whale Cove.

Currently in the middle of a renovation, it was a grand, old hotel from the thirties; the place to see and be seen by Portland's elite. Founded by a Frank Collins and his wife, Rowena, it took full advantage of the repeal of Prohibition by including a good-sized dance hall next to the hotel, complete with a fully-stocked bar.

Running across the end of the bar, the long counter reflected the abundance of natural resources and the profligate attitude of the times in which it was harvested. Edged with bark, and coated with resin, it ran forty feet long, carved whole from a towering Douglas Fir. This was when the coastal range was so packed with trees that running out of them was inconceivable, and no one had even heard of the spotted owl.

The Collins Hotel held court atop a magnificent, oceanside cliff on the south end of town, just past a couple of smaller inns and houses over the bridge. The spread of pictures that had accompanied Sam's article in the News Herald showed Art Deco rooms with fantastic views of the bay and a long deck fronting the dining room so guests could watch seals, sea lions and migrating whales at their leisure. Sea otters, or *elakha* as the indigenous people called them, were once plentiful on the Oregon coast, but had long since disappeared. The article said the last sea otter in Oregon was killed in Newport in 1906. Its pelt sold for $900.

Getting back to the humans, Logan remembered from Sam's article that the oldest living member of the family, the matriarch, Charlotte, still lived there. Wife of Frank and Rowena's only child, Emerson.

Sad that she died, but why would Sam's paper want her to rush? What was the urgency? An old woman, even a wealthy one, dying from some end-of-life disease or just plain old age in her family hotel didn't seem to warrant the grim look on Sam's face.

"What did she die of? Did she have cancer?" Logan asked.

"No, Charlotte is—was—only thirty-two—and as far as I know, until today, was in perfectly good health."

11

Logan assumed at some point this would make some sense. Without asking anymore questions, she pressed on the gas, praying no one parked along the highway would back out of their parking space into her lane. Four minutes later, they almost missed the turnoff, but Sam pointed it out in time. Just past the bridge, the drive to the hotel dipped steeply down and to the left, widening into a small parking area. Fifty feet beyond was the main entrance, flanked by two impressive, stone planters filled with sea grasses, daffodils and pansies. The flowers must be grown inland or in a greenhouse, then brought here, Logan thought. Too cold and overcast for them to be in season now.

An Oregon State Police (OSP) patrol car, a fire truck, and an ambulance were lined up nose to tail on the right, leaving room in the middle for emergency vehicles to maneuver in and out. Crime scene tape wrapped the hotel in bright, yellow ribbon, as if a present for someone's birthday. All it needed was a candle.

Making sure to leave the central area open, Logan parked on a small parking area on the left.

"Thanks!" Sam said, jumping out, notebook in hand.

Logan waited in the car. Her brother being a cop in California, she knew enough to stay out of the way. She looked around and saw only three other unofficial cars. One, a late model SUV, was from a rental company in Portland. Then there was a beat-up truck and a Porsche. Registered guests? Was the hotel open during remodeling? She couldn't remember.

Tapping her steering wheel, Logan wondered how long Sam would be. She decided to at least get out and stretch. She'd stay out of the way, but maybe she'd hear what was going on. It beat sitting in the car twiddling her thumbs.

Thirty-two. Wow. Not much older than Amy. Sam had explained that the Charlotte who died was the namesake and granddaughter of the family matriarch, Charlotte Collins. Logan wondered if the young woman's parents were alive—they weren't mentioned in the article, so maybe not. She also wondered who discovered the body, then chastised herself for being gruesome. To get her mind off of that, she focused on Sam, who was talking with the uniformed patrol officer on duty.

She must have known him, because he hadn't told her to go away. In fact, he was still talking and she was still taking notes. Logan strained to hear, but they were too far away.

Just then, another car pulled in. This one was a dark gray sedan of some kind. She wasn't good with makes and models of cars. She was good with faces, though, and she recognized the one belonging to the man getting out of the car. Detective Monson of the Lincoln County Sheriff's Department.

Last summer, Detective Monson had pulled her away from Ben's beefy cheese enchiladas for some heavy questioning—as a homicide suspect. She still hadn't quite forgiven him. Ben's enchiladas were legendary.

Monson had an unhurried air about him. Slightly rumpled suit. No rush as he ascended the stairs, nodded at the patrol officer and let himself into the hotel. About six feet tall, Monson was somewhere in his early sixties, paunchy and pale, still sporting a full head of wavy black hair. Logan didn't know if his tired attitude was a conscious projection, but she knew it hid an active mind. If she'd been guilty of murder, his skillful questioning of her that night would have pulled a confession out of her for sure.

Before she had time to wander very far down that memory lane, Logan's attention was drawn to the large, picture window to the left of the hotel entrance. From where she was parked, she could see most of the hotel lobby and part of the check-in desk beyond.

But what caught her attention wasn't the luxurious lobby, but a tall young woman with stick-straight, light-brown hair that skimmed her shoulders who was being escorted to a green, velvet couch by Detective Monson. She wore an open, waffle-weave, white spa robe over a dark blue, one-piece bathing suit, but her hair wasn't wet. Taking a chair opposite her, Detective Monson pulled out a notebook and pen.

Logan had only seen her picture on the website, and the window was a good twenty yards away from the parking lot, but still—that had to be her.

Olivia?

What was Olivia doing here already? She wasn't supposed to get here until the morning.

12

Without thinking, Logan raced past the crime scene tape and the patrol car. She made it halfway up the stairs before she was stopped by the young officer manning the entrance—the one Sam had been interviewing. Before she could whiz past, he reached over and blocked her way with a beefy arm.

"Ma'am! You can't go in there—this is a crime scene," he said.

"That's my sister!" Logan said, pointing to Olivia through the window. "I don't see any dead bodies in the lobby. There's no reason why I can't go in there!"

Unsure, the officer looked back up at the window, where the woman Logan was pointing at was being interviewed by Detective Monson.

"Who are you?" he said.

"She's with me, Rob," Sam said.

Then, as if welcoming guests at a dinner party, she added, "Logan McKenna, meet Robert Ollis."

Introductions over, Sam said, "That's her sister, Rob. She was expecting her tomorrow. Looks like she came in early. We didn't know she was here."

Sam couldn't resist asking a few more questions.

"Was she here when the body was discovered? she asked.

Rob ignored her question this time and turned to Logan, a doubtful look on his face.

"How do you not know when your own sister is coming in and where she's staying?"

Logan couldn't begin to explain her convoluted family, and it was none of his business anyway. Instead, she folded her arms, took a military stance and huffed her defiance.

Sam had much better people skills than Logan.

"Her sister's name is Olivia. She's from New York, just drove down from Portland, she wasn't sure when she was coming in," she said, "Could you just maybe see if Detective Monson will allow Logan to come sit with her? If she promises not to say anything? She looks pretty upset."

"You know I can't do that, Sam," Rob said. "Monson doesn't like to be interrupted. But I'll let him know she's here as soon as he's done."

That was the best they were going to get out of him for now, so Logan returned to her car. Sam tried to talk with one of the EMTs coming out to the ambulance, but it didn't look like they gave anything more than a short response. They yanked a gurney down and rolled it back inside, disappearing into the hotel.

Logan wondered where the dead body was. Obviously not in the lobby.

Monson released Olivia from the small couch after about thirty minutes, but it was another half hour before she emerged from the hotel, fully dressed, with a small rolling bag at heel. Officer Rob pointed to Logan's car and Sam walked her over. Behind Olivia, Logan could see Detective Monson moving on to the next interview, this one with a dark-haired man about

Olivia's age. Another guest?

"Hi, Logan," Olivia said, smiling weakly, "Not exactly how I planned our first meeting."

"Why don't we get you something to eat? We can come back for your car," she said.

Olivia nodded and got in, putting her bag in the back.

Logan leaned her head down to look out the window at Sam, "Do you need to stay?"

"No, I got everything I can for now," Sam said. "I'll check back with Rae when she finishes up."

A local EMT for the last seven years, Rae was one of Sam's best contacts.

"Okay, hop in," Logan said, "McKenna Uber—at your service, where shall we go?"

"How about Spouting Horn?" Sam said.

"Sounds good," Logan said.

Logan was sure Sam wanted to start firing questions at Olivia, but to her credit, she resisted.

"Have you eaten anything?" she asked Olivia.

"No. I usually swim before breakfast. I went down this morning to the pool . . . that's when I saw her," she said.

So that's why they couldn't see any crime techs gathering evidence in the hotel. They were all downstairs. The hotel must have an indoor swimming pool on a lower level.

Sam wasn't taking notes, but Logan knew her. She was listening. Sam had a talent for memorizing almost every word she heard.

Olivia looked pale, but maybe she always looked like that. This was the first time Logan had seen her in person. With the sunlight slanting in, Logan noted a light sprinkle of freckles across her nose. Without mascara, transparent eyelashes fringed hazel eyes.

"We can talk about that later—if you want to," Logan said. "Right now, let's get some food into you. Then we can figure things out."

That's what her dad always did. All problems could be solved over food. Memories of sitting at the beat-up kitchen table, her father tending to her and Rick's many skinned knees and a few broken hearts, always followed by big bowls of chili or double grilled cheese sandwiches brought back a flood of warm memories. She wondered what Olivia's childhood had been like. She knew their mother was a cold fish; she'd never met Olivia's dad. Maybe Olivia hadn't led the charmed childhood Logan had imagined. Money couldn't buy everything.

Logan's current food supplies were limited to beef jerky, pre-packaged pudding, and a few apples. Not exactly warm, rib-sticking comfort food. She'd mostly been eating out until the kitchen was done, with only an ice chest/cooler for backup.

Since it was January and a week day, parking was open. They got a space right in front. Olivia and Logan followed Sam upstairs and they were shown to a table along the wall of windows overlooking the highway to the bay. It was only spitting rain at this hour, but the temperature had dropped dramatically. A pale, almost colorless sky stretched over a choppy, gray sea, speckled with foam. It felt good to be inside, warm, and out of the wind.

Over cheeseburgers and fries, Olivia brought them up to speed. With Olivia's permission, Sam took actual notes this time.

First, Olivia apologized for not letting Logan know she'd driven down early. It was a last minute decision and already late when she got to the hotel last night.

She'd found The Collins Hotel online, but almost didn't call because the website said they were in the middle of a remodel. But the woman who answered said they were keeping a few rooms open during the renovations and yes, as long as she could get there by 10:30 p.m., she would hold the room.

She stopped for dinner in McMinnville on the way in. After that and getting lost a couple more times, it was about 10:15 p.m. before Olivia pulled into the parking lot. She was in bed by 10:45. The only other person she saw that night was the middle-aged woman who checked her in and told her about the available amenities, including an indoor lap pool in the lower level, open from 6:00 a.m. to 10:00 p.m. daily. She could reach the pool by a set of stairs at the end of the hall. The price of the room would be reduced because the full dining room was not open. There would be, however, a continental breakfast set up on the buffet table along the south end of the lobby, served from 7:00 to 9:00 a.m. Coffee and tea were in the rooms.

Logan fidgeted a little, wanting to ask more questions, but controlled herself and let Olivia catch her breath before continuing. She'd get to the dead body soon enough.

13

EARLIER THAT MORNING
THE COLLINS HOTEL LOBBY

Two down, three to go.

"If you think of anything else, I can be reached at these numbers," Monson said, handing the young woman his card. She had already given him her cell phone number in case he had more questions while she was still in town. She was only planning a short stay—visiting family.

As his mother had taught him to do every time a woman left the room, he stood as she exited. He knew it was old-fashioned, and probably not even welcomed by this young woman. You never knew. Since it was a habit so ingrained, he couldn't stop it, but he'd learned to make it seem casual, just in case. He no longer included a nod of his head and a "Ma'am" with the gesture.

He waved to the young man waiting in an overstuffed armchair near the door. He checked his notes. The fiancé. After he finished taking his statement, he just had the grandmother and the manager to talk to. Grandma was on her way right now, driving back from Portland. Should be here by the time he was done with this guy.

The crime scene techs were working downstairs at the pool and he'd already talked with the two kitchen workers. The uniform was keeping out the press and any curiosity seekers that would undoubtedly show up as word of the young woman's death got out.

"Hello, I'm Detective Monson, please sit down," he said, indicating the loveseat across from him that the young woman had just vacated. "Let's start with your full name," he said.

He knew, of course, who the young man was, but he knew these banal, softball questions would help him get through the interview as painlessly and accurately as possible.

"Wade. Wade Ellis," he said.

"I know this is a difficult time for you, Wade," Monson said. "I understand the woman who drowned was your fiancée."

"Yes—we were planning on getting married . . . at the end of the month," he said. His eyes watered. Trying to blink away the tears that fell down his cheeks anyway, he sat rigid, fists clenched in his lap.

"I am sorry for your loss," Monson said. "I'll try to make this as quick as possible. I just need to ask you a few questions for my report."

"When did your fiancée . . ." Monson began.

"Charlie," Wade said, his eyes filling again with tears. He was barely keeping it together.

"I thought her name was Charlotte," Monson said.

"Charlotte was her grandmother's name. She was named after her, but has always gone by Charlie," Wade said.

"Of course, Charlie . . . when did you last see Charlie?" Monson asked.

"Last night," Wade said. "She loved to swim. She always did her laps at night. It was her way of unwinding before bed."

"What time was that?"

"Nine. Nine-thirty? I'm not sure. I wasn't paying attention," he said.

"You don't swim?" Monson asked.

"Sometimes, but not very well. Charlie's a lot faster—was a lot faster than I am," he said.

"So, she was a good swimmer?"

"Yeah, she learned to swim here in this pool—she lived here in the hotel during high school—that's when we met," he said. "Charlie loved to eat, so she was always hanging out in the kitchen. My mom worked here back then. Most of the locals worked here at some time or another."

"Charlie never took the lifeguard test," he added, "but she could have passed if she had. Her grandmother didn't think it was ladylike for a girl to be athletic."

"Getting back to last night," Monson said. "How long did Charlie usually swim? Did you expect her back at any certain time?"

Monson listened carefully without appearing to place any particular importance on Wade's answers. He knew this would be a sensitive area. If the young man had anything to do with Charlie's death, he might pick something up in his response. And if he had fallen asleep instead of checking on her when she was late coming back to bed, Wade would feel horribly guilty. But he needed to verify the timeline, the sequence of events, so he plowed ahead, asking the question again.

In response, Wade looked stricken.

"Normally, it only took her about a half hour to do her laps," he said, "I should have been awake."

"Did she call you or come back to the room at any time?"

"No, I mean . . . I don't know. I don't think so. I must have fallen asleep," Wade said, breaking down into tears, hunched over, holding his head in his hands.

Monson waited until he regained control. He could be faking it, but probably not.

"I understand," Monson said. "You fell asleep. When did you wake up? When did you learn she had drowned?"

"It was early," he said, "in the morning. Around seven, I think. Something like that. Amanda called and told me."

"Amanda?"

"Charlie's older sister, and the manager of the hotel here," Wade said.

Monson mentally went through the checklist of people he still had to speak with. He had two more. The owner of the hotel, the grandmother, who was on her way back from Portland. Amanda was the one who'd made the 911 call. He would get to her later. For now, he wanted to keep Wade on track. Things went faster that way and people did better if they could tell their story all at once.

"What did you do when you got the call?" Monson asked.

"I remember feeling confused. I think I patted the bed next to me to wake Charlie up. I assumed the call was for her because it was on the hotel phone, not my cell. When I finally answered, Amanda told me Charlie had been found in the pool . . . that she was dead. I remember dropping the phone, running around the room, checking the bathroom, thinking Charlie must be there somewhere. That there must be some mistake."

"Then what did you do?"

"I ran out, down the hall to the stairs to the lower level where the pool is, but an officer was standing there, outside the door.

He wouldn't let me in. I guess I wasn't the first person Amanda called, because the police were already here."

Monson asked a few more questions, noted Wade's personal contact information, then handed him his card as they stood, giving him the same instructions he'd given to Olivia, the one who'd found the body. To call if he thought of anything else. He told Wade he was welcome to wait in the dining room— they'd set up a table and some food and coffee in there. He said an officer would escort him back to the room, so he could get his car keys and a change of clothes. Everything else needed to stay until the room was cleared. They would notify him.

Monson watched him go. Accidents weren't as bad as suicides, but they still created a gaping hole in the lives of those who loved the one who'd died. Always tragic when they were so young. He expected this to be an accident report, but he was thorough. His training officer years ago drilled it into him to process every scene that didn't exhibit an immediate, obvious cause of death as a potential homicide. You never knew. Better to have all the evidence collected properly in case you wound up having to investigate a murder.

While he was wrapping things up with Wade Ellis, he heard gravel crunching. When he looked out the window, he saw a well-dressed, but slightly disheveled elderly woman emerge from her Mercedes and hurry into the hotel. Must be Mrs. Collins, the grandmother.

14

Monson had seen it all, but the devastation on the woman's face was so complete, he wasn't sure she'd be able to withstand even the most basic questions he needed to ask. Red-rimmed, faded blue eyes looked blankly past him as Mrs. Collins lowered herself carefully onto an upholstered, Queen Ann chair in front of her desk. Monson took the large armchair across from her and Amanda, the manager and granddaughter, who had gone to get some tea, perched on a side chair on her return. After scootching her chair closer to Mrs. Collins and dunking the teabag up and down several times while blowing on it, she placed the teabag in a small saucer next to a plate of cookies she'd brought along from the kitchen as well.

Monson assumed the cookies were for all of them, but wasn't sure, so didn't take any. One looked like lemon shortbread, his favorite, but he'd wait until offered.

Amanda gathered a slim, mint cookie with chocolate filling in a napkin and gave it to Mrs. Collins, who meekly accepted it, then put it down on her lap.

So as not to stare, Monson looked around the room. The woman sitting before him bore little resemblance to the confident photos on the wall picturing her at various ribbon cuttings, galas, and hotel events. One featured her smiling proudly, bending over a rose bush covered in yellow blossoms, cupping one in her hand to display it at the most advantageous angle for the camera. In all of these photos, her hair was neat, her makeup perfect, and her smile wide. She wasn't a flashy dresser, but even to his untrained eye, her clothing and jewelry looked expensive.

Sitting here now, she looked nothing like that confident woman. She looked twenty years older, frail, and pale. White, papery skin, etched with a network of fine lines stretched over still prominent cheekbones, sagged at the jaw. Her face was without makeup, but he could see a faint residue of bright, red lipstick in two or three of the smoker's lines radiating up from her mouth.

Meekly, she barely noticed when her granddaughter placed the mug of hot tea in her hands and coaxed her to wrap her fingers around it so she wouldn't drop it. How she'd managed to drive herself all the way back from Portland without getting in a wreck Monson could only imagine.

He would have preferred interviewing them one at a time, but in this case, he allowed Amanda to stay. He didn't want to upset the older woman any more than necessary.

"Mrs. Collins," he began, "I am very sorry for your loss, but I need to ask you a few questions. I promise to keep them brief. Once I establish the facts, we can finish our business here and leave you and your granddaughter in peace."

The word granddaughter made her squeeze her eyes shut and brought on the tears. The older woman must have thought he meant the granddaughter who had drowned in the pool. He meant the one sitting right here beside her. He waited until she regained control.

"Mrs. Collins," he continued, "Are you able to continue?"

LIES THAT BIND

He thought he may have to summon the EMTs in to administer some kind of tranquilizer for her, but with great willpower, she pulled herself together and looked him in the eye. He took that as a good sign.

"Just for the record, you are Mrs. Charlotte Collins, is that correct?"

"Yes," she said.

Turning to the woman seated beside her, he said, "And you are Amanda Daspitt?"

"Actually," she said, "it's Amanda *Collins* Daspitt. I'm Mrs. Collins' granddaughter."

It was hard to see how these two women were related. In her eighties at least and in the middle of overwhelming grief, the older woman still had more vibrance and color than the younger one. Amanda was kind of a beige, boneless blob. The word *sycophantic* came to mind. His college English professor would be proud.

Monson turned back to the older woman.

"I understand you were away at a conference in Portland," he said.

"Yes, the Pacific Northwest Gardening Society," she said.

Monson added this to his notes.

"Grandmother was the keynote speaker," Amanda added, proudly, even though no one had asked.

"Yes, that's correct," Mrs. Collins said dully.

That kind of thing probably didn't matter at a time like this.

"When did you leave for the conference?" he asked. "You drove yourself?"

"Monday," she said, "Yes, I drove myself. It's not that far— only a couple of hours or so, depending on traffic. I go every year. I ate an early breakfast here, drove up, then checked into my hotel in time for the orientation."

"Do you stay at the same hotel every year?" he asked. Not wanting his questions to sound like an interrogation. Just a friendly question.

"The Sentinel," she said. "It used to be called The Governor. That's how I always think of it."

"And when was the last time you spoke with your granddaughter?" he asked.

Amanda butted in. "Grandmother and I spoke every day, sometimes several times. I kept her updated on the progress of the renovations. There was always something that needed to be seen to. It was my responsibility to hold down the fort—keep things running smoothly while she was away," Amanda said.

"I meant Charlie, your other granddaughter," Monson said softly, already regretting his decision to let Amanda stay.

15

Keeping his attention on the grandma, he asked, "When was the last time you spoke with Charlie?"

"The night before I left," Mrs. Collins said. "Saturday evening. And her name is Charlotte. She was named after me. Charlie is a boy's name. I never liked it, but for some reason she insisted we call her that."

"And you didn't speak to her on the phone, or call or text while you were away, during the last few days?" Monson asked.

"No," she said. "I assumed we would talk in the morning, but I had to leave early and she wasn't up yet."

"That was Wade's fault," Amanda said. "He was the problem. He was the wedge between Charlie and our family."

Mrs. Collins roused somewhat from her misery and looked at the woman sitting beside her as if seeing her for the first time.

"And what was the problem there? Why wouldn't Wade want Charlie to be close to her grandmother, or to you?" Monson asked.

"He wanted her to himself," Amanda said, leaning forward. "Wade was only in it for the money. He didn't have any, so he decided to marry Charlie for hers."

Well, this chat just got more interesting.

He turned to the grandmother. Asking questions out of left field often jolted people into revealing more than they wanted to about private family matters.

"Do you have any reason to believe your granddaughter's death was not an accident?" he said. "I understand she was an excellent swimmer."

Mrs. Collins took only a second to reply. Looking him directly in the eyes, she answered.

"Yes, she was, but she'd had the flu a few days before. Amanda told me when she called. Charlotte swam most evenings, but this time, she must have become ill again while she was in the water. With no one there to help her . . ."

"Do you know of anyone who would want to harm her? Had she had any problems with anyone? A former boyfriend, maybe? Any recent visitors?"

"No."

"Did you notice any changes in her behavior recently? Did she seem worried about anything? Had she had any disagreements or confrontations with the staff or anyone in town?"

Mrs. Collins shook her head, but Amanda chimed in.

"Wade did this," she said.

Monson let the silence lengthen. He wondered what her logic would be. If Wade was a gold digger hoping to marry into the family fortune, it didn't make sense to kill his fiancée before they tied the knot. Once married, he would be entitled to half of whatever money she had or might inherit. Before the wedding, he got nothing. Why kill her? He had no reason to.

Mrs. Collins remained silent, but Amanda sat back, arms folded triumphantly.

"They had a fight," she said.

Well, this certainly sheds new light on things.

"What about?" he asked.

"Like Grandmother said, the night before she left, we were all having dinner together. Wade invited himself, so he was there, too. There was a heated discussion."

Monson was having trouble keeping this woman on track. He'd asked about Wade's argument with Charlie, but now it seemed she was talking about an argument Charlie had with her grandmother.

"What about?" he asked.

"It was the same thing they always fought about. The Collins," she said. "Grandmother generously offered her a role in running the hotel, now that she'd put her through college."

"And Charlie didn't want that?" Monson said.

"No. Under Wade's influence, she wasn't interested," she said.

Grandma straightened up and, speaking in a stronger voice, her tears under control, explained.

"It's true. Wade filled Charlotte's mind with unrealistic plans to go save the world," she said. "One poor village at a time. Or so he said. But Wade was just a dreamer. None of that would have lasted. She would have tired of it eventually, but not before getting malaria or dying of a snakebite in some god-forsaken, filthy village. I raised Charlie. She was used to nice clothes, a warm bed, and more than just a roof over her head. Wade couldn't provide for her. He didn't want what was best for her."

"Which brings us back to Charlie's argument with Wade," Monson said. "When exactly did this happen? Can you describe exactly what you heard? Did you observe their disagreement directly?"

"It was earlier that evening," she said, "after dinner."

Mrs. Collins listened attentively. This was apparently news to her, too.

"What time was that?" he asked.

"Like I said, it was just after dinner, so around 6:30 p.m. I was at the front desk. They were around the corner in the hallway, just about to take the elevator up to her room—it was Charlie's room, he shouldn't have been here, but he always snuck in to stay with her whenever you left town, Grandmother."

Mrs. Collins nodded. This did not seem to be news to her.

"But the elevator was stuck. It's one of the things they're working on. You have to keep hitting the button to get it to go back up and come down again, then it works fine. So, they were standing there, waiting for it, when Charlie told him she'd changed her mind. Said she'd been thinking it over and was going to accept Grandmother's offer. Stay and run the hotel. Family came first. She said she just didn't love him enough to leave it all for him."

"What was Wade's reaction?" Monson said.

"At first he tried to talk her out of it," she said, "but then he went ballistic! Said he was tired of her family interfering with their lives, that he would never allow it."

"Did anyone else hear them?" Monson asked. "This must have been a pretty loud argument."

"No, I don't think so. Everyone else had gone home," she said. "And we had no other guests. Just that one woman who checked in late. She didn't get here until much later."

"This was Ms. Landers?"

"Yes."

"So, what happened next?"

"Nothing," she said. "I mean, the elevator finally got there. I heard the bell ding and the doors open, then their voices fading when they got in. But I could still hear them yelling at each other when the doors shut."

Monson sat back and got out a fresh notebook. This was going to take a while. He wondered if he should ask for more tea. And cookies . . . he'd finally given in and eaten three.

16

Detective Monson had continued badgering them with questions about Charlie for another hour, going over everything she'd already told him, but then wanting to know all about Wade's relationship with Charlie and what arrangements she had made for Charlie to inherit and take over the management of the hotel.

She saw no reason to withhold any of this information from him. To do so would only arouse suspicion. Yes, Charlie would have inherited quite a lot of money if she'd decided to stay and run The Collins.

The last thirty minutes of the interview, Monson directed most of his questions to Amanda and the argument she said she had overheard between Wade and Charlie Tuesday night. During all this, Mrs. Collins, claiming she needed more tea to settle her nerves, sat back and observed.

She had been such a fool. Deep inside, she knew Charlie wasn't coming back. She knew Charlie loved Wade and was strong enough to withstand a few mosquitoes and floods. She probably would have charmed the mosquitoes into pets and, with a wave of her hand, diverted the flood waters around the village. That was Charlie.

Charlie was never going to take over the hotel. She knew that now. It was a mistake to try to mold her favorite grandchild into someone she didn't want to be, force her to live a life she never wanted. Her dreams for Charlie were just wishful thinking. She could see that now. The thought made her infinitely sad.

So why was Amanda lying? Why was she pointing the finger at Wade? Was it to please her? She had to admit, that was pretty quick thinking on her part to invent that story. And, of course, she had. Wade and Charlie never argued.

And if Amanda had lied, why? To protect her? She couldn't possibly know about the poisoning, could she? Bootlicker that she was, she probably would lie to protect her, but how could she know she had accidentally poisoned Charlie? And did she know the rest? Did Amanda know why she fought so long and hard to keep Wade and Charlie from ever marrying and producing children?

Just how much did Amanda know?

Replenishing her tea from the thermal pot on the small table where Amanda had placed it, Mrs. Collins studied her eldest grandchild surreptitiously over the top of her mug, while sipping the scalding tea.

Amanda and the policeman's voices blurred and faded into the background as a long-ago memory began to surface.

○ ○ ○ ○ ○

It was the summer of 1999. Both girls had been sent out to stay with her for the month of August, as usual, by their mother, Dorothy. And she supposed, their father, Robert Schmitt, although he probably just rubber-stamped whatever his wife wanted. Not a bad man, but as far as she could tell, he was a distant and ineffectual father. Neither girl ever got homesick.

LIES THAT BIND

Charlie must have been about twelve. Amanda had just turned fifteen and had the pimples to prove it.

That summer was unusually warm for the coast and Charlie spent every waking minute outdoors—swimming, fishing and exploring. Tree climbing was a particular specialty. Amanda, on the other hand, preferred watching television or doing puzzles. When she wasn't in her room, she could be found hanging around the lobby, trying to ingratiate herself with the adults, guests and employees alike.

Charlotte wished Amanda, pudgy since birth, would spend more time in the fresh air—it would help her complexion she was sure, but summers were busy and she couldn't keep an eye on her granddaughters as she would have preferred, leaving them to their own devices.

But she always made sure they took dinner together in the private dining room. Just her and the girls. Emerson was sometimes there, but often had 'meetings' or other vaguely phrased business obligations that kept him away until late. She had no problem with his nightly wanderings. They'd kept separate bedrooms for years now.

That night—it must have been a Tuesday, because the weekenders had left and there was a slight lull between bookings, Amanda was at her place at the table on time—they always ate at 5:30 p.m. sharp—but Charlie's chair was empty.

"Where's your sister?" she asked.

She'd never forget the odd gleam in Amanda's eyes. It chilled her to the bone. But her face was all innocence.

"I don't know, Grandmother Charlotte, I haven't seen Charlie all day."

Then Amanda began loading up her plate from the dishes on the table.

"This dinner looks delicious, Grandmother Charlotte! It's rude of Charlie to be late."

Not knowing what to think, she checked in her room and then took the gardener with her to search the grounds. No Charlie. It stayed light a long time this far north, but the sky was definitely darkening. Soon they wouldn't be able to see her. Where could she be?

Just as panic started to set in, the gardener spotted a flash of white on the rocks off the back deck. She raced to the edge and leaned over the railing.

Lying motionless on a shelf of rock about thirty feet down, Charlie's white t-shirt glowed against the slick, black basalt. Her right arm bent underneath her at an odd angle.

There was no easy way down, but two of the hotel guests, a young man and his wife from California, were rock climbers and had mountain-climbing gear in their SUV. They had been sitting at a table on the deck, enjoying a glass of wine and the last remnants of sun when Charlie was discovered. Within minutes, they'd retrieved what they needed and rappelled down the cliff to bring her up. In the meantime, she had summoned the doctor in town. As a general rule, Dr. Cramer no longer made house calls, but he did for the Collins family.

He arrived just as they got Charlie into the house and onto the couch in the lobby, carefully avoiding moving her arm. She had come to and cried out with every jolt. She screamed even louder when the good doctor yanked on it. After examining her for any other injuries, Dr. Cramer straightened up and pronounced she was fine.

"Kids are amazingly resilient, Mrs. Collins," Dr. Cramer said, "Just a dislocated shoulder. Had the wind knocked out of her, that's all. Bring her to the office tomorrow morning. For tonight, just make sure she gets some rest."

Turning to his patient, who was now seated on the couch, he added, "What were you doing out there, anyway, Miss Trouble? Climbing around on those rocks is dangerous."

"Yes, I know," she said, darting a look at Amanda, who was seated primly next to her, hands folded in her lap. It was just a flicker, but for the first time ever, she saw fear flash briefly across Charlie's face.

"Promise me you'll be more careful, Charlie," Grandmother Charlotte remembered saying.

"I'll be more careful," she said, "I promise."

◇ ◇ ◇ ◇ ◇

Detective Monson stood up, handing Amanda his card.

"Well, that should be it for now," he said. "Feel free to call me at that number if either of you thinks of anything else over the next few days. Any time is fine."

"Allow me to express my condolences once again, Mrs. Collins," he added, reaching down to shake her hand.

Standing to show him out, she asked, "Where is she? When will we be able to . . . ?"

"She's temporarily located in a funeral home in town," he said. "Just procedure. Shouldn't need to be there long."

He took back his card and scribbled something on the back.

"Call this number," he said. "You can tell them where you'd like her taken, if you prefer a different funeral home."

17

An early riser, Olivia said she was up and in her bathing suit by 5:30 a.m. She made herself some coffee in her room, then, throwing on the white, waffle-weave spa robe she found in the closet, pushed her feet into flip flops and just before 6:00 a.m., went down the stairs at the end of the hall to do her laps.

"Were there any other guests? Did you see anyone else?" Logan asked.

"No," Olivia said. "If there were other guests, they must have been in bed or at least in their rooms already. I didn't see anyone."

Logan held back her barrage of questions, allowing Olivia to tell the story at her own pace.

Olivia said she found the pool area easily. Other than a restroom and some locked doors she assumed were storage closets, it was the only room on that level. Her key card opened the door, but the lights didn't come on. With the weak light from the hallway, she located a manual switch to the left of the door near a water fountain and flipped it on.

The pool wasn't as large as the Olympic-size pool she swam

in back home, but it was long enough for laps. She was looking forward to this swim.

Grabbing an oversized towel from a stack on a shelf next to the water fountain, she removed her robe and laid it over the back of one of two aluminum chairs nearby—the kind you always find at pools, bottom and sides woven from those strips of water-proof vinyl. The other chair already had a towel folded neatly on the seat. Blue, with a white stripe. A key card rested on top. She looked around, but the water was still and at first glance, she didn't see anyone else in the pool. Shrugging off her robe and kicking off her sandals, she walked over to the hand railing that led into the deep end of the pool.

That's when she saw it. Bobbing gently in the corner was a woman's body, mostly submerged, floating face down, probably pushed there by the artificial current directing debris to the filters. Short, dark hair fanned around her head, waving slowly, like a sick halo.

"I knew she was dead," Olivia whispered, "I did summers as a lifeguard—I mean, I was pretty sure, but I just couldn't leave her like that."

She hauled the body out of the pool, checked for a pulse just in case she was alive, then ran back to get her cell phone and dialed 911. The call wouldn't go through, she didn't have any bars so she ran back up the stairs to either get reception or find a phone.

Completely off topic, Logan wondered where there was a beach in New York. Maybe Olivia had been a pool guard. How funny that her sister had been a lifeguard, too. She and Rick had both certified. An unexpected point of similarity. Somehow it didn't fit her image of an uptight, desk-bound, New York attorney.

Olivia paused, fiddling with a French fry. She hadn't eaten much of her hamburger.

"That's about it, really," she said, squeezing her shoulder blades, letting out a breath.

"What time was that?" Sam asked, "What time did you try to call 911?"

"Uh, must have been just after 6:00 a.m.—she consulted her phone—6:07 a.m. It didn't go through."

"What did you do next?"

"Like I said, I ran upstairs. I needed to find a landline if I couldn't get cell reception," she said.

"Was anyone up? Who did you find to tell?" Sam asked.

"No one was at the desk yet, so I went into the dining area. I could hear people working in the kitchen, so I went back there. There were two people that I could see. A Latino man, the cook, and a young blonde girl. I really didn't get a good look at either of them. I was pretty rattled. The girl called 911 and the man got on a house phone and called the manager. She came right down. She was the one who let the police in when they got there," Olivia said.

"Did you catch her name?" Sam asked.

"Daspitt, I think. Amanda Daspitt. I heard her tell Monson she wasn't the official manager. The woman who normally handled the desk had gone down to Brookings to visit family during the remodel. Mrs. Daspitt was helping out while she was away," Olivia said. "It was odd, she may have been in shock, or I could have heard her incorrectly, but I think she said she was Charlie's sister, but I could be wrong."

"Short, sort of shaped like a fireplug? Dishwater blonde hair, dresses like a bank teller?"

Olivia nodded.

"That's her," Sam said, "I've only met her once. Cold fish that one. She's the older sister."

"Was anyone else there?" Logan asked.

"A man named Wade," Olivia said, "Charlie's fiancé."

Sam looked over at Logan, "Isn't that who you bought your house from?"

"Wade Ellis?" Logan asked Olivia.

"I didn't catch his last name. Black hair, average build, kind of ruddy cheeks?" Olivia said. "Is that him? Do you know him?"

"No, well, sort of. I mean we met him, but only once for the walk through, before Ben and I signed the papers for the house. He seemed like a nice guy. This must be awful for him."

Logan felt bad for him. She'd been through the death of a loved one and wished she could save him the pain. No one should have to go through that. Wade had just contacted her last week and said he'd come by to clear out a few boxes left up in the attic. They still had to arrange an exact time, but he was supposed to come out sometime tomorrow.

"He just fell apart when he heard," Olivia said. "He started running down the hall, tried to go down to the pool level, but they held him back before he made the stairs. The man was a mess. One of the officers took him in the bathroom to get himself together. He stayed with him until the EMTs got there. They were still checking him over and calming him down when Detective Monson arrived. I guess that's why he interviewed me first."

Logan noticed that Olivia seemed to be recovering slightly from the shock of discovering a dead body first thing in the morning. An intelligent curiosity, that must have served her well as an attorney, was asserting itself as she recalled the details of her experience.

"Who else was there?" Logan asked.

Olivia counted them off on her fingers, "Mrs. Daspitt, Wade, the two people in the kitchen, I don't know their names or what their jobs are or when they arrived or if they have rooms there, too. Those are the only people I saw. There could have been more somewhere else or people in their rooms that hadn't come down yet."

"What about the grandmother, Mrs. Collins?" Logan asked. "Where was she?"

"I didn't see anyone else. No older woman," Olivia said.

Sam spoke up, "I asked Rob the same thing. He hadn't seen her, either, but he had been outside for a while. She could have been upstairs. He was first to arrive, but after calling in the troops, he stayed outside, cordoning off the area. Since then he's been at the entrance securing the scene, checking people in and out."

"So she could have been in there—maybe up in her room?" Logan said.

"I don't know," Olivia said. "Even an elderly woman couldn't have slept through the scream Wade let out when they told him about his fiancée."

"Charlotte Collins is far from frail," Sam said. "If she were there, she'd be downstairs taking charge. Charlotte's a force to be reckoned with."

18

By the time they finished lunch, the sun was well over the yardarm.

Sam's boyfriend, Tim, finished with his errands in Lincoln City, swung by to pick her up. She said her goodbyes, making sure it was okay with Olivia to quote her in the full article. Tim was going to drop her off at The Collins. The newspaper photographer was meeting her there in a few minutes. Sam had already posted the pics she took with her phone and the bare bones story she had so far. Jerry would be very happy.

The News Herald was a weekly print paper, but due to Sam's encouragement and a forward- thinking new publisher, the Herald had been increasing its online presence in the last couple of years. This story would help. It was Sam's fondest dream to help drag the little paper into the twenty-first century.

After Sam left, Logan paid the bill while Olivia went to the bathroom. Now she just needed to decide what to do with her. Olivia was going to need a place to stay tonight. The Collins hotel, now a crime scene, was obviously out and her place was hardly fit for company.

Logan started thumbing through her phone for options, but when they got in the car, Olivia surprised her.

"Look, I know you said your place isn't finished yet, but you've got the essentials, right? Running water, electricity . . . flush toilet? I am absolutely okay with camping out on the floor."

Logan thought about it. She had Ben's cot, her cot, and some sleeping bags. There were plenty of blankets. And with the new water heater, they wouldn't run out of hot water. Coming from the big city, she figured Olivia would be a pampered, picky New Yorker, but she was proving to more down-to-earth than expected.

"Well, if you don't mind roughing it, you're more than welcome," Logan said. The fireplace works, so it's toasty at night. Are you sure you don't mind? Depoe Bay's hotel offerings are limited, but I'm sure we can find you a nice place here or in Lincoln City or Newport if you'd rather."

"Are you kidding? What's the fun in that? I came down here to get to know my big sister. I can't do that very well by staying in a hotel." Olivia flashed a perfect smile.

Orthodontia and laser whitening, no doubt, Logan thought ungenerously. Their father couldn't afford orthodontia after Sofia left. Rick had always been self-conscious about his distinct overbite. Still, that wasn't Olivia's fault.

"Well, okay. If you're up for it, the house isn't far from here. Do you want me to drop you off so you can lay down for a while? I need to make a quick run down to Chester's to stock the ice chest—I eat out for most meals, but I've got a cooler for backup. No refrigerator yet, the kitchen's still torn up."

Technically still in Depoe Bay, Chester's was a small market about fifteen minutes north of town, kind of in the middle of nowhere. Ten feet off the highway, other than an adjoining coffee shop, its nearest neighbors were cedars and pines.

"I'm good. I'll go with you," Olivia said. "Do you mind if we pick up my car first?"

"Not at all," Logan said, turning left instead of right on Highway 101. Chester's was north.

"I don't trust the police," Olivia explained.

Logan raised her eyebrows and looked over at her. Typical attorney response. She wondered if Olivia knew her half-brother, Rick was a cop back in Jasper.

"There's no reason for them to go through my car, but I know the police. Even without a warrant, they'll comb through whatever's around, looking for whatever they can use."

Logan couldn't argue the point. She knew how a lot of cops—Rick being the exception—operated. Look now, get warrant later. Shave the corners to make the pieces fit. Well, at least find pieces that mostly fit and make a good picture, even if it wasn't the right one.

At Chester's, Olivia put fruit, granola, and yogurt in the cart. Logan added a big hunk of Tillamook cheddar cheese, crackers, and Oreos. In a nod to health, she threw in some oatmeal cookies. She wanted ice cream, but knew the cooler wouldn't keep it cold enough. She liked her vanilla bean rock hard.

They did agree on the wine, however. Olivia insisted on buying and seemed to know what she was doing, so Logan let her pick out a red and a white she'd never heard of, but were from the top shelf. All above her budget, so they were probably good.

On the way out of the store, Olivia asked if she knew of anyplace that had good caramel corn. Logan grinned. Ainsley's had *great* caramel corn. She was addicted to it.

"Absolutely, we can pick some on the way back so it'll be fresh," she said. "Follow me, it's not far."

Wine and caramel corn—she might like this sister thing after all.

19

"It's a girl!" the nurse said, smiling down, smoothing a couple of strands of hair off her young patient's slick forehead. "You did very well, Mrs. Ellis."

A small, resigned nod was the only indication Mrs. Irene Ellis had heard.

It being his fourth delivery of the night, the doctor had nothing to add. He cut the umbilical cord and handed the newborn off to his nurse to clean and wrap for presentation to the mother, then dragged his sleepy self to his next patient. There was nothing more for him to do. This was her second child. She hadn't torn and he hadn't had to do an episiotomy.

The new mother's reaction—or lack thereof—was odd, the nurse thought, but maybe she was just exhausted. It had been a tough delivery, on top of seven hours of hard labor. But still, most mothers couldn't wait to see their new babies. Most mothers' eyes hungrily searched for that first glimpse, and to a woman, couldn't wait to hold their precious new infant.

Not this mother. Nurse Taylor shrugged and went briskly about her business. A few minutes later, when she returned with the freshly swaddled newborn, Mrs. Ellis kept her arms stiffly by her side, fists clenched, and turned her head to the wall. Squeezing her eyes shut for good measure, she refused to even look at her child. A few hot tears rolled down her face onto the pillow.

Well, you never knew.

Obviously, there was a story here and from the looks of it, a sad one. But whatever the story, this beautiful baby was no part of it. It wasn't her fault her mother didn't seem to want her. This innocent, new life did not deserve to be rejected. Like all children, she deserved to be loved! Whatever sad burden this young mother carried—and after her seventeen years at Salem Hospital, Nurse Taylor had no doubt it must be a truly terrible one for her to reject her own child—this was her daughter, and like women before her, she needed to square her shoulders and take care of her. This tiny baby girl deserved a chance. And it was her job to make sure she got it.

Wisely, Nurse Taylor followed her regular routine, introducing mother and child, without additional comment. A junior nurse had already freshened the bed and seen to Mrs. Ellis.

First, she tucked some pillows behind the woman's back and shoulders until she was more or less in a seated position. Then, without asking for permission, lay the infant against her mother's breast, guiding her mouth to the nipple, which was already dripping. It didn't always happen this easily, but this little girl began sucking greedily on her first try.

LIES THAT BIND

Excellent!

Mrs. Ellis' body knew how to love the child, even if her heart didn't, yet.

Satisfied she had done all she could do for now, Nurse Taylor left mother and baby alone to get to know each other. An eighteen-year old girl had just been admitted. First-timers always needed hand holding. She'd try to come back by to check on Baby Ellis and mother at the end of her shift.

❁ ❁ ❁ ❁ ❁

NOVEMBER 24, 1932
DISCHARGE DESK
SALEM COMMUNITY HOSPITAL

Blowing on the paper to dry the ink, Irene looked at the momentous lie she held in her hand.

Certificate of Live Birth
Child's Name: Mara Ellis
Sex: Female
Date of Birth: November 13, 1932
Father: Jacob Ellis
Mother: Irene Amanda Ellis
Place of Residence: 354 Barber Road, Depoe Bay, Oregon

She clamped her mouth into a firm line and handed it back to the clerk.

Well, most of it was true, anyway.

Irene didn't like being untruthful, but given her options, she felt she'd made the right decision. She'd had nine months to think about it. Touching the ink with the pad of her finger to make sure it was dry, she handed the official document over to the clerk behind the counter, who was saying something about her receiving the official copy in the mail in the next few weeks. Sometimes it took a while, so she was to watch for it.

At least she'll have a name.

Irene looked down at the tiny infant sleeping in her arms.

Mara *Ellis.*

Having this baby wasn't her first choice. Her first urge had been to get rid of it, this unholy life, to scrape the filth from her body as quickly as possible. But it wasn't that easy. She had Aaron to think of. Her four-year old son needed her. And then there was the threat. If she told anyone what he'd done, Frankie said he would tell everyone she was a willing participant. She had been too afraid to tell anyone what happened at the time. Now, who would believe her?

She wouldn't have known where to go, anyway. There were rumors about a doctor in Tillamook who could be persuaded to help girls who got in trouble. But she had no money to pay for the procedure and no way to get there even if she did. He probably wouldn't help a married woman, anyway, especially one whose husband couldn't give his permission, because he was missing.

Irene had also heard the gruesome stories. Sometimes girls died after the trip to Tillamook. She couldn't risk having Aaron lose both his father and mother in one year. Her parents would care for him, of course, if anything happened to her. But they were old, and her father had little patience for children, particularly rowdy, headstrong little boys who ate strawberries off the vine in his garden, then laughed and ran away, no matter how many times she told him not to.

She didn't know what she would tell Jacob if he ever came

home. She couldn't imagine what he would do if she told him the truth. For starters, probably kill Frankie.

So, she settled on the lie—told everyone she was expecting Jacob's child. For any old biddies doing the math, it would add up well enough. Jacob hadn't been missing a week when Frankie showed up. Frankie hadn't lost any time taking what wasn't his.

Just thinking about the afternoon Frankie weaseled his way into the house made her sick. Jacob had been missing for a week. He stopped by, he said, to see if Jacob had come home yet or if there was anything he could do. He'd brought a box of groceries, so she let him in to put it on the table. He must have timed it so her in-laws weren't home and Aaron was with her mother. Or maybe he was just lucky. She certainly hadn't been.

No sooner had he put the groceries down on the table, then he was right there in front of her. The sheer menace emanating from him rooted her to the floor. Leaning slightly forward, a cruel smile playing on his lips, he started walking her back into the bedroom. The slanting rays of the afternoon sun lit up his shock of red hair and glinted off the bright blade of the long knife he held in front of him, aimed at her stomach. She'd been stunned, and so afraid. She drew in a breath to scream, but he waggled the knife. He said if she yelled or resisted him in any way, he'd tell her son and Jacob's folks that she had tempted him into her bed. It still caused a wave of shame and anger to pour over her so powerful it made her shake.

She'd never liked Frankie. She'd tried to talk Jacob out of associating with him, but they'd been friends for a long time. He said he wasn't so bad once you got to know him. A couple of months earlier, Frankie told him about a job down in Florence he could get him every other week or so. It was boring, just making some deliveries, but Jacob was grateful for the work. Jacob said the work was easy and it paid well. He promised her he would just do it until he could find something steady closer to home.

And they didn't waste the windfall. They saved every penny they could. Irene knew how badly Jacob wanted to move out and get a place of their own. Jacob already put a down payment on a piece of land which they were planning on turning into a motor lodge. There was a second building on the lot where they could add a small grocery store. Jacob said they should add gas pumps out front, because so many more people were driving to the coast now, it would pay for itself in no time.

All that was gone, now. When Jacob hadn't been able to make the next payment, she went to see the owner, Mr. Woodrow. He met her at the door with folded arms. Wouldn't even let her inside. Said he would only deal with her husband. And since her husband had chosen to disappear, the down payment would be forfeited. Told her he had no intention of doing business with a woman, even if she were to come up with the rest of the money.

20

With the fourth of July just a few days away, preparations for Depoe Bay's holiday bash were in full swing. Red, white, and blue bunting brightened the bridge, shops were fully stocked and festooned with American flags, and this year The Collins Hotel had even imported special fireworks from Liuyang, China.

Most holidays attracted vacationers from Portland to the coast, but the Fourth of July could usually be counted on to at least double the population of the coastal towns of Depoe Bay, Lincoln City, and Newport. All the hotels and inns were booked months in advance, but for anyone who was anyone, the luxurious Collins Hotel was the place to see and be seen.

The proprietor, Frank Collins, was a lively host. Also, the town mayor, the man's wiry form, topped by a shock of red hair could be easily spotted around town, yakking it up with locals and tourists alike. Frank did more schmoozing than governing. His wife, Rowena, ran the hotel.

Rumor had it the only reason the Fitzgeralds, a prominent logging family in the area, allowed Frank to marry their eldest daughter was the fact that he had already established himself as an up and coming young man of some means. Frank didn't come from money and he never seemed to work very hard, but somewhere along the line, he'd gotten his hands on a small fortune. No one seemed to know or care how. A lot of fortunes were gained and lost in the rough and tumble thirties.

Frank's money and Rowena's taste made The Collins the showpiece it was. When Prohibition was repealed, Frank added an expansive dance hall, making it an even more popular destination.

Frank could usually be found holding court at the bar. The couple was rarely seen together, as each had established comfortable roles for themselves in the town. Quick with a smile and endowed with tons of energy, Frank could be counted on to buy the house a round or impulsively gift someone a new boat if he were in the mood. Rowena stayed in the background, chairing various charitable committees and running the hotel. She made sure to employ as many locals as possible. In turn, they were pretty much accepted as Depoe Bay's first family.

Rowena's main job, though, was spoiling their one and only child, Emerson. Everyone has a blind spot. Emerson was hers. Never constrained or made to work, the boy had copious amounts of free time on his hands and was given the run of the town. Subsequently, he didn't have many friends. Most kids his age were children of hard-working locals: commercial fisherman, charter boat captains, or shop owners. They went to the small public school on the south end of town, helping out in their family businesses after school and on weekends.

Once, a fisherman caught Emerson setting a fire on the deck of his boat, just for the fun of it. The fisherman didn't report him to his parents or the police, just whooped his butt good. The boy wouldn't be bothering his boat again. The kid was a bad egg, but he wasn't stupid. He knew even his mother couldn't buy him out of that kind of trouble.

"Idle hands are the devil's workshop," the fisherman told his wife.

Bringing the full force of her ambitions for him to bear, Rowena hired private tutors for Emerson. When he was old enough, she drew upon family connections back east and, after making a generous Collins arts endowment, eventually got him into a good college. Not Yale, which was her first choice—his grades just weren't good enough for that—but one with some East Coast polish on the diploma.

The town was glad to see him go.

The Collins Hotel always put on a good Fourth of July show, but this year they were also celebrating Emerson's graduation and engagement. After five years, he'd finally managed to accomplish both feats, squeaking by with a general business degree, and securing the promise, if not the affections, of a beautiful but impoverished southern belle named Charlotte Lee Abbott of the Georgia Abbotts. The diminutive, raven-haired young woman knew exactly the kind of man she was getting.

A pragmatic steel magnolia, as the years passed, she would keep the hotel mainly as it was, only adding a greenhouse out back to indulge her love of flowers, and bringing soft, Southern touches to the property, inside and out. But for now, she would keep a low profile and be the obedient daughter-in-law.

For the next two days, though, Emerson was on his own. Charlotte would be arriving in time for the main events, but was still making the trek across country from Georgia. Rowena was sending him in a car to pick her up in Portland.

❍ ❍ ❍ ❍ ❍

Leaning against the doorway to Room 19, scotch in hand, Emerson admired the generous backside before him. Mara Ellis. Quite the little worker bee.

After being away for several years, he almost hadn't recognized her. She wasn't much taller, but she'd filled out. In all the right places.

He'd known Mara since they were kids. He remembered a scrawny little girl who used to tag along and help her mother, Irene, clean the rooms. He hadn't seen the mother in years. Probably too old to handle the heavy lifting. Rowena Collins didn't keep anyone on who couldn't keep up with the work, and there was always plenty of that. His mother squeezed every last ounce of labor out of all of her employees. Tough boss.

Needless to say, their families didn't socialize. Now that he thought of it, his mother hadn't allowed him to socialize with any of the children in town.

He turned his attention back to Mara. She still had that fire engine-red hair, a single, thick braid down her back, just waiting to be grabbed. One of Irene Ellis's two snotty kids who never seemed to have properly fitting clothes. They had a father, but he had deserted the family before Mara was even born. Left his wife and two kids without a penny to their name. Just disappeared one night—no one ever heard from him again.

Emerson didn't like red hair. He was glad his father's copper mop skipped a generation with him. He was grateful to his mother's side of the family for his sandy-colored, if thinning, hair.

But for Mara, he'd make an exception. The blue maid's uniform pulled tightly over her equally tight bottom as she bent over to pick up some trash behind a potted schefflera next to the window. Mara was nothing like the languid, long-legged Southern women he'd been bedding at college the last four years. No, Mara was straightforward and intense. She seemed hungry for something. Her compact body made him want to take her—violently—each time he saw her. And although she put up a fight the first time, since then, she'd let him take her whenever and wherever he wanted. She was a simple creature. There was no nuance or manipulation with Mara.

Each time they rutted, he saw the naked ambition in her eyes, on her face. She probably had the hilarious thought that by putting out so willingly, she would soon become Mrs. Emerson Collins! Well, the *real* future Mrs. Collins would be here tomorrow. But Mara didn't know that. His mother was planning on making the announcement at the party.

Emerson smiled, set his glass down on the dresser, and closed the door behind him.

Better make hay while the sun shone . . .

21

In spite of—or maybe because of—all that happened yesterday, Logan slept soundly and woke with the sun. She still couldn't believe that poor young woman had drowned in her family's hotel pool or that Olivia had made the grisly discovery.

She put Olivia in the downstairs bedroom, giving her some privacy, but they'd wound up dragging both makeshift beds in front of the fireplace in the living room last night.

Still bundled in her sweats, Logan padded across the bare floor to the bathroom. It was freezing, but a hot shower helped. On his last visit, Ben had rigged a shower curtain around the inside of the white enameled, clawfoot bathtub. It worked great. They'd put in a forty-gallon hot water heater, but Logan kept her shower short in case Olivia wanted to take one. She made sure there was a clean towel folded on the corner of the tub, got dressed, and went back into the living room.

Stoking the embers, but waiting to throw on a new log, Logan looked out of the window to check the weather. There was a gray haze of clouds, but at least it wasn't raining. She'd have to see if Olivia was up for a run before breakfast. She wanted to get to Pirate's before they ran out of breakfast burritos.

They'd stayed up well past midnight, sitting opposite each other on their cots, as close to the fireplace as they could get, wrapped in jackets and sleeping bags. Warmed by the fire and the wine—it was excellent—they had filled each other in about their respective lives, still careful to avoid any talk which might bring up the touchy subject of their mother, Sofia.

To their mutual surprise, they discovered that in spite of being fourteen years apart in age and brought up on opposite coasts of the United States, they had a lot in common. Both were athletic, good at math, and weren't into sororities or doing their nails. They both worked what used to be considered non-traditional jobs for women—lifeguard, musician, technology—Logan in the computer business she started with her husband before he died and Olivia in law offices. Although it was no longer unusual in 2020 for women to be lawyers, Hale & Patterson was almost entirely male—all the partners were, at least. Olivia said someone would probably have to die for her to be brought in. She knew it was a boys' club going in, but it was a good firm and she was getting a lot of experience in different areas of the law. Currently, she was working a lot of criminal cases. She said she'd stay another two years and then move on if things didn't happen for her there.

In turn, Logan shared her recent disastrous foray into public education. After Jack died, she'd tried being a teacher, but quickly realized she wasn't cut out for it. She loved the kids, she just didn't get the petty, bulletin board wars between some of the teachers and the constant focus put on test scores over the well-rounded education she felt all students deserved. Luckily for her, she landed on her feet directing Fractals. It was a much better fit.

When Olivia asked her what her program was all about, Logan groaned. This was the toughest part of what she did—trying to explain it to people. She started by telling Olivia how a lot of brain research showed that music and math are intricately connected, and that learning both skills together builds new neural pathways—making your brain work better in lots of other areas, too. Research also showed that kids learn and retain more of what they learned when learning is fun!

So, with grant writing and the generous support of a few inspired private parties, Fractals ensured kids from kindergarten through high school in the program received music instruction—including composition as well as performance, played math/music games on their computers, developed true numeracy through mental math competitions, created their own musical instruments, and coded new software programs. Last year, Logan had even wrangled a professor at UC Irvine into offering a cross-cultural music course for high school seniors wanting to earn college credit focusing on the commonalities and differences in musical forms and functions across cultures.

"What about you? Do you play?" Logan asked.

"Not really. I took piano lessons as a kid, but never went much beyond Für Elise or Clair de Lune," she said. "Once I got into swimming and track, that's all I wanted to do. In law school, there wasn't any time."

"Do you?" Olivia asked. "I assume you must," she nodded toward the violin case in the bedroom. "Is that yours? I'm afraid I can't serenade you with chopsticks—no piano—but I'd love to hear you play. If you don't mind."

Far from minding, Logan was itching to play. Music was her go-to stress reliever. Lately, she'd been playing her violin, Bella, every night. Being up here alone, she'd even had time to do some composing. Something about this area made her need to express something—convey the sight of graceful cedar branches dipping and waving in the wind, the feel of the delicate, soft western hemlock leaves—or were they needles? The spongy layer of leaves, moss, and earth mounded along the forest floor behind their house. And the ocean . . . another whole feeling. She didn't know how or what would come of it, but the Pacific Northwest was definitely spurring her to create.

She didn't have anything ready to share yet, so after tuning up, Logan rolled through some of her favorites. The night felt close and the stars could not be seen out the window. Flames leaped and crackled behind the grate. Olivia pulled her sleeping bag tighter around her shoulders. The soft darkness called for songs in a minor key. For the next hour, Logan became one with Bella, lost in the music, playing melancholy ballads and the plaintive, Scotch lullabies Amy loved when she was little. Tales of faraway lands, mystical *selkies* teaching *bairns* to swim in the *faem*.

When Olivia woke, she scored points by only taking a few minutes to do her morning ablutions. Logan was already waiting by the door, zipping up her jacket. For a moment, she caught their reflection, standing side by side in the long, entryway mirror. Straight and tall, they definitely looked related. Logan marveled again at having a sister, even if technically, she was only a half-sister.

Slightly slimmer and an inch shorter than Logan, Olivia's smooth, caramel brown hair fell forward as she bent over to tie her shoes. Her skin was pale, almost milky white. Logan, on the other hand, was tan year-round, with a smattering of freckles sprinkled across her nose, cheeks and the tops of her shoulders. Both sisters were in good shape.

Another thing the two shared was a healthy appetite. They'd polished off the caramel corn in front of the fire and planned to pick up some more to fuel a movie marathon tonight. African Queen, the Maltese Falcon, or Casa Blanca . . . anything they could find online would do. They'd have to watch it on one of their laptops since she didn't have cable yet, but neither of them minded. For now, Olivia was staying on at least another couple of days and Logan was determined to do her best to help her forget the tragedy she'd witnessed at the hotel.

22

Logan wasn't sure whether to lock the house while they went on their run, or leave it open. She still hadn't heard from Wade. He was supposed to come by sometime this morning and clear out a few remaining items in the attic, but given the fact his fiancée just died, she didn't know if that was still on. She would certainly understand if he didn't make it. In the end, she decided to leave the house unlocked just in case, but she and Olivia locked their laptops in the car and took their ID and phones with them.

Taking the lead, Logan started at an easy pace down Baird, then picked up speed as they ran along the spine of the town via Williams, down Collins and across Highway 101. Other than a few cars and trucks when they got to the highway, they had the streets to themselves. They found a comfortable, easy rhythm, ending their run at Pirate's. Gloves and hats stuffed in their pockets, they ordered, then took their coffee and breakfast burritos out to the sea wall to look for whales.

Logan was hoping one would show itself, but there weren't any yet. They must still be enjoying the warm waters of Baja. Hopefully they'd be cruising by in March with their calves.

She promised to send Olivia pictures if she didn't get to see any while she was here.

Even if it was only for a few days, Logan was glad she and Olivia had some time together. She worried Olivia would be traumatized by what she had seen yesterday—finding that young woman drowned must have been awful—but she seemed to be handling it.

They returned to the house around 9:00 a.m. and got to work in the living room. It was still chilly, so Logan stoked the fire and brought in more wood. Nothing like the smell and crackle of a real wood fire. She'd need to ask Clay where she could get a good deal on firewood. He probably knew someone—Clay knew everybody in town.

With Logan and Ben's help, Clay had ripped out all the old carpets, revealing usable hardwood floors in several of the rooms, including this one, which Logan had sanded and stained. The new baseboards looked great, but the subcontractor put them in only primed, not painted. Clay assured her he'd have him come back and do it properly, but the guy had already taken another job and it would be three weeks before he could fix it. Not wanting to wait, Logan said she'd handle it. Olivia said she'd help, so that's the project they tackled this morning.

They laid tarps across the gleaming floors to protect them, and with windows open and Prime Music filling the house with Tchaikovsky's piano concerto No. 1 in B-flat Minor, dipped one-inch brushes into the glossy paint, transforming the baseboards from chalky white to a rich color called appropriately, Ivory Keys.

Forty-five minutes later, Olivia sat back on her heels. They'd made it more than half way around the room. Logan got up and opened the door to let in more light so they could admire their handiwork.

"Oh, yeah!" Logan said.

"That looks great!" Olivia agreed.

Just then, a shadow fell across the floor. They turned to see a dark-haired man leaning slightly in, knocking on the open door.

"Hello?"

Logan squinted into the bright light to see who it was.

"Oh, Wade, please, come in," she said, laying her paint brush down across the top of the paint can she'd been using.

When he saw Olivia, Wade hesitated.

"Oh," Logan said. "Sorry. Wade, this is my sister Olivia. Olivia, Wade Ellis."

Olivia waved her paint brush at him.

"Good to see you, Wade. We sort of met yesterday," she said. "At the hotel."

"Yes, the detective talked to you just before he interviewed me," he said.

Logan took a step toward the door, gesturing to Wade. "Please, come in."

Wade stepped gingerly onto the tarp, looking awkward.

"I wasn't sure you were coming," Logan said, "after all that happened."

She reached over and tapped on the key pad of her laptop to pause the music. "I am so sorry. I can't imagine how you must be feeling. We can do this another time if you want. Or I can have someone pull out whatever boxes and things are up there and have them delivered to you."

She didn't know where he was staying since he'd sold her his house. It probably wasn't The Collins, because according to Sam, Wade was *persona non gratis* there. The grandmother hadn't approved of his engagement to Charlie.

"I wasn't, either," Wade said. "But there's nothing else I can do right now. They're taking care of all the funeral arrangements and everything. It's going to be a big service, I'm sure.

"Not what Charlie would have wanted," he added.

His eyes watered and he looked at loose ends. Logan felt sorry for him. She knew from experience that pity and gushes of emotion were the last thing people needed at a time like this. After Jack died, one kind word could undo her.

She took charge.

"Well, I was just about to take a break here, anyway," she said. "Let's you and me go tackle that attic. There's a ladder in the garage I think will be tall enough."

Olivia said she'd finish the last length of baseboard, while they still had plenty of daylight.

Getting everything down from the attic wasn't too difficult, but there were more boxes than could fit in Wade's car. Logan opened the garage door and he backed his car in about half way. After stuffing the back seat, trunk, and the front passenger seat, they stacked the remaining boxes in a corner of the garage, under a small, side window.

"I'll come back tomorrow to get these," he said.

"Do you have a place to stay tonight?" Logan asked, unable to stifle her mothering instincts. The young man looked so sad and alone.

"I'm fine, thanks," he said, "I'm staying with a friend of mine in Newport. He said I could camp out there until after the funeral."

"Well, at least come inside for a drink first," Logan said, "I've got a cooler with Coke, bottled water, or beer. I think Ben left a Sam Adams."

Wade accepted the offer and followed her back inside. Olivia had finished the baseboards and they all stood around, drinking their beverage of choice as Wade answered Logan's questions about the house. His childhood reflected some of her own, growing up in a small, oceanside town, although Depoe Bay was more remote than Jasper.

Before he left, Logan asked if he'd like to take a walk through the house and see the work they'd done so far. They were heading back down the stairs after seeing the three-quarter bathroom she and Ben had added upstairs, when they heard a car come into the driveway, blocking Wade's car. Doors opened and gravel crunched as the occupants walked up to the house, then clomped up the wooden stairs. Unfortunately, Logan recognized them.

"Ms. McKenna," Detective Monson said, nodding to Logan.

Then to Olivia, "Ms. Landers."

Logan recognized the second, younger man as Detective Grant. He stood slightly behind and to the left of his partner, remaining silent.

Neither was smiling—and they were looking over Logan's shoulder into the house, directly at Wade.

23

APRIL 1972

OREGON STATE HOSPITAL

SALEM, OR

"**I** can't handle him, anymore," she said, erupting into tears.

Handing her a tissue, Dr. Weston sat back in his chair and waited for the woman to compose herself. One of the managing directors of the Oregon State Hospital (OSH), he didn't usually meet with family members of incoming patients, but recently decided he needed to get back in touch with the real work of this place—not just the paperwork. He hadn't become a doctor to push paper.

He looked at the mother sitting across from him. He'd given her son a complete examination, but he needed to learn more about the family before he decided on a final diagnosis. Mental illness wasn't caused by a bad home life, but it often went hand in hand. He glanced down at intake report. Mother—late thirties. Unmarried. Probably didn't help.

Clenching the tissue tightly in her hands, she startled him with a surprisingly direct gaze, "He wasn't always like this," she said.

"No, I'm sure he wasn't. These problems don't always manifest until the child hits puberty," he said, looking down at the intake form. "Your son is . . ."

"Fifteen, he turned fifteen years old last October, on the twenty-first," she said. "Everything was normal then. It was a lovely dinner," she added. "It's just the two of us and I always make his favorite on his birthday, chicken and dumplings. And carrot cake. He loves the cream cheese frosting."

Dr. Weston's assessment of the boy's home life shifted just a little. Carrot cake was his favorite, too. He leaned forward.

"All right. Start from the beginning. When did you first notice a change in your son, in . . . ," he looked down at his paper, ". . . Archer?"

He pulled out a legal pad to take notes. "And please don't hold anything back. I can't help your son if I don't know everything."

"Well, like I said, he's always been normal. Then, he just started changing. He used to be a regular, happy boy. Had friends, loved to fish and play ball. It was just after Christmas, I noticed it. He started getting tired and sad. He'd stare off into space—almost like he wasn't there, like he he'd gone someplace else. Didn't want to go to school or play with his friends. Wanted to sleep all the time. Wouldn't change his clothes or let me wash them.

"When I tried to talk to him about it, he got really mad—started yelling at me and stomping off, slamming the door. Other mothers complain about their children being disrespectful, but Archer and me—we've always gotten along. He never talked back to me. Like I said, it's been just the two of us. But, now, it's like he's someone else."

She looked down at her hands in her lap, "A lot worse than just talking back."

"Anything else? What made you decide to bring him here?" Weston asked. He knew he hadn't gotten the full story.

For a minute, nothing. Then, a simple statement.

"He came at me with a knife."

The admission almost undid her, but she held it together. He had to admire that about her. Strong woman. She might make it through this.

"He'd been getting worse. I'd taken to locking him in his room at night, but last week our neighbor, Mr. Nichols, said something to him about the garbage piling up on the side of our house—told Archer he needed to clean that up before rats got in. That's always been Archer's job. He used to keep our place nice, took pride in it—but the look he gave Mr. Nichols. I was so scared. Mr. Nichols is a large man, but even he clamped his mouth shut and went back inside. His last words to me before he shut the door were, "You've got to do something about that boy.""

Archer just stood there, shaking, talking to himself. I finally got him to come back inside, but he grabbed a knife from the kitchen counter where I'd been making dinner and came after me, his face all twisted like I've never seen it."

Dr. Weston quickly looked her over for injuries, but didn't see any.

"How did you stop him?"

"I didn't. The neighbor was watching and ran over and knocked the knife out of his hand," she said, "He wrestled him to the ground and I ran for the doctor. Doc gave him a shot that calmed him down so we could drive him out here."

She looked at him imploringly, "What is wrong with him, Doctor? What does he have? Is it something you can fix or is this . . . will he always be like this? I can't bear the thought of him living in a place like this . . . I just want him well enough to come home."

Dr. Weston decided to be honest with this woman about her son's condition.

"Miss Ellis," he said, "let's take this one step at a time. "I've given your son a full, medical assessment and from my exam and what you've told me today, my preliminary assessment is that Archer very likely has paranoid schizophrenia."

He let this sink in. Mara Ellis's eyes brimmed with tears.

Dr. Weston leaned forward. "I know that sounds frightening, but we are learning more and more about schizophrenia every day and this is a treatable disease, assuming the patient receives help in a hospital such as ours, and follows the treatment protocols."

A glimmer of hope shone in Mara's eyes.

"There are new drugs we are finding effective, such as chlorpromazine. An antipsychotic, it helps with the voices, which your son says he hears."

"Voices?"

"Yes, your son's view of reality is not the same as yours. Paranoid schizophrenics often hear voices telling them to do things or simply harassing them," he said.

He waited to gauge how much more this mother was able to hear.

"But, please don't give up hope. We have many treatments here—not just drugs—electroshock therapy, and a whole hydrotherapeutic wing. I am starting a work rehabilitation and training program for patients just like Archer. Work is very good medicine for these patients, Miss Ellis. Some of our patients can eventually earn grounds privileges."

"So does that mean he can be cured? How long will it take?"

she asked. "Will he be able to come home? Will he ever be able to live a normal life outside?"

"Let's take it a day at a time, shall we?" Dr. Weston said. "We want to make sure he is stabilized and is not a danger to himself or others before even talking about that. This is not a quick process."

He began gathering the papers on his desk, tucking them back into the file folder labeled Archer Ellis. He needed to make his rounds soon.

His patient's mother sat up a little straighter in her chair, waiting for his attention again. When he looked up, she asked, "What about payment? How much will all this cost? I can send some, but I don't have much. I work as a maid on the coast. We live out in Depoe Bay."

Dr. Weston's face brightened, "Depoe Bay! My family used to summer on the coast every year . . . Agate Beach . . . filling our buckets with clams, pulling mussels off the rocks. Great memories!"

Then he stopped himself, realizing this woman didn't want to hear about his family vacations.

"As for the treatments, it's true some require extra fees, but we can talk about that if it is decided Archer needs those therapies," he said. "This is a state hospital, and as you and your son are residents of the state of Oregon, the basic costs of treatment are covered. And as I said, as soon as he is able, Archer will be working to earn his keep."

"It gives them a sense of pride," he added, ushering her to the door.

He tried to sound positive, but he knew it would be a very long time before Archer Ellis ever came home again, and when he did, things would never be the same. Life as she had known it was over.

24

After carefully taking his seat on the wobbly, plastic chair, twenty-three-year old Wade Ellis looked over his shoulder across a sea of mortarboards behind him and spotted his mother, shielding her face from the sun with one hand, fanning herself with a program with the other. She and Suzi had arrived early, so got front row seats in the family section.

Mother was wearing the same dress she'd worn to Suzi's high school graduation last week—her new Easter dress. She usually wore jeans and sweatshirts on the coast, where it was cooler, but Easter dresses were non-negotiable. One of the few luxuries she allowed herself. Even at her age, his mother was a striking woman. Her dark hair was shot with gray, but still full, and although he couldn't see them, he knew his mom's eyes were shining with pride.

Eighteen-year-old Suzi, arms folded, long legs sticking straight out from under a tight, belted mini-dress, punctuated with some kind of clunky, boot shoes—he had no idea why those were in style—slouched on her mom's left. His sister, still gangly, had the same coloring as her mom, but had yet to grow into her mother's good looks. He was sure Suzi would rather be out with her friends than sitting through a graduation ceremony, but pouting or not, he was glad she was here. He needed to spend more time with her. He'd come home when he could, but he'd been so busy the last four years.

He waved at her, but she was looking at her phone.

He was surprised they'd made it at all. Dad was getting worse; his mother had said. He wasn't well enough to make the trip. He'd need to be recommitted soon.

If he'd just take his medicine . . .

But Wade knew this was a pointless wish. Archer Ellis had a mind of his own. It was the same every time. When he first got out of the hospital, he'd promised to follow all of the doctor's instructions. He loved his wife; he loved his family. He wanted to come home and stay home. But after a year or two, he didn't think he needed the pills and the cycle would repeat itself. Eventually, Mom would be calling the doctor and she and Wade would be driving him out to the local hospital where he would be transported to Salem. Sometimes, the sheriff's office had to help.

Wade didn't know how his mother did it. Mrs. Pamela Fowler Ellis was a saint. Who else would have stayed with a man diagnosed with schizophrenia? And it wasn't like she didn't know what she was getting in for. She knew about his illness when she met him. He could have hidden it from her— he was in a good place, then, but he'd been up front about it even though his illness wasn't manifesting at the time. Wade had to give him that. His father had been honest.

Well, he probably didn't have much choice, it would become obvious soon enough—his dad couldn't have kept it hidden from her forever. The highs were always followed by the lows. He had her meet with the doctor up in Salem, the one who knew Archer best. He was retired now, but mom said he'd told her the unvarnished truth, that Archer Ellis was a good man—a good man with a serious mental illness, but a manageable one. The question she had to ask herself, he said, was if she could handle it.

Way ahead of her time, his mother was. Even now, mental illness had a stigma, and he couldn't imagine what it was like back then.

That was love.

He could only hope to find someone as solid and giving someday as his mother. And she'd done it all with a smile. In spite of Archer's illness, their home was a happy one most of the time. There were birthday cakes and Monopoly games and family fish fries at the beach. When he was well, his dad taught him how to catch lingcod and salmon. He still remembered those short summers—his mother skipping down the beach, running in and out of the waves with their old lab mix, Rusty, throwing sticks of driftwood into the incoming tide for him to fetch.

Mom knew how to live in the moment, long before mindfulness was a thing.

Wade's row of graduates got up and filed to the front, slowly stepping up the wooden stairs and walking across the stage, timing their arrival for their handshake and diploma.

"Cameron Jude Ebert . . . Monica Jeneane Edingham . . . Wade Archer Ellis . . ."

He only had his mother and sister there, but he could hear them clap and holler when his name was called—one loud and proud, one perfunctory. Suzi felt enthusiasm was uncool.

Wade insisted on taking them both to a late lunch after the ceremony. He wanted to spring for a hotel, too, but knew his mom was anxious to get home. Depoe Bay was only an hour and a half away, she said, and she really wanted to sleep in her own bed. Wade knew she was just trying to save him money, and, of course, was worried about leaving Archer alone for too long. He had to turn in his cap and gown, anyway, and take care of a few other details, but promised to drive out first thing in the morning.

Once they got Dad squared away, he needed to sit down with Mom and Suzi for a family meeting. He knew how much his mother wanted him to become a doctor, but he was glad she didn't know how that was accomplished. Not only were his grades not good enough to get into med school, but if he had applied anywhere, which he hadn't, that process would have started months ago.

It's not that being a doctor wasn't a noble profession, but he'd known for a while now that he wanted to do more than help one person at a time. He'd started thinking of how we are all connected and how we are no longer single individuals.

He was considering different majors when he met a visiting grad student from Duke. He'd gotten excited about the work he was doing in environmental technology. It opened up a whole new world of possibilities. Ways he could help whole villages get clean water, survive drought, or deal with pandemics—all of which were happening right now all over the world.

Being a doctor felt like cleaning up the mess the world was in after the fact. He just didn't have the patience for that. Preventing illness and poverty seemed much more efficient, even if it meant giving up the financial rewards of being a doctor. Scrounging for research dollars, living in poor villages around the world—it all made sense to him, but he still hadn't figured out how he was going to explain this to his mom, who'd worked so hard to give him what she viewed as a good life.

After Mom and Suzi got on the road and Wade was back in his room, he went through the closets and bathroom one more time to make sure he hadn't forgotten anything. He put his bags by the door then lay on his bed, hands behind his head, staring up at the ceiling. There really wasn't any rush to tell his mom about his change of plans. He knew she'd object, but he was planning to work for a while before applying to graduate school anyway—help Suzi pay for college and his mom pay for his dad's continued care. Insurance and the state never covered it all. Besides, she'd figure it out eventually, when his summer job stretched into fall and no acceptance letters to medical school arrived. He had it all mapped out.

25

"Wade Ellis?"

"Yes," Wade said, coming to the door. "I remember you from yesterday, Detective Monson. How can I help you?"

"Hello, Mr. Ellis, we'd like you to come down to the sheriff's office with us," Monson said. "We have a few more questions we'd like to ask you. Just a few details to clear up."

"Why?" he said, "I don't understand. I told you everything I know yesterday."

"We just have a few more questions, Mr. Ellis," Monson said. "Clarify a few specifics about your and your fiancée's activities that night."

"Wait . . . why?" Wade said. "There's nothing else to tell. Like I told you, we had dinner, she went down to do some laps and I fell asleep. I didn't know she hadn't come back up to the room until the phone rang the next morning. I mean . . . what more do you want to know? It was horrible."

The two detectives body language changed only slightly, but Logan and Olivia picked up on it right away. With surprising quickness and ease, Olivia stepped in front of Wade, extending her hand.

"Olivia Landers, Detective Monson. We met yesterday."

Logan didn't know what was coming, but she was impressed with her little sister's take- charge attitude.

"I believe Mr. Ellis already answered your questions, detectives," Olivia said.

"What exactly do you need to talk with him about?" Logan asked.

"I think you're overreacting a bit here, ladies," Monson said, not sure which protective she-wolf to address first.

Hands out in front of him, palms out in a defensive gesture, he said, "We just have a few items to clear up. It won't take long."

"Well, here he is, gentlemen," Olivia said, looking over her shoulder at Wade. "If you have any questions to ask, I'm sure Mr. Ellis would be happy to answer them—right here, right now."

She leveled her gaze at Detective Grant, the younger of the two, who shifted uneasily on his feet, putting his hands in his pockets. Detective Monson remained as he was, gazing placidly past his attackers to Wade, "Son, are you refusing to come with us?"

Wade looked at Olivia and then Logan, who was clearly in charge at this point.

"No, he's not coming with you," Logan said. "Ask whatever questions you want to ask right here."

Monson took a moment to consider his options, then tipped

his virtual hat and left.

After they got in their car, Wade asked, "What was that all about? Why do they want to ask me more questions?"

His voice had a tinge of panic in it. Logan felt sorry for him. He'd just lost his fiancée and now the police wanted to question him. Never a good sign.

"Notice they didn't come out and ask if I was your counsel," Olivia said. "Detective Monson knows I'm an attorney. He asked me my occupation when he talked to me at the hotel yesterday. Once it's official that you've 'lawyered up' they know they can't ask you any more questions without me present."

"Yeah, it's weird he didn't ask why Wade was here, or knew he would be. The house is sold and Wade doesn't live here anymore. I wonder how he tracked him down?" Logan said.

To Wade Olivia said, "Don't let them talk to you without an attorney present."

"I don't have an attorney! Why would I ever need one?" he said, clearly alarmed.

Olivia sighed, "No one ever thinks they need an attorney until they do."

Logan went into Mom mode and herded everyone back inside. It was way past noon, so she cobbled together something resembling lunch—beef jerky, salami, peanut butter and crackers, a couple of cut-up apples. She dug out the last two bottles of beer for Olivia and Wade, and a Pellegrino for herself. A Snickers bar cut three ways constituted dessert. She'd have to go shopping.

"Okay," Logan said, once they were all more or less full. "Why do you think they want to talk to you?" She hated to ask Wade to think about the details of Charlie's death, but she forged ahead, "Was there any reason to think Charlie's drowning was anything but an accident?"

"I don't know," Wade said. "Charlie was a good swimmer—an excellent swimmer—but she'd been sick, she had a flu bug a couple days earlier. Stomach cramps, diarrhea, throwing up, but it was just a 24-hour thing. She still didn't feel great, but wanted to swim. She rarely missed doing her laps. Swimming was a great stress reliever for her."

"Did she have any big stress in her life? Was she going through anything?" Logan asked.

"Nothing new. She and her grandmother, Charlotte Collins, got into it a few days earlier, but like I said, nothing new," Wade said.

"What did they fight about?" Olivia asked.

"The usual. For one thing, her grandmother always wanted her to take over the management of the hotel," he said.

"I gather she didn't want to," Logan stated. "What did Charlie want to do?"

"We were going to save the world," Wade said, with the saddest expression Logan had ever seen.

"Charlie was a cultural anthropologist. She already had her PhD. We're the same age, but I took a couple years off for work, so started my program later. I am just starting my dissertation. I've done all the course work; I just have to gather data and write it up. We were headed to a small village on an island off the coast of India to do my field work."

For a moment, a spark of enthusiasm lit Wade's eyes. "I designed this water filtration and desalinization system that can be scaled. We were going to test it in several villages and towns. Clean water is more important even than food to so many people. And with sea levels rising, seawater incursion is a real problem. Of course, the pumps will need adjustments and refinements, and we still have to find distribution channels to get this technology where it is most needed, but . . ."

"What was the other thing Charlie fought about with her grandmother?" Olivia asked, bringing him back on point.

"Me," Wade said simply, spreading his hands on the table top. "Charlie's grandmother was completely and adamantly against us getting married. I have no idea why, other than that my family doesn't hail from proud, Southern landed gentry like hers—or any landed gentry that we know of. Going back three generations, the Ellises were all poor, blue-collar workers—fishermen, carpenters, house cleaners. My grandmother Mara was a maid at the Collins hotel."

"But Charlie didn't see you that way," Logan stated.

"No, Charlie had a mind of her own. She saw people as they were, not as the world saw them," Wade said.

"She sounds like a good person," Logan said. "I wish I could have met her."

"She would have liked you guys, too," he said, smiling at the two women. "Thanks for taking on the cops for me."

Turning to Olivia, he added, "What do I do if they show up at my friend's house?"

Olivia retrieved her bag from the bedroom, pulled out a card and handed it to Wade.

"Have them call your attorney," she said, her brown eyes smiling.

26

After making apologies for the police showing up at her house, Wade told Logan he'd be back tomorrow for the rest of the boxes. For now, they'd be fine in the garage. Logan closed the garage door and went back inside, where Olivia was cleaning up their impromptu lunch.

"That was nice of you, offering to help Wade like that, but don't you have a job to get back to?" Logan asked, "in New York?"

Secretly, she was proud of her sister for looking out for the underdog, but Olivia wasn't a partner in her law firm. It was Hale & Patterson . . . not Hale, Patterson, & Landers. Not yet. Logan doubted Olivia had much leeway in deciding what cases to take on. She didn't want her sister to take time off she couldn't afford.

"No worries. Hale owes me," Olivia said.

Logan raised her eyebrows and helped herself to some more beef jerky.

"Do tell," she said, looking forward to hearing this story. The atmosphere was ripe for it.

While they were talking, a surly sky god had pulled some

ominous clouds over the sun. A breeze kicked up, threatening rain. Even though it was only one-thirty in the afternoon, the two sisters adjourned into the living room, closed the window, and settled in front of the fire, just in time for a brief, but heavy downpour. Logan was getting used to these and kind of liked the way they kept the air always fresh.

"I got his kid community service on a breaking and entering charge," Olivia explained.

This didn't sit well with Logan. She hated that only the rich and connected kids got the breaks.

Olivia quickly clarified.

"His girlfriend's mother pressed charges—which were unfounded. Her parents were holy rollers. The kid didn't break and enter *anything*. His girlfriend snuck him and his laptop into her room, so they could watch a movie together. The girl wasn't even allowed to have a computer or phone in her room. She was only permitted to use the family dinosaur desktop computer in the dining room—and that only for homework. When her mother saw her baby girl with a computer AND a boy, she went over the edge," Olivia said, sitting cross-legged on the hardwood floor. "It didn't matter that the movie they were watching was E.T., the lights were on, and they were fully clothed. According to the mom, he was out to corrupt her baby girl. Lord, save us all! We were lucky the mom didn't cry rape," Olivia added, "She's that kind of awful, that one."

Logan nodded. It was obvious Olivia had more experience with this than she did. Logan thought in terms of black and white, right and wrong. The legal system—the world of lawyers—resided in a big swath of gray. Having the police show up at her house pissed her off. She hated to see anyone badgered by the cops. She'd made a quick decision and landed on Wade's side. If Olivia helped the kid charged unfairly back in New York, maybe she could help Wade.

"What about your license being from out of state? Can you represent someone here in Oregon if your license is in New York?" Logan asked.

"For now," she said. "He's not under formal arrest or anything. And if necessary, we have a small office in Portland. I could work with someone there who is licensed in the state. Also, if this were to go forward, I can petition the court to represent him until he can find someone local. I've worked some criminal cases, but he would need an experienced defense attorney. And someone good, preferably local, who knows the judges, the DA's office, the prosecutor, has a good investigator . . . all of that."

Logan doubted Wade could afford any attorney, good or otherwise. He'd be stuck with whatever wet-behind-the-ears public defender they assigned him.

"What do you think the police were after?" Logan asked.

Olivia laid back on the floor and stretched out, warming her feet in front of the fire, a studious expression on her face.

"I don't know. They must have some reason to suspect Charlie's death was not an accident," she said. 'If it was something more routine, they could have just called him, or they would have talked with him here."

"But what else could it be?" Logan said.

"I have no idea and no way to find out—not without contacts here. I have people back in New York that help me out with some of my clients—an investigator, some of the county clerks, a forensics tech."

She paused, then said, "No, Len's probably out—we're not dating anymore."

Logan smiled, then thought of something.

"What about Sam?" she said. "She has contacts. Sam knows everyone around here—and whoever she doesn't know, her boyfriend does. He's lived here his whole life."

When they were finally able to get Sam on the phone, she said she'd meet them at The Horn around six for dinner. That was the soonest she could get away. They'd fill her in then—see if she had any ideas.

After cleaning up the paint brushes and trays and changing clothes, Logan and Olivia set up work stations in front of the fire, powering up their laptops. Logan tacked a sheet over the large picture window in the front room to minimize the glare on their screens. The storm had passed. Within minutes, Olivia was lost in her own world, tapping intently on her keyboard, then jotting notes on a yellow legal pad. Not wanting to interrupt her with constant questions, Logan caught up with her own work, signing off on a grant proposal and checking in with Huey about a new math animation game he was adding to the Fractals program, called Dolphin, for primary age students.

Around three o'clock, with nothing left to do until five-thirty, Logan straightened up the kitchen, then went out to the garage to check on Wade's boxes. She kicked herself for not remembering to move them when it rained. The window had leaked a little on one corner. Well, she'd just have to move them now. Mop up whatever water there was and maybe put the boxes up on some loose boards in case it rained again. She made a mental note to tell Clay about the leak.

Most of the boxes looked dry. She began moving the three boxes in front, which looked relatively new. None of them were taped, just secured in the usual over/under system of interlocking flaps every college student knew how to do. Blocky black letters announced the contents of each: Canning Jars, Boots, Archer-Fishing. Peeking inside, the contents in each box were as advertised and dry. Logan closed them up again and pushed them to the side, revealing a much more interesting container—an old army footlocker. The box on top was okay, but the water had run down the wall and at least half of the locker sat in a pool of water.

Nothing fancy like the leather and brass-trimmed trunks she'd seen in antique stores, this one was unembellished and battered, with a simple metal latch. The paint had faded from what must have been the original drab, Army green. On the top of the lid, return and recipient addresses were printed in thin, white paint—like on an envelope.

Logan pictured a young soldier, far from home, carefully painting each letter, trying to keep the lines straight and legible to make sure his trunk got to where he was sending it. Even with his best efforts, some letters came out wider than others and she could see where sometimes the brush ran out of paint before the letter was finished. Sharpies must not have been invented yet.

In the upper left-hand corner only a name and serial number could be read. An outfit was below that, but that part had gotten rubbed off. Pvt Aaron Ellis, ASN 13001337. In the center of the lid was the name of the person this trunk was being sent to—probably his mother. Just a name and town. Back then, that was probably all the postman needed to find someone if the town was small. And this one was.

Mrs. Irene Ellis of Depoe Bay, Oregon

27

Curiosity getting the better of her, Logan undid the latch and pushed up the lid.

Inside, the unlined trunk was only half full, but each item was neatly placed and dust free. On the right, old uniforms were carefully folded and stacked on top of a pair or Army boots. She removed the clothes and draped them on a tool rack behind her, then placed the wet boots to the side. A mottled, round, cardboard hatbox trimmed in worn, saddle-stitched leather took up all the space on the left and sat in a puddle of water. Reaching in and grabbing it by the sides, Logan lifted it out. It felt too heavy for a hat.

Journals—five or six that she could see, along with a large, manila envelope on top. Lifting everything out one at a time, Logan spread the contents out in the center of the garage floor to dry. She then turned her attention to the manila envelope. There were several loose documents inside. First, a birth certificate. On August 18, 1927, Jacob and Irene Ellis welcomed a baby boy, Aaron Jacob Ellis, into the world.

Next came a small packet of letters home, arranged in chronological order from May, 1943 to September, 1945—and a Western Union telegram dated September 5, 1945. Private Ellis' trunk arrived safe and sound, but he would never come home. September fifth. If Logan remembered her history correctly, that was just three days after the Imperial Emperor of Japan formally surrendered. Short and to the point, the telegram stated that on September 4, 1945, Private Ellis had been killed by a land mine in France. They regretted to inform them that his body was not able to be recovered.

Tears sprung to Logan's eyes.

How awful!

To worry every second for two years about your son being in mortal danger, then finally, hearing the war was over and being able to breathe a sigh of relief, thinking he was safe now, on his way home to you, only to get the dreaded telegram telling you he died. She couldn't imagine how his mother must have felt.

Wiping tears away with the back of her hand, Logan placed the papers back into the envelope and tucked them under the journals where she found them. She wondered if Wade knew about this tragic part of his family history. Should she even bring it up when he came to get the boxes? Given the recent loss of his fiancée, she was hesitant to dredge up sad memories, or spring new ones on him if he didn't already know. But she felt obligated to let him know these records existed, so he didn't inadvertently throw them out.

"What's that?" Olivia asked, looking over her shoulder.

"Just an old Army trunk," Logan said. 'Listen to this . . .'

She proceeded to tell Olivia what she'd found.

"Irene must be Wade's great-grandmother," Logan said. "I wonder if he's ever seen these."

"No way of knowing," Olivia said.

"Should we tell him? I mean, I don't want to share more sad news. Poor guy," Logan said.

"It's not like he knew him," said Olivia, "He would have died long before Wade was even born."

"Good point," Logan said. "But still . . ."

"What's in these?" Olivia asked, picking up one of the journals. This one had a green, cloth cover with brown, leather corners. It was wet, but the water hadn't soaked through to very many of the inside pages yet.

Since Logan wanted to know what was in them anyway, she didn't object to Olivia's snooping. It was her turn to look over Olivia's shoulder as she carefully turned the first page. The writing was attractive and deeply slanted, filling the pages with even, neat lines, as if not to waste paper.

December 27, 1931

We had a good Christmas. I was able to find a beautiful fresh orange for Aaron's stocking, and fill the rest with nuts and almost a full cup of hard candy Jacob brought back from Florence. He also brought back two large chickens for Christmas dinner. Mother was so pleased. Father made no comment.

Mother made Aaron a warm, new coat, which he loved immediately and wore all day, even indoors! He wouldn't even take it off when it was time for bed, but finally, Jacob coaxed him out of it, promising he could wear it in the morning. He is such a good boy and the light of our lives. We hope to give him a brother or sister soon, but Jacob wants to wait until we are in our own home.

To make this dream come true sooner, Jacob and I did not exchange gifts this year. We put those monies toward The Ellis Lodge, our fancy name for the motor lodge we hope to own someday. Jacob says that in a few months, we'll have enough to make the full down payment. Then he can buy the land—it has a building on it now—and we can start the renovations.

We hope to be open in time to welcome visitors this summer!

Father is not keen on the idea. He doesn't think Jacob capable of running a business, but he'll see. Jacob is a lot smarter than Father thinks.

Most of all, I'll be very happy when Jacob doesn't need to work with Frankie anymore. I've never liked him. But he is Jacob's friend. And Jacob promises me it's only a couple more months. Once we open the lodge and are on our own, we won't need anyone's help. Not father's or Frankie's.

"This is awesome!" Olivia said. "It's like looking into someone's mind that lived almost a hundred years ago. Imagine getting excited about finding an orange for your kid for Christmas. They must have really been poor."

"Yeah, but that was during the Depression. A lot of people were poor. And even if you had the money, oranges on the Oregon coast must have been hard to come by," Logan said.

Just then, the gathering clouds let loose and it began to rain in earnest again. Olivia weighed the book in her hand.

"We've already started this one . . . ," she said, looking down at the rest of the journals and back up at Logan, waggling her eyebrows.

"Can we, Mom, can we?" she begged.

"Well, we're not going anywhere in this weather," Logan pretended to sigh. "Shame to waste a warm fire when we have such good reading material here."

Doing a little happy dance, hugging the journal to her chest, Olivia led the way.

Logan grabbed the other two notebooks, then followed her in.

"As long as we put them back," she said. "I don't see what harm it could do. They'll dry better inside near the fire anyway. And we don't have to be at The Horn for a few more hours."

28

For the rest of the afternoon, Logan and Olivia got lost in the 1930's world of Irene Ellis. Before cell phones. Before the internet. And, as a reminder of how lucky they were to live in the twenty-first century, before women had many rights and even less power.

They took turns sharing interesting entries as they found them.

One passage in particular struck Logan as almost unbelievable.

"Listen to this one," she said to Olivia.

February 12, 1932

I don't know what to do. Mr. Woodrow won't budge. I went to see him this morning, to let him know the rest of the payment might be late, but we'd make it. We still want this piece of property, even if it only has one run-down, boarded up building on it. Jacob can fix anything and we're not afraid of hard work.

That hateful man! Mr. Woodrow just stood there in his doorway, folded his arms and said straight out he'll only do business with Jacob. Says he has no contract with me. I explained Jacob's not here and I don't know what's happened to him or when he's coming back. Woodrow said he'd give Jacob until Friday, but if he didn't show up with the rest of the deposit by then, he would forfeit the rest.

All that money, just gone! I tried to reason with him. I told him that was our money and I would make good on the rest if he just gave me some time. But he said he didn't do business with women. Period.

And when I tried to stand my ground, he told me my best bet was to find another man if Jacob didn't come home. Like Jacob had run off or something! I wanted to scream and cry at the same time, but I wouldn't give him the satisfaction of doing either.

When I told Father, he said Mr. Woodrow is within his rights according to the law. I don't know what I expected. I think I wanted him to offer to help. He could pay the rest of the deposit and put the property in his name until I could pay him back. But he refused.

Father always thought we were foolish in buying that property. This just seemed to harden his opinion against Jacob further. He said Aaron and I will always have a roof over our heads, clothes on our backs, and food on our plates. As if that was enough to keep someone alive.

I don't mean to criticize him. Father is a good man. I know he and mother sympathize with our situation, but secretly, I think he is pleased that Jacob is gone and hopes he never returns.

I will live, but only for Aaron. As for me, I will just have to learn to live without dreams.

"Wow," Olivia said. "Hard to believe men could get away with that crap back then. What was that, about eighty years ago?"

"Eighty-eight," Logan said. "Not that long ago, when you

think about it."

Logan stirred the fire, adding another log. Olivia got up, stretched and brought back a snack. Cheese, crackers, olives, and a bottle of Willamette Valley Pinot Gris. They settled in for some more reading.

"Here's one . . . ," Olivia said, furrowing her brow, "Listen to this . . ."

NOVEMBER 1932

Well, it's done. I'm home. And finally, alone.

The last nine months have been exhausting. At first, I was hoping it would just go away or I was mistaken and just had some kind of growth. I tried to lose it. God knows I tried. This unholy thing inside me. But nothing I did worked.

Eventually, I started to show, Mother was overjoyed. Said at least I'd have something of Jacob's to remember him by. She doesn't think he ran off like Father does. She thinks, as I finally had to, that he met some tragic fate. Fell off a cliff or was killed by vagabonds on the road—buried somewhere we'll never find him. We'll never know. All I know is that I am alone.

What's worse is I suspect Frankie had something to do with it. I just can't prove it.

Keeping a smile on my face, pretending to be excited and happy about this baby is the hardest thing I've ever had to do.

When Mara was born, I saw it right away—she had that fiery red hair, the mark of the devil. She is his child, but he wouldn't take her, even if I asked, which I won't because the shame would kill my mother.

And I wouldn't wish that on any child, even this one. I will do my Christian best to raise her, but I don't love her. I can't. I gave her Jacob's name so she wouldn't have to go through life as a bastard. I hope I am not damned to hell for lying about that.

I miss Jacob so much! I know I must not wallow in self-pity. I am grateful to have a home. Mother and Father provide for us now, but I will need to find work as soon as I'm strong enough. Mother can tend this baby and Aaron is in school now.

Now that I am home, I feel somewhat like Ruth, except that it is my own parents I will care for when they are old, just as they have cared for me and my child. And this new one.

I must stay strong. For Aaron. And for Jacob, in case he ever returns to us.

o o o o o

Olivia lowered the journal to her lap, keeping her place with her thumb.

"Wow," she said.

"Poor woman," Logan said. "It sounds pretty clear she was raped."

"Does she ever say who it was?"

Logan quickly skimmed the next few pages.

"Not here," she said, "but maybe in one of the other journals."

"If this happened now, we could do DNA. I'd love to nail that bastard to the wall!" Olivia said.

"Yep, things were definitely different then," Logan said. "Victims of rape were either not believed or blamed."

Learning these secrets made Logan feel like she'd overstepped her bounds and intruded on Wade's family's privacy. She put the journals back into the hatbox. While Olivia was changing, she texted Sam to double check their arrival time at The Horn.

Can't make it tonight, but how about Pirate's tomorrow? I'll fill you in then.

29

Charlotte Collins sat at the desk in her well-appointed corner room, savoring a second cup of her favorite tea—Earl Grey—in front of a warm fire. She always brought her own electric kettle so each cup was piping hot.

The conference was going well. Her speech had been well received. It always was. All in all, she was pleased with the life she had built for herself. She had health and wealth. That was what mattered. Happiness was overrated. The key was to not look ahead, but to focus on the here and now. Do what you needed to do and the rest would follow.

She did allow herself a moment this morning to look ahead, to anticipate the joy of having Charlotte home again, all to herself. To her granddaughter taking over The Collins. As intelligent as Charlie was, she didn't know what was best for her.

And Charlotte had to admit, although she didn't mind hard work, she was eighty-two years old now and slowing down. It gave her a great deal of satisfaction to know she could let go in a few months, maybe spend more time in the greenhouse, spend her last decade or so with her beautiful flowers. She closed her eyes, savoring the Earl Grey's fragrant steam with the faint scent of bergamot rising up, warming her face.

Then she allowed herself a brief review of all she had accomplished over the last year—all the efforts that would soon culminate in bringing Charlie back into her life.

o o o o o

Last October, just as the season began to turn, she'd gone to a place she knew, up an old logging road, and parked her car. Basket in hand, she then walked fifteen minutes into the forest until even that narrow trail petered out. An easy hike. Almost eighty-two, she was careful, but she knew if she took her time and avoided the blackberry brambles she'd be fine. And she had no doubt she'd find what she needed. She knew these woods.

She hadn't always known them. She'd come from softer, more settled lands. The rocky, Oregon coast was a far cry from gentle Savannah, Georgia, with its broad, leafy shade trees and nannies pushing baby carriages in the park. Here, nature came with stickery needles, rough terrain, and, this far in, sometimes bears.

Placing one foot at a time carefully on the spongy, fern-filled undergrowth so as not to twist an ankle, Charlotte smiled. The carpet of leaf litter exuded earthy smells. Somewhere to her left, a pileated woodpecker tapped steadily against a tree, and low-hanging cedar boughs brushed against her skin as she passed their regal trunks.

The basket she held reminded her of ones her mother used when gathering cut flowers for the table back in Georgia. Memories flooded back to the day she first arrived in Depoe Bay to marry Emerson. She made him wait to marry until after they both graduated. Abbott women had degrees. They just never used them.

With nothing but one trunk—a trunk filled with the best trousseau her family could afford—she'd made the three-thousand-mile journey in only three days. She'd done the best she could to freshen up before they pulled into the station. From the look in Emerson's eyes when he saw her, she knew she'd succeeded. When he lifted her down the steps, Charlotte Lee Abbot looked every inch the delicate, wasp-waisted, dark eyed, ivory skinned, southern belle she was raised to be. Her soon-to-be-husband pulled her close, crushing her against him. Emerson was always ready to rut, but Charlotte extricated herself skillfully. There'd be plenty of time for that. "Later," she'd reminded him gently, "your family is waiting." Depoe Bay was a good two-and-a-half-hour drive away.

Charlotte's job, as her mother reiterated to her before she left, was to meet and impress her new family so they loved her and made sure their unreliable son went through with the wedding. But she was also to take stock of her surroundings—make sure the financial situation was as Emerson had advertised. Marriage was an important step. It paid to be careful. Once that ring was on her finger, Charlotte would begin to shape her new life. With Emerson's money and her good breeding and style, she was confident she could make it work. She had to. There was no going back.

Her family in Savannah had pooled their last resources to send her off to a good college where she would meet eligible men and find her future husband. And she had. Out here in the hinterlands no one knew the Abbot fortune had dwindled so far over the years they could barely pay their taxes. Once she was established on the Oregon coast, maybe after her first son was born, she could send money back home and help the Abbots regain their rightful place in Savannah society.

This was her duty as a daughter of the south and she'd been very successful at it, if The Collins Hotel was any indication. She'd taken gentle, but firm control of the finances, which Emerson was happy to relinquish. As long as he had his single-malt in hand and guests to impress, he was happy. All she had to do was look the other way when those attentions strayed to the help. Her husband was particularly enamored of a certain, earthy, red-headed maid. Charlotte got rid of her, of course, but unfortunately, not in time. That was one weed she hadn't been able to root out completely.

Thus, her trip today. Even though Emerson had been dead and gone for years—the result of his inordinate love of those bourbons—she was still cleaning up the man's messes.

Charlotte squared her shoulders and refocused on her mission. Up ahead was the break in the trees she'd been looking for. She made her way up the last incline in that direction and thought back over the years—over her life—of how that path had led her to this one.

30

As she walked, Charlotte continued reflecting on her life.

She had been a good wife—it didn't really take too much effort. She eventually was able to send money home to her family in Savannah to lift them back onto—if not the highest, at least the middle rungs of the social ladder.

Emerson had been Emerson. But she didn't complain. She knew what she was getting when she married him. Women were always throwing themselves at him. Like that slut, Mara. At least he left her alone to run things. She learned the business from her mother-in-law, Rowena. They became quite close.

A few years after her father-in-law, Frank Collins, died, Rowena developed lung cancer. Charlotte cared for her until she died. In those last days, under the influence of quite a cocktail of drugs, the old woman whispered things about Frank into Charlotte's ear that should have surprised her, but didn't. It turned out Emerson hadn't fallen far from the family tree.

Frank's sins were worse, but only by degree. His other sins, the two Rowena only hinted at, were much darker, but if she was correct, were the foundation of the family's wealth, the very cornerstone of The Collins Hotel. Charlotte knew she could have gone to the authorities or done something to help the people whose lives Frank had ruined. But what had been done was done. Probably couldn't prove anything now, anyway. And what if Rowena was wrong? Better to leave things as they were.

Rowena never told her son and instructed Charlotte to keep the secret as well. But that was all a long time ago. Emerson was dead now. No one missed him or his reprobate father.

A memory of her father-in-law floated into her consciousness. He'd cornered her once in the stairwell, before they'd had the elevators installed. She smiled to herself. He only got to try it once. A knee in the groin had done the trick. Steel magnolias didn't start with the movie. Every southern woman knew how to manage men.

Charlotte stepped over an alder that had fallen across the path in the last rain, then decided to sit down on it for a few minutes and rest before continuing to her destination.

She didn't miss them—men—that was for sure. When Emerson died, she didn't go looking for his replacement. For a long time, now, it had just been her. Her and The Collins. She'd poured her heart and soul into this hotel. She had hoped to leave her legacy to her daughter, Dorothy, but Dorothy turned out to be a milk toast disappointment. The little mouse married young and faded away into the Midwest somewhere. Insurance salesman.

But Dorothy gave her one good thing.

Dorothy had two daughters. One just like her, a sour-faced girl, and the other, two years younger, a little bundle of energy the spitting image of her grandmother. To no one's surprise, Dorothy hadn't been able to handle either of them.

LIES THAT BIND

When Charlotte, named after her grandmother, became a strong-willed teenager, it didn't take too much convincing to talk her mother into letting her come live with her. She was so spirited!

Just like me.

She, of course, loved Amanda—blood was blood—but everyone knew Charlie was her favorite.

All through her high school years, Charlotte groomed Charlie to take over The Collins. She planned on leaving it to her when she became too old to run things—someday—she wasn't planning on leaving anytime soon. She sent her to college, of course. She didn't really care what she majored in. All well-bred women in the south received good educations. It was just what one did. One did what was expected.

Last year, Charlotte had her attorney draw up the paperwork to turn the hotel—and all her assets—over to Charlie. She was done with her schooling. It was time. Oh, Charlie talked about going off to help villagers get clean water or some such nonsense, but Charlotte knew her granddaughter would come to her senses. In anticipation of her arrival, she'd grown some lovely tea roses in the greenhouse to grace Charlie's room and had the cook make her favorite dinner—pork chops and gravy, fresh green beans, mashed potatoes and apple pie a la mode for dessert. But nothing went as planned.

First, Charlie insisted on inviting that horrible Ellis boy to the celebration and she'd had to eat cook's fabulous dinner with him. Even worse, he had been there—had witnessed her humiliation when she unveiled her surprise, a framed deed to the hotel, and watched as Charlie threw it back in her face! Well, not literally, but she said flatly she didn't want it.

How could she not want it?

Charlotte vividly remembered sitting there, stunned, while ice cream pooled on her plate, looking at the rejected gift, laid carelessly on the table, a gift she'd worked her whole life to give. How could Charlie not want it? It would provide her a solid future, one not dependent on any man.

Then Charlie dealt the final blow.

As if things couldn't get any worse, Charlie again began prattling on about being in love with Wade—they were in love with each other and they were going to get married. Whether she liked it or not. Wade got the nerve to speak up, too. He said they hoped she would come around and be at their wedding. It would be small, not a big blow-out wedding the whole town was invited to. They would love to get married right here in The Collins, just the family, if that was okay with her.

A sudden rage had filled Charlotte's body. Wade Ellis? No. This was definitely not okay with her. Charlie could absolutely not marry that man.

Bringing herself back to the present, shaking her arms out and rubbing her right knee, Charlotte rose stiffly from the log and set about her business. Not a pleasant business, but she needed to get on with it.

It didn't take her long to find the place. After just a few minutes of hunting, she spotted a small grouping under some ferns. Yes! This spot never disappointed. She didn't need many. A few would do. Cutting them carefully at the base of their stems, she placed the milky, white treasures in her basket. When she had enough, she turned and walked back to the car, reveling in the crisp, fall air. She would begin drying them when she got home.

Charlie graduated this year. She'd be home this summer. If she didn't come to her senses by then, Charlotte knew she'd be ready.

o o o o o

When the phone rang, breaking the silence, Charlotte didn't jump. She'd been expecting the call. She'd planned this, after all, down to the last detail.

Shaking off the memories, she calmly reached for her phone. It's not that she hadn't tried. She'd exhausted all other alternatives, but Charlie wouldn't give in. What she had done, she'd done for Charlie. Arranging her face into relaxed lines, she answered the call in her most gracious, Southern hostess tone of voice. They would never suspect a thing.

"Hello?"

31

Somehow Charlotte Collins managed to stuff her things into her suitcase, check out of The Sentinel, and get on the 405 without getting in a wreck. According to her Mercedes GPS, which she didn't bother to consult, she'd be home in two hours and fourteen minutes. She knew these roads. She'd make it in an hour and a half.

Not believing what she was hearing at first, she hadn't asked Amanda for details. All she could manage to say was that she was on her way. Maybe there was some mistake. But in her gut, she knew there wasn't.

Now that she was on the road, with nothing more to do than drive, the shock began to wear off. A searing pain filled her chest and tears began to flow. She gripped the steering wheel and willed herself not to pass out.

How had this happened? How could her Charlotte be gone?

Charlie was an excellent swimmer, but Amanda said she had drowned. A horrible accident. Said Charlie had the flu Sunday, must have gotten sick again and not been able to make it out of the pool. Why hadn't anyone called her?

She answered her own question. When she left, Charlie

wasn't talking to her. Wade certainly wouldn't call, and there would be no reason for Amanda to. After all, she thought it was just the flu.

But if only someone had called her, if only she had known, she could have done something! Even if it meant her own actions would be discovered, she would have done anything to save Charlie!

She reached for her purse for a tissue, but it was out of reach. She wiped her eyes with the back of her hand as best she could, almost missing her turn. Backing off the gas, she tried to calm herself. She made the turn. It was okay.

But nothing else was. Nothing was okay if Charlie was gone.

And if what she thought had happened actually had, this was all Wade's fault. The thought of his stupid, earnest face at the dinner table the night before she left, taking Charlie's hand, taking possession of her—inviting her to their wedding! As if he had the right! Wade Ellis didn't have the right to breathe the same air as Charlie!

She had done everything in her power to dissuade them from marrying. Not only did Charlie belong with her, with The Collins, but the Ellises and the Collins could not join. Not ever. Not again.

She had hoped reason would prevail, but no. Wade would not give up and Charlie seemed hell bent on throwing away her legacy to go save idiots in India. She'd had no choice! And now her Charlie was gone. She would never forgive him. Never! She pressed down on the accelerator.

✿ ✿ ✿ ✿ ✿

"Grandmother!" Amanda cried, reaching out to embrace her as she hurried up the steps.

"Where is she?" she demanded, pushing Amanda aside,

walking unsteadily across the entrance toward the hallway and the stairs that led to the pool. "I want to see Charlie!"

"She's not there, Grandmother," Amanda said, talking now to her grandmother's back. "They've already taken her."

This news stopped Charlotte in her tracks.

"Where?" she asked, suddenly seeming confused.

"I don't know exactly," Amanda said. "They said they'd call later. We can't go down there, now. They're still doing things."

A large, dark-haired man with a serious expression suddenly materialized, stepping in front of her, preventing her gently from going any further. She had seen him when she came in, sitting in the striped, velvet chair in the lobby. He had been speaking with a young woman she didn't recognize.

He reached out his hand. Reflexively, she took it and limply shook.

"Mrs. Collins?" he said. "My name is Detective Monson. Let me say first how sorry I am for your loss. You've had a big shock. I am speaking with one of your guests right now, but will be with you shortly. Is there somewhere you can rest for a few minutes? Then I will need to ask you a few questions. I promise it won't take long."

The hated Wade was slumped into one of the side chairs. Charlotte could not bring herself to speak to him yet. She nodded to Monson and allowed herself to be herded into her private office by Amanda, who was making soothing, clucking noises at her elbow. Once she was deposited into her favorite Queen Anne side chair, Amanda said something about getting her some tea. As if tea could fix any of this.

At least it would give her a minute to think. She needed to decide what to say—how much to say—before the policeman returned. His eyes had been soft with sympathy, but sharp with intelligence. She couldn't afford to underestimate him.

So far, no one suspected anything. This was just a horrible accident. And in a way it was. She certainly had not meant for Charlie to drink Wade's protein shake.

Why? Why had she? Charlie hated those shakes! She was always teasing Wade about his green pond scum, which he insisted tasted great when mixed with grapefruit juice and cured everything from colds to cancer.

They thought she didn't know, but she was well aware Wade stayed with Charlie at the hotel whenever she was out of town. He arrived the minute she was gone. Amanda ratted her sister out every time. Hence the canister of protein powder Charlie kept for him in the kitchen cupboard. God forbid he should go one day without it. He had one every morning for breakfast.

She spotted the container one day, tucked behind the plastic food containers when looking for something to put leftovers in. The idea came to her instantly. It had been easy to slip some of the ground up, dried mushrooms into it. Between the awful taste of the protein powder itself and the grapefruit juice mixer, he'd never notice the taste. She thought it would be safe. She'd be long gone before the poison did its real damage. No way she'd be connected to his death.

But Wade hadn't died.

She still couldn't work it out. There was no way Charlie would have had any on purpose and she definitely wouldn't have mistaken it for anything else. And even if she had somehow had some, why hadn't Wade been poisoned? There was absolutely no reason for Charlie to drink it and certainly no reason for Wade *not* to.

It just didn't make sense. Or was it a wild coincidence and really just a case of the flu that came back around and Charlie was too weak to get to the edge of the pool?

Either way, her Charlie was gone, ripped away from her.

The breaking of her heart all but overwhelmed her, but right now, she needed to focus. She needed time to think everything through. With the policeman coming back—what was his name again? Monson. She'd have to slip back into numbness. He wouldn't expect her to know anything, but still, she would have to be very careful until she could regroup.

And as soon as possible, get rid of that canister.

32

Finally, the detective finished his questions and the police techs wrapped up their business and left. Grandmother was in her room. After first making sure everything was locked up, Amanda walked down the hall to her own room—which was on the first floor, with no view at all, but conveniently located near the front desk and office, where she worked—for nothing. With trembling hands, she let herself in and locked the door.

With muffled giggles bordering on hysteria, she threw herself onto her bed and did a silent, screaming cheer, pumping her fists into the air repeatedly.

She'd done it!

Things couldn't have gone better if she'd planned them this way! Two days ago, she'd resigned herself to forever playing second fiddle to her sparkling, vivacious sister, waiting for whatever crumbs Grandmother threw her way. But, in less than twenty-four hours, with absolutely no preparation, she'd gotten rid of Charlie, fixed the blame squarely on Wade, and now had Grandmother all to herself!

And she felt not a shred of guilt.

That whole bit about Wade and Charlie getting in a fight? That had come to her in a flash of brilliance. Grandmother hadn't looked totally convinced, but that stupid detective sure fell for it. Amanda had always been a good liar. She considered it one of her best gifts.

Bouncing off the bed with maniacal energy, she planted herself fiercely in front of the full-length mirror she usually avoided, and for once, liked what she saw. No longer the mouse people saw when they bothered to look at her at all, Amanda Collins Daspitt was now a lion!

She had done it! And not through dumb luck. She'd used the intelligence and strength she always knew she had, but everyone else seemed to dismiss, to make her *own* luck. She'd seen the brass ring and grabbed it!

Sure, there were some glitches. Some things she'd have to work out. When she was over the initial shock of Charlie's death and thinking more clearly, Grandmother might doubt the Wade and Charlie argument and Charlie deciding to stay, but there would be no question her death was an accident. Conveniently, Charlie had the flu a few days ago, which made her drowning very believable.

Now that she was alone, Amanda caressed and savored the memory.

It had been a long, boring day.

It was Amanda's job to man the desk, manage the kitchen staff, communicate with the contractor and repairmen, and at the end of each day, make the rounds, secure the building and lock everything up. Organized and systematic, she always did the lower level last, then walked up the short flight of stairs to her room, which was on the lobby level, the first one on the left. It was the one Grandmother always gave her when she visited. Again, the least desirable room because of the noise created when people went up and down to the pool during the busy season. She used it now out of habit.

Momentarily surprised the pool was in use, she'd entered, intending to ask Charlie to finish up so she could lock up behind her. It had to be her in there. Charlie did laps several times a week. Sometimes she swore her sister did things just to make her life difficult. Irritated, she'd walked over to the edge of the pool to get her attention.

Immediately, she spotted some kind of bloody fluid floating in the pool—vomit? diarrhea? Maybe both—and just a few feet in, Charlie was struggling, jackknifing into a severe cramp then arching back, greedily sucking in more air. Obviously disoriented, she was just a few feet away from the stairs, but was facing away from her, toward the deep end.

She'd had a pretty bad bout of the flu a few days ago; she must have cramped up and because she was in the water, gotten herself into trouble.

Idiot.

Without hesitation, Amanda quickly stepped down the cement stairs into the water. She only had to go in a little ways. She could reach her from the second stair and pull her to safety. She would be Charlie's savior. That had its advantages.

But when she got there, another thought surfaced. A cold rage. It almost felt pleasurable.

Instead of grabbing an arm, or even pulling her sister by her hair to drag her up and out, Amanda felt her fingers moving of their own free will, forming a claw, fiercely gripping the top of Charlie's head. It didn't take much. All she had to do was push down and continue holding Charlie's head firmly under the surface of the water until she stopped struggling and went still.

Her beloved little sister was already weak and half dead from cramps and vomiting that must have hit while she was trying to do her laps. She probably would have died anyway. Amanda just helped.

And the beauty of it was there was absolutely nothing to connect her, no reason to suspect Charlie's drowning was anything other than a tragic accident.

Cramps were the bitch, as everyone knew.

Revved with adrenaline, she'd flipped off the lights, locked the door, and had gone upstairs to change out of her wet slacks. Her shoes were probably ruined, but she'd see if they were salvageable after they dried. She almost went to bed, but then remembered she had a late-arriving guest, a young woman driving in from Portland. On automatic pilot, she'd checked her in and then gone to bed herself, where she lay for hours, going over every delicious detail of her sister's demise.

True, she wouldn't get the hotel and all the money right away. But it was hers. She would prove herself invaluable. Grandmother would come around.

She'd start tomorrow. Grandmother usually got up early, but she'd be up earlier. Prepare her favorite breakfast: English Breakfast tea, two slices of sourdough toast, and a soft-boiled egg. She could picture it all in her mind. The two of them . . . the grand dames of The Collins Hotel. Grandmother would still be grieving, but she'd gently bring her around, remind her of her obligations to The Collins. Appeal to her strong, southern sense of duty.

She'd bring her up to date on the renovations, making a few slight changes along the way, like a larger room for herself—or maybe she could take over Charlie's room. It wasn't big, but had the best view.

Around midnight, the initial rush had subsided and Amanda went over the whole event again in detail—comparing it to what she'd told the police. She could find no flaws. It was the perfect cover story. If the police ever did get their heads out of their asses and realize Charlie was murdered, the finger was already strongly pointed at Wade.

Who had a more perfect motive than the jilted lover? Who had a more perfect opportunity? He was staying right there with Charlie in her hotel room. He knew she was going to the pool. There were no other guests except that one woman, who had arrived late, and was a stranger and therefore had no motive. And as luck would have it, the guest ended up using the pool that morning and discovered Charlie's body, thus removing her, Amanda, even further from suspicion.

No, it would make sense that Wade killed her, then snuck back to his room. As for her own opportunity, locking up at night, even if they thought of that, she wouldn't be suspect. Wade would have turned off the lights after he killed her. There would be no reason for Amanda to even enter the pool area. Like she told the police, the room was dark and she just locked the door as usual, assuming Charlie was done with her laps, like she always was by that hour.

No one would suspect her. She had no motive. She didn't directly benefit from Charlie's death. In Grandmother's will, The Collins went to Charlie, and any remainder to her Gardening club. She'd gone snooping one day and found the will in Grandmother's files in the office. She'd only left Amanda a mere pittance of $25,000. A slap in the face, but the police didn't know she knew about the will. No one did.

No, she was the innocent. The distraught sister, the diligent, good granddaughter, the one taking care of everything.

33

"**M**onson," he said, picking up the landline.

"Gary," she said, "Jean here, have you got a minute?"

Hanging his jacket on the back of his chair as he sat down, Monson rolled his office chair closer to his desk so he could take the call and drink his coffee at the same time.

"Shoot," he said.

He didn't bother flirting with Jean. The Lincoln County Medical Examiner was a very attractive woman, but they were friends from way back and it wasn't his style. He left that to Grant, who was good at it.

"I might have some news for you on the Collins drowning," she said.

"Official?" he said.

"Not yet," she said. "I'm still catching up here. Borgia did three DBs while I was out and . . ."

"Oh, welcome back, by the way," he said, feeling bad he hadn't thought to say that when she first called.

When she wasn't busy being a full time doctor and a part time medical examiner, Jean and her husband, Lee, were huge baseball fans and had just returned from a trip to the Baseball Hall of Fame and Museum in Cooperstown, NY. Monson was more of a basketball fan himself.

"Thanks," she said. "The thing is, I think he may have missed something on this one. I'm going to go over his notes one more time, but I spotted some bruising at the base of the skull. Easy to miss in the initial," she added, not wanting to cast blame on her assistant. "Tough to see under the hair."

Monson sat up.

"What kind of bruising?"

"Area of hemorrhage could be a grip mark . . . possibly from a thumb," she said.

"Were there others?" he asked, assuming if there were a thumb print bruise, there would be more from the other fingers.

"No," she said, "but that's not unusual."

The ME's voice rose to an excited 'isn't-this-fascinating' teacher tone Monson recognized. He'd have to cut her off if she went on too long.

"Push the skin around on your scalp. It moves around to help prevent brain injury. Sort of deflects any blows. There's also a thick layer of gristle under the skin that adds another layer of protection. Blood vessels are under that, so even if someone gripped the top of the head hard, there wouldn't necessarily be a bruise. You'd almost need to whack someone with a two by four to leave a mark."

Monson held his breath, waiting for her to elaborate. Jean was very careful with her words. His patience was rewarded.

"But, lower down on the neck there wouldn't be that layer of protection. It's just skin and blood vessels there. A firm grip would bruise—leave a mark. If someone had gripped the top of her head, they'd only leave a thumbprint at the bottom of the skull at the top of her neck."

"Okay . . . ," Monson said. "What's the bottom line?"

"The bottom line is someone may have pushed this girl's head underwater and held it there until she drowned," Jean said.

He knew it! He had a feeling this wasn't going to be an accidental drowning. Now, he just needed definitive proof and a way to connect the killer to the act. He'd have to comb through the crime techs' goodies from the scene.

"When will you know for sure?" he said.

"Give me 'til lunch," she said. "I'll call you back. There's something else I want to check."

Monson felt the rush of adrenaline, but kept a lid on it. Only on TV did cops run off half-cocked and catch the killer in thirty minutes. His solve rate was what it was because he took his time, built his case. He made a quick call to a Lincoln City cop who was a whiz at writing requests for both search and arrest warrants. Since it was Friday, time was of the essence. Judge Pritchard would be gone fishing by four, off to his favorite lake for holdover trout.

In the meantime, Monson needed to talk with his one and only suspect, Charlie's fiancé, Wade Ellis. He reached for the phone again.

"Grant," he said, "Monson. You free?"

34

Monson hadn't wasted any time.

While waiting for the ME to call him back with ammunition for the warrant requests, he made a beeline for the friend's house where Wade said he was staying. Knowing he had to handle this just right, Monson went by himself, driving his personal car and took the "So sorry to bother you this morning, but whenever there's a death, I have to fill out all these forms" approach.

"They'll make me keep coming back to bug you, so if you could just come down with me and help me out with this paperwork, it would sure make my life easier and with that out of the way, allow you to grieve your loss in peace."

Yada, yada, yada . . .

The kid bought it and here they were. Monson was surprised he didn't ask for an attorney, but sometimes you just got lucky. If he could get Wade to slip up, give him anything, he could serve those warrants, call out the Major Crimes Team, and get this done. The phone call from the ME definitely moved this into the possible homicide column and made everything more urgent. And if it wasn't this guy, they didn't have much time to find out who killed that poor woman. The trail was already growing cold.

He flipped to a fresh page of his notebook. This conversation was, of course, being recorded, but he still liked taking his own notes. Grant was on the other side of the one-way observation window.

He'd worked with Grant before on other homicides and trusted the younger man's judgment. The sole detective for Newport, Grant was overworked and underpaid, but promised to be there for this. Monson wasn't surprised when he arrived five minutes early, sharply dressed, clean-shaven and every strand of his light brown hair neatly in place.

His own suit pants and long-sleeve button-down were clean, but Monson already looked rumpled and sported a 5:00 shadow even though it wasn't even 10:00 a.m.

Hoping Grant was still in place and hadn't been called out for a robbery or some other reason, Monson continued.

"Were you just visiting, or were you staying there with your fiancé? I understand Charlie is the granddaughter of the owner, Mrs. Collins."

Wade's squeezed his eyes shut and opened them. They'd been at this for over an hour already.

"I just told you that," he said. "Didn't you say you had some forms for me to sign?"

Monson smiled apologetically, "They're being prepared now."

Wade let out an exasperated sigh and continued.

"Yes, Charlie is short for Charlotte. She was named after her grandmother, Charlotte Collins. Up until she went away to college, she lived there. Her grandmother always kept a room for her when she stayed."

"How long was her visit this time?"

"This time she'd been there a couple of weeks."

"Were you staying there, too?"

"Not exactly," Wade said. "Not at first."

Monson waited.

"I wasn't exactly welcome there," Wade said. "Not since last summer, anyway."

"But you were there *that* night, correct?"

"Like I told you before," Wade said, looking somewhat ashamed at the admission, as if he were the help, sneaking into her window at night, "I only stayed over when her grandmother was out of town. Mrs. Collins left for one of her gardening conferences over in Portland earlier this week. That's when I came over."

Again, Monson waited. He knew all about how Mrs. Collins felt about Wade, but now he needed to know how Wade felt about her and the ultimatum she laid down for Charlie that night.

Again, Wade filled in the silence.

"Mrs. Collins didn't like me. Actually, it was stronger than that. She hated me. Probably because my family was poor. We didn't run in the same social circles. Charlie was Mrs. Collins favorite grandchild. She had big plans for her and those plans didn't include me."

"How did Charlie feel about all this?" Monson asked, although he already knew.

"Charlie loved her grandmother, but she was an independent adult. She had room in her heart to love both her grandmother and me."

Since he was the only one in the room, Monson had to play both good and bad cop. With one question, he shelved Mr. Nice Guy and brought out The Interrogator.

"Did Charlie ever express any doubts about your plans to

marry and for you to take her away?"

"They weren't *my* plans; they were *our* plans. I wasn't taking her anywhere, we both wanted to go," Wade said.

"Are you sure you want to stick with that story?" Monson asked. "It seems to me that Charlie had a very strong relationship with her grandmother and very few people turn down the kind of wealth and opportunity her grandmother had to offer. *You* couldn't offer her that, could you, Wade?"

Wade looked as if he'd been slapped.

"No," he said, fumbling, "But Charlie didn't care about those things—the money and all. She didn't reject her grandmother, just the hotel and staying here to run it."

"I don't believe you," Monson said flatly.

"Well, I don't know what else I can say," Wade said. "It's the truth."

"Women can be fickle. Charlie may have started out liking the idea, but being back here, seeing all she was giving up, spending the summer with her grandmother, seeing all the new renovations, she must have started to waver, to have doubts, when she saw that Mrs. Collins was pouring some serious money into this place. It was going to be a gold mine for Charlie, but only if she stayed—and dropped you."

"It wasn't like that!" Wade said.

"It must have been very hard for you," Monson said, "Thinking it was all wrapped up, that you were going to marry into one of the wealthiest families around, and still have Charlie all to yourself. You didn't know her grandmother would disinherit her if she chose you, did you, Wade? I bet that bit of news came as a surprise. I bet knowing she was going to be cut off changed Charlie's mind in a hurry. Why would any woman choose you over a family fortune?"

"I wasn't marrying Charlie for her money. Charlie loved me.

She didn't change her mind. Why do you keep saying that?" Wade's voice rose.

"Because," Monson said. "It's the truth. We have an eyewitness who's willing to testify she overheard Charlie and you arguing. Loudly. She was leaving you. That must have infuriated you. You couldn't take it, so since you weren't going to get Charlie or her money, you killed her."

"What? I'd never hurt Charlie! I loved her! Charlie was everything to me!" Wade said. "No one could have heard her say that because she never did!"

Although the veins on Wade's neck were starting to pop out and he wasn't restrained in any way, Monson wasn't worried. He may have more fat than muscle, but he still outweighed the younger man by thirty pounds. He could take him. And he knew Grant was right next door.

Monson looked him straight in the eye, "I can't help you until you start telling the truth, Wade."

His face darkening with rage and frustration, Wade shoved the table, which didn't budge, as it was bolted to the floor. He only succeeded in unbalancing his chair and almost tipping himself over, which didn't improve his mood. Shaking, he could barely control himself. Fists clenched together in front of him now, he stared in stony silence at his right thumb rubbed the left one over and over.

Monson continued, "Look, we know you didn't plan this. It wasn't calculated. It's not like she told you last week and you bought a gun and shot her."

"I didn't do *anything* to Charlie! This is insane," Wade said quietly between gritted teeth.

"When did you find out grandma dropped the bomb and was disowning Charlie if she didn't leave you?" Monson asked. "Grandma must have told Charlie before she left for Portland.

She wouldn't have delivered that message over the phone. When did Charlie tell you? Over dinner?"

"She didn't tell me. She never said anything like that," Wade said.

"It must have been that night, at dinner, but it doesn't matter. It could have been anytime those last two days."

Wade held his head in his hands, breathing heavily.

"You probably thought you could talk her out of it, convince her to still come with you," Monson said. "But there must have come a point when you realized. You realized she wasn't going to change her mind. Wasn't going to marry you. Wasn't going to turn down her grandmother. You were going to lose it all."

"No! No!"

"You probably argued for hours, then because she wanted to get away from you and you wouldn't leave—did you refuse to leave, Wade, knowing she'd never let you back in? Into her life, into her room, into her bed? Maybe when there was nothing left to say, she got away from you by going down to do her laps, hoping you'd be gone by the time she got back. But you didn't go, did you, Wade? No, you couldn't let her go."

Wade ground his forehead into the palms of his hands, rocking back and forth in his chair.

"The ME said the time of death was somewhere between nine and eleven. That fits, doesn't it, Wade? You couldn't accept her decision. You knew where she was and that she'd be alone. You went down, went into the pool area, maybe watched her swim for a minute, remembering how great things were between you and how it had all gone horribly wrong. Then you waited until she came to your end, and you just reached out and—you're pretty strong, aren't you, Wade—you reached down and held her head under water. It didn't take much. She must have been exhausted from arguing for hours, then doing laps. And still weak from the flu she had earlier that week. Was that how it happened, Wade?"

"No," Wade said, wearily rubbing his face.

Then, as if he'd just remembered something he sat up and his demeanor changed. He reached into his pocket, pulled out a card and pushed it across the table at Monson.

"I don't know where you're getting all this, but you're wrong. I want my lawyer."

35

Althought pain lived deep in her eyes, in every other respect, Mrs. Collins was totally composed. Neat clothes, full makeup. Tasteful jewelry. She greeted Logan at the door with a thin smile. Very much the southern lady Sam wrote about in her article. Gracious, even in grief. She stepped aside to let Logan in.

"You must be Miss Landers," Mrs. Collins said, "The police called and said you would be stopping by to collect his—that man's—things."

Those last few words dripped with disgust.

Logan stepped into the lobby, following her hostess into the entryway.

"It's Logan, actually. Logan McKenna," she corrected. "Olivia is down at the jail. She asked me to come in her place."

She was just here to collect Wade's things, not get into it with this woman.

Even though Charlie's death had been an accident, the police were thorough and processed her hotel room, hallway, and stairwell as well as the pool area as a crime scene. Wade had been informed he could return in a day or so to pick up his things, but of course, now, being held at the jail, he was not at liberty to do so. The police had been interrogating him, apparently for hours until he had them call Olivia.

Olivia acted quickly. Before they got a warrant to sweep in and grab whatever they wanted, Olivia wanted Logan to get Wade's things—his laptop in particular. She believed Wade was innocent, but didn't want to give them any ammunition. She would have come herself, but needed to meet with her client. If Logan was lucky, she'd be in and out before the police arrived. Wade wasn't formally under arrest, at least not yet.

Mrs. Collins nodded and set off at a brisk pace toward the elevator. Their path took them directly through the lobby, past a massive fireplace. A large family portrait hung above it and dozens of pictures, some in color, most black and white, of what must be important guests and events were scattered along the wide mantle.

The phone rang back at the front desk and while Mrs. Collins walked back to inform whoever was on the line that the hotel was temporarily closed and took their contact information, Logan took a minute to look more closely at the portrait.

It had been taken in front of the hotel. From Sam's description of the various family members in the article, she recognized the patriarch, Frank Collins, seated next to his wife down in front. Even though he was an old man in the portrait, his red hair thinned and faded, his blue eyes burned out at you directly.

He and his wife, were seated in two straight-backed chairs, the rest of the family arranged around them. Behind Frank's wife stood a classically handsome, light-haired man, next to a petite, dark-haired woman Logan recognized immediately as her host, Mrs. Collin. Still attractive, maybe in her late fifties or sixties in that picture.

On the right, behind Frank, a younger, plain-looking woman stood stiffly next to a doughy man with harshly trimmed hair and a prominent cowlick. An impish looking dark-haired preschooler with a brilliant smile was seated cross-legged at the matriarch's feet, right in front. A lighter haired girl, a few years older, stood next to her mother on the other side. Must be the sister.

Something about the portrait gave Logan a strange feeling. It was as if the artist tried to put elements together that just wouldn't go. But it was more than that. Something in the back of her mind was tugging at her consciousness. Just as she started to pull the wispy strands of thought together, Mrs. Collins' call ended and she came back to gather her charge.

"Is that you?" Logan asked, pointing at the attractive woman in the portrait next to Emerson.

"Yes," she said, hurrying her along, "many years ago."

After a very short elevator ride—there were only two floors, if you didn't count the pool level underground, which Logan was sure was not on the tour—they arrived at Room 202. Mrs. Collins unlocked the door and let her in.

"Please don't disturb anything of Charlie's, just remove his things. All of them," she said. "I want nothing of his to remain."

"Absolutely," Logan said.

"Do you need any bags?" she asked.

Lifting the empty duffel bag she had brought with her, Logan said, "I'm good. Hopefully everything will fit in here."

Mrs. Collins nodded curtly. "I'll be back in ten minutes. That should give you enough time."

Jeez! Here's your hat, what's your hurry?

With her deadline set, Logan got to work. Wade had given Olivia a list of the things he could remember he had taken with him when he went to stay with Charlie. A change of clothes, toiletries. Shoes. His laptop. His phone. Working as efficiently as she could, Logan started in the bedroom, stuffing clothes around the electronics and a pair of shoes, then went into the bathroom. Still plenty of room left. There was an electric and regular toothbrush, a man's kit bag, and a couple of combs on the counter and a razor in the shower. Not knowing which combs or toothbrushes were his, she stuffed both of each in the kit bag. She left the razor and the face cream. The razor was pink and she didn't know of any men who used face cream.

Doing a final walk-through, knowing Mrs. Collins would be back at any minute, Logan took a moment to survey the room. How strange to think that just days ago, this room was just a room, holding two young, vibrant lives. There were no hints of sadness here. No hints of death for one and jail for the other. Just disheveled sheets, where they had probably recently made love, she thought sadly.

She looked over at Charlie's work space, a desk near the window. Several inexpensively framed photos perched on the sill. A snapshot of Mrs. Collins, pruning roses, every hair in place. A selfie of Charlie and Wade in full-on hiking gear, next to a magnificent waterfall. Both were beaming carefree smiles. Charlie's eyes sparkled. Wade, his arm around her, looked like a different man than the grieving one she'd seen through the window at The Collins that awful morning, or later, at the house.

Given Mrs. Collins's attitude toward Wade, she didn't think she'd mind if she took it. She added the photo to her stash, tucking it into a side pocket for protection.

Hoisting her now full bag up onto her left shoulder, Logan turned to leave just as Mrs. Collins arrived to escort her back down and out. The emphasis on out. It was obvious she wanted her off the premises as soon as possible. Of course, if her granddaughter has just died, Logan would want to be alone, too.

Suddenly, Logan saw this woman as a grieving grandmother. She wanted to say something. Something to express her condolences, but the right words wouldn't come. As she stepped out onto the porch, she noticed the two impressive blue, ceramic pots bordering the entrance, planted with bunches of bright, colorful flowers.

"These are beautiful," she said, gesturing to the blossoms. "How do you get such delicate flowers to grow in this climate?"

Softening an iota, Mrs. Collins gestured to a small path just beyond the parking lot on her right, leading to a sturdy, brick building with mullioned windows.

"The greenhouse," she said. "I grow them there."

"Ahhh . . . ," Logan said. "Well, they're very beautiful."

She hesitated, then added, "I'm very sorry for your loss, Mrs. Collins."

Lips pressed together in a firm line, Mrs. Collins stepped back, nodded curtly, and shut the door.

36

"In here!" Logan called from the kitchen, as she put a new liner in the trash can. "Did you get my message?"

The front door slammed.

"Sorry! Hands full! It's the wind—"

Logan looked out the window. An afternoon squall had blown in and she could hear Olivia kicking off her shoes in the entryway. Probably so she wouldn't track in mud. Until she got some landscaping or bark chip out there, the short walk from the gravel driveway to the front porch would be an issue every time it rained. When she turned around, Olivia was standing in the doorway, holding up two plastic bags that smelled delicious, reminding Logan she hadn't eaten lunch.

"Yeah, the takeout line at the Sea Hag was super fast. Where do you want it?" Olivia said. "Need any help?"

"Nope, I'm almost done," Logan said, "Just put it on the table. I'll be right out."

Logan came out with paper plates, utensils, paper towels for napkins, and a bottle of Willamette Chardonnay with two plastic wine glasses.

"Thanks for going over to The Collins to pick up Wade's stuff. Did you have any trouble?" Olivia asked.

"No," Logan said. "I wasn't exactly welcome, but it went okay."

A half hour later, fish and chips dispatched, Olivia stoked the fire and topped off their glasses. She spread a blanket on the floor between their chairs while Logan went to retrieve her duffel bag.

"Okay, what'd you get?" Olivia asked.

Logan removed the contents and spread everything out, more or less organizing it into piles.

"Nothing exciting, but I hope I got everything," she said. "I don't think Mrs. Collins is going to let me back in again."

Olivia went right to the laptop and flipped it open, but the battery was dead, so she found the charger for it and plugged it in the nearest wall socket. Putting the rest of the things back in the duffel, she thanked Logan again and said she was sure Wade would be grateful.

"Okay," Logan said. "Your turn. Spill! What happened at the sheriff's station or jail or whatever? Is Wade under arrest? Is he in actual jail?"

Olivia sat back in her chair.

"Yes and no. He's not under arrest—not yet, anyway," she said. "But they're holding him for now."

"Can they do that? How long can they keep him locked up? This is ridiculous!" Logan said.

"It varies, but I'm hoping to get him out tomorrow," she said.

"What did he say happened? Why did they want to question him? Do they think Charlie was murdered? I thought it was an accident," Logan said.

"Wade said Monson thinks he and Charlie argued, that she was dumping him," she said. "That would give him motive, but I don't think they have any physical evidence. And Wade of course, denies it. I couldn't get any answers out of the Sheriff's office. But I don't think this is over. If they do determine it's a homicide, they'll keep digging until they find something to pin on him."

"What do you think? Do you think he could be guilty?" Logan asked.

"My gut tells me no, but everyone's guilty of something," Olivia said. "I'll know more when I can get into his computer. People put their whole lives online. If he's guilty of anything, it'll show up in there."

"Did he formally retain you?" Logan asked, "Do you think he needs an actual lawyer yet?"

"No, for now I'm just advising him," she said, "keeping him out of trouble. Hopefully, he won't need me formally. The police are probably just doing their due diligence."

Both women sat in thoughtful silence for a few minutes, watching the fire.

This wasn't exactly how Logan thought her first visit with her half-sister would go, but it didn't feel odd or uncomfortable. It was as if they'd always known each other. She was glad Olivia was here.

Logan's phone rang. Smiling at the screen, she tapped it and took the call.

"Hi, honey!" she said, then mouthed to Olivia, "It's Amy."

Just hearing her daughter's cheerful voice transported Logan back home. For the next few minutes, she listened as Amy relayed all the family news back in Jasper, CA. She and Ian were over at Logan's place, checking on the house and watering the plants. Well, she was watering and Ian was digging in the mud.

It was good to hear about events that had nothing to do with death or police interrogations. Amy's job as education coordinator for the Sea Otter Center in town was going well and Liam, her Scottish botanist husband, was having a lot of success with his sea kelp restoration projects, strung like green jewels just off the coast from La Jolla to Jasper.

Ian was growing like a weed. Logan was starting to shop for his present. She hoped Sofia, Logan and Olivia's mother, would stick to her policy of buying appropriate gifts for her great grandson's upcoming birthday. After abandoning Logan and Rick years ago, Sofia had only recently reentered their lives. Being wealthy, great-grandma could have tried to buy her way into Ian's affections, but so far, had resisted.

She asked Amy what Ian was into now. She'd seen a couple of things online he might like. Her tow-headed grandson heard his name and insisted on getting on the phone to talk to 'Gamma Logan'. His smiling face filled the screen—albeit upside down—and he babbled excitedly for a few minutes, pointing at Marmo, the neighbor's English Cream Golden Retriever, who was wagging his tail, head cocked, listening to the conversation. Ian continued relaying some tale of adventure they'd gotten into—all in one, long, streaming sentence. Marmo was short for Marshmallow and he spent almost as much time at Logan's house as his own. Everyone loved Marmo.

Seeing his buddy wander off into the next room, Ian dropped the phone and toddled after him. His mom came back on the line and they chatted for a few more minutes before Amy said she had to go—it was way too quiet in the other room! Logan laughed and said she'd call again in a few days.

Which reminded her, she needed to call Ben. They weren't attached at the hip, but if he didn't hear her voice at least every few days, he said he started going through withdrawals. She wouldn't admit it, but Logan felt the same way. Good to be loved. She needed to update him, anyway. She'd been keeping him in the loop since all this started and appreciated his calm take on things. She was definitely the more reactive of the two and wanted to get his opinion about the last few days' events.

While she was on the phone, Olivia had gone over to the Army trunk they'd dragged in from the garage to dry out yesterday. They'd stacked the journals next to it and spread out a few that still had damp pages. Olivia brought a couple of them back.

"Do you think they're dry enough to put back in?" she asked, handing one to Logan.

Logan reached up and took it, fanning through the pages. It was the green one she'd been reading before, where Irene confided to its pages the story—or at least the reference to it—of her rape. Knowing she probably shouldn't, but wanting to know if Irene ever revealed who the perpetrator was, Logan answered by beginning to read, picking up where she left off.

Within minutes, both she and Olivia had lost themselves again in the 1930s and '40s—the early days of Depoe Bay and the intimate lives of the Ellis family. It was strange to think that for the last eighty years, up until she and Ben bought this house from Wade, no one but Ellises had lived here. High on a hill, its back against thick forest, this humble home had sheltered Irene, her children and the generations that followed. They'd sat on that deck, looked out that window, watching fishing boats go in and out of Depoe Bay, sea lions bark on the rocks, and gray whales swim placidly by.

In this house, Irene had raised her two children, Aaron, the son of her beloved Jacob, who never came home, the other the unwanted result of a violent assault, a little girl named Mara. If she did the math right, Mara must be Wade's great-grandmother.

Logan lowered the journal onto her lap and gazed out the window.

Whatever happened to Mara?

37

"**I** love it!" Samantha said, walking into the living room, placing the booty from Pirate's on a table in the kitchen. She'd picked it up at a second hand store. She planned on using it outside once the deck was refinished. That was Clay's next project. After Logan filled her in yesterday, Sam had arranged this little get together at the house.

A tall, striking woman followed Sam in. Her thick, black hair was gathered into a chic French twist and sported a distinctive, white skunk stripe. Logan's French foreign-exchange-student would have called it a classic chignon. Logan admired the smooth style, but knew there was no way she could get her hair to do that. She'd tried.

Before removing her calf-length leather coat, the tall woman placed two large containers of hot coffee on the table with four cups. Logan hoped one of those was all for her.

In answer to Logan's raised eyebrow, she said, "I don't know about you, but one cup of coffee just doesn't do it for me. And if you can't roast your own, Pirate's has the best."

Logan smiled, "Absolutely! Not complaining. Let us know what we owe you guys for the goodies."

Sam made the introductions, identifying her guest as Dr. Jean Pullman, the local Medical Examiner for Lincoln County, who also happened to be her boyfriend Tim's big sister. Logan knew who she was. She'd talked Sam into bringing her over so they could maybe get the scoop on why the accident part of Charlie's accidental drowning death was now in question and what the police thought they had on Wade.

Olivia was checking out her black and white ensemble and blue shoes.

"Louis Vuitton?" she asked.

"Ferragamo," the woman smiled, "Got 'em in red, too!"

While Olivia and Jean talked designers, Logan got paper plates and a small bowl for the creamers and sugar packets, Sam put the pastries and breakfast burritos in the middle of the table.

"Didn't know what everybody wanted, so got a little of everything. Help yourself!" she said.

Everyone dug in. Between bites, they learned that Jean had a regular family practice in town as well as serving as the local ME.

"Harvard, top of her class," Sam told them. "Jean was offered a position at Johns Hopkins."

Olivia asked why she didn't take that position—it would have meant a much more lucrative and higher status career.

Jean wiped her mouth, then answered. "There's a need here. It's still hard to attract and keep doctors in small towns on the coast. Lack of professional opportunities to advance dissuade the younger ones. But I wouldn't want to practice anywhere else. I come from a commercial fishing family. Saltwater's in my blood."

Logan nodded. She'd always lived near hers. Now that her family included Olivia, it made her feel sad to know she would probably never have as close a relationship with her, since she lived 3,000 miles away in New York.

She learned more about Olivia's law firm when she described her work there to the other two women. She noticed Jean glancing at her watch, a plain, black Timex. So, she wasn't all about status symbols. She must just like good shoes. Sam glanced at her watch, too.

"When do you need to be back?" she asked.

"I've got another forty minutes before my first appointment," Jean said. "Like I told Sam, I can't promise anything, but I'll listen. Where do you want to start?"

"Well, we don't know much, but everyone seems to have a piece of the puzzle, how about if we go around and share what we know, then decide what to do next?" she said.

"As I said, I can't promise anything," Jean said, "but I'll listen. I'll share what I can."

"Olivia, why don't you go first?" Logan said.

"As most of you know, Wade Ellis called me—unofficially— to come down to the jail. We met briefly yesterday afternoon, but I'm going back there today to review what the police have—whatever they'll share with me—and try to get him released."

"Have they charged him with anything yet?" Sam asked.

"Not yet, but I don't want him down there. I told him not to say anything, but he already talked with them for a long time before he had them call me. It doesn't matter how innocent he is, they have a lot on tape. They can twist those words however they want. No one's memory is perfect. Their tactic will be to hammer him with the same questions over and over, have him give them a sequence of events, for example. Any inconsistencies from one telling to the next makes it sound like he's lying."

Everyone at that table knew this to be true. They were all law-abiding citizens who respected the police and the work they did, but they also knew how cases were closed. Jean and Sam both worked with law enforcement and Rick, being a cop, had often told her if she was ever detained by the police to keep her mouth shut.

"My goal today is to get him out." Olivia said. "They either need to charge him or let him go."

Sam reviewed the basic backgrounds of Wade and Charlie, information from the feature she'd done on The Collins Hotel up to Charlie's death Tuesday night. Something she said caught Logan's attention. She only half-listened to the rest of her summary of the two families while her brain tried to grasp the faint connection she felt was important but didn't know why. She couldn't put it into words and had nothing new to add, so passed the baton when the conversation came around to her.

Up to now, Jean had been listening intently, not commenting or reacting to everyone else's input. They all looked at her expectantly, but she shook her head.

"I'm sorry, but I can't share anything," she said. "Not yet, anyway. I've been out of town. I'm catching up with my regular patients—the live ones. I won't even be able to get back into the morgue again until Monday. I shouldn't even be talking with you about an ongoing case."

"So, there *is* a case?" Logan and Olivia both asked at once.

Jean remained silent.

They hadn't really expected her to share sensitive, official information, but still, Logan was disappointed. The police had to have some reason for suspecting Charlie's death may not have been accidental and suddenly wanting to question Wade more aggressively. That kind of information could only have come from the medical professional who examined the body.

Not wanting to push her any further and possibly alienate her, Logan said she understood. She thanked her for coming and started to clean up. Hopefully, Olivia would get Wade released today and they would never need to know what information pointed the finger at him.

For the next few minutes, Sam steered the conversation into lighter territory, talking about a kayak trip she and Tim planned on taking in the spring.

On her way out the door to her car, Jean looked back over her shoulder at Logan and added, "I can say this much. Your friend, Wade, may or may not be involved, but the police have a good reason for looking at Charlie's death a little closer."

38

Olivia called from the jail. The news was not good. Far from being released, Wade had been formally arrested. The police were keeping him. They charged him with murder. First degree. Senior Deputy District Attorney Kazinski had been assigned to the case.

Not only that, but in the initial arraignment that afternoon, the judge refused to set bail. He considered Wade an escape risk because he and Charlie had airline tickets to leave the country for India next week. Unfortunately, those tickets included a layover in Vietnam, a country without extradition. Wade's explanation that he and Charlie were leaving the country to do humanitarian work and so he could begin his field research for his PhD fell on deaf ears. The judge said he would review the documentation once the defense received and submitted it, but in the meantime, better safe than sorry.

The next court appearance date was set. Hopefully, they would determine there wasn't enough to bring the case to trial. Olivia told Logan they needed to prepare as if they were going to trial, because they probably were.

They?

When she got home that night, Olivia explained the use of the plural pronoun.

Wade had spent hours talking with the police before he asked for a lawyer. Who knew what they had or thought they had? Olivia would have to go down to the jail and go over everything with him again. She'd already called her firm in New York and took two weeks of vacation she had coming. Wade would need a local lawyer, but she'd help in the meantime. Hopefully, before the two weeks were up, this would all be resolved and Wade would be free.

With a limited amount of time to prepare, Olivia said she'd need all the help she could get, so Logan was invited to the party. To make it official—which was the only way the guard would let her into the jail with Olivia to meet with the prisoner, Olivia printed out a form and handed it to Logan with a pen.

"Sign here," she said.

Logan looked at her warily, but did as instructed.

"Congratulations!" she said, taking the form and shaking her hand. "You're now my legal assistant. Welcome to the team!"

At some point they'd know what the DA's office had, but for now they were on a fact-finding mission which started with Wade. They would meet with him first thing in the morning. Logan's job would be to listen and take notes.

The Lincoln County Courthouse took up about one square block—just a few bulky rectangles in downtown Newport, hooked together with indoor and outdoor walkways. Once they made it through security and their bags were pawed through and returned, a guard came out to lead them to a meeting room where they could consult with their client.

On the way, they passed the entrance to the DA's office.

Logan scowled at the door. Kazinski was probably in there right now, thinking of ways to lock Wade up for the rest of his life. Logan couldn't help her reaction. Until evidence proved otherwise, Wade was innocent.

This was an experience Logan could have lived without, but she couldn't help it—in spite of the dismal, gray surroundings, the security check, the single file walk into the bowels of the jail, and the thick, metal door that just clicked shut behind her, Logan felt excited.

After what they'd read in Irene's journals the night before, she had questions, and hopefully, Wade had answers.

But it was a truly dispirited man Logan saw seated at the metal table when they walked into the tiny room assigned them. Without thinking, she almost went around the table to wrap Wade in a big, fierce, Mama Bear hug. But she resisted. The guard hadn't left yet. Legal assistants probably weren't supposed to hug their boss's clients.

Once seated, Olivia took the lead. She took out a couple of yellow pads from her briefcase for each of them. Logan was impressed with her little sister's professionalism and composure. She radiated confidence.

Wade seemed to absorb some of that and even though he still looked tired, he sat up straighter and looked ready to aide in his own defense.

For the next hour, Olivia had him go over every aspect of his relationship with Charlie—how they met, what she was like, who her friends were. Then she built a precise timeline of the events of the week leading up to Charlie's death.

She had explained her process to Logan on the way over in the car. For now, she wouldn't ask any leading questions, just let him relay the events and give his opinions fresh and without prejudice. She didn't try to direct the process, because she never knew what information might prove valuable for his defense. Cases could turn on one little detail. A discrepancy in time, a hint of motive, a thread of deceit—any of these could set them on the right path. Until they knew what the police had, they'd just have to scattershot it and collect everything.

Now, Olivia was going back over Wade's answers, asking specific questions about points she felt needed more attention, particularly everything he'd done and said from the time he and Charlie were seen downstairs at dinner until the next morning when Olivia found her body. He went through it all again, from the conversation they had with Grandmother Charlotte Saturday night to the next morning when he brought his things over to stay until she returned from her conference.

"What time did you arrive at the hotel?" Olivia asked.

"Around 7:30 a.m. I left Pete's house as soon as she called to tell me the coast was clear. His place is only about twenty minutes away," Wade said.

Logan recorded the address.

"What did you do when you got there?" Olivia asked.

"Well, after I put my stuff in the room, we went downstairs to have breakfast. We were going to go on a hike later, but Charlie said she was tired," he said.

"This was when she came down with the flu?"

"Not yet," Wade said. "It wasn't full blown yet, I thought maybe she was just run down. She hadn't been sleeping well with all the arguing with her grandma. So I made her my protein shake. It's got all kinds of good stuff in it. It usually fixes me up—there wasn't enough powder left for two shakes so I had cereal."

"When did she get sick?"

"A little later," Wade said, "She had a fever but seemed to feel better after she threw up a couple times. It was just a twenty-four-hour bug. She was fine by Monday night. We did a shorter hike Tuesday morning."

"Maybe we overdid it," he said. "Do you think that's what made her get sick again that night? Maybe we shouldn't have gone . . . if I had known . . ."

Olivia got him back on track, asking about anyone he may have talked to or who may have seen him that evening to establish an alibi, to prove he was anywhere but the pool area during the critical time period. But other than some texts he'd exchanged with his friend, Pete, around 8:30 p.m.—she'd get the exact time from his phone records, later—he hadn't spoken to or seen anyone but Charlie.

Next, Olivia focused on motive. Could he think of any reason why the police would think he had anything to do with Charlie's murder? Did he benefit in any way from her death? But Wade could think of nothing, other than the non-existent argument Monson kept insisting he and Charlie had had.

"If I was after Charlie's money and was going to kill her for it," he said, "I'd have done it *after* we were married, not before!"

He sat back with a frustrated huff.

"This is all so insane!" he said. "I *loved* Charlie. How can anyone think I would hurt her? If it wasn't an accident, they need to be looking for who *did* this!"

It was clear Wade was exhausted and they'd gotten everything they could out of him for now. They gathered their things and Logan knocked on the door to let the guard know they were ready to leave.

As the guard hooked him up again and guided him around the table to walk him back to his cell, Wade asked them not to forget to check on his dad, Archer Ellis. He usually visited him every few weeks and was supposed to have gone over to the state hospital in Salem this weekend.

Something clicked in Logan's brain. She and Olivia made it

through all of Irene's journals last night. In the last one, Irene said something about her daughter, Mara, when she was pregnant with Archer. She hadn't named the father, but if what Irene alluded to was true, it would go a long way to explaining why Grandmother Charlotte was so against Wade and Charlie ever marrying.

She wasn't sure how it fit into Wade's defense, if at all, and it was only one piece of the puzzle, but Logan had a gut feeling that if they could just unravel the secrets held close for so long by both families and find out how they were connected, they could help the earnest, frightened young man being marched away from them down the hall—helpless, grieving the woman he loved.

More than ever, Logan felt determined to get to the truth. On the way to the car, an idea began to take shape. She shared it with Olivia on their way to meet Sam at the Tide Pool Pub in Depoe Bay for some pizza.

39

Sitting just a few feet off Highway 101, The Tide Pool Pub and Pool did not dress to impress.

Light blue shake siding, badly in need of a paint job, was graced by a sign proudly proclaiming its main offerings—Full Bar, Lottery, and Pizza. A two-by-four railing strung with last year's Christmas lights bordered a plywood ramp that angled up to the entrance. A gravel-filled flower bed was decorated with colorful, battered fishing buoys. Inside, ripped Naugahyde bar stools and threadbare carpet didn't make the place look much better.

But locals knew if you got past all that and ordered, you were in for some of the best pizza on the coast. Skilled bar tenders, local wines, beers on tap, a fireplace and free pool. What wasn't to like?

Sam sat in back, near the fire, anchoring a table for four, enjoying her usual, a tall, black-and-tan. Logan and Olivia were arriving in a few minutes and Jean said she'd stop by for a slice and a beer on her way home. They'd order once everyone got there.

The bar didn't start hopping until later, but the kitchen was pretty busy already with takeout orders and early diners.

The door whooshed open and several people came in at once. Sam spotted Jean immediately. Her distinctive skunk stripe was hard to miss. She smiled as her future sister-in-law slipped off her raincoat and made her way over. A crewneck, ivory cashmere sweater topped her usual slim, black slacks. Today's shoes were jade green and looked butter soft. How she managed to keep them dry and unscuffed in all this rain was a mystery.

Taking the seat across from Sam, she waved down a server and ordered a beer. When her Rogue brewery Outta Line IPA arrived, she took a long pull and smacked her lips.

"I needed that!"

While waiting, they talked family and fishing. Tim had one of the 315 crab permits given out in the area and had been bringing in pretty good hauls this year. He'd been out for a couple of days already, so would be back in tomorrow to deliver to the seafood processing plant in Newport before going back out again. Crab was on the menu for Sunday dinner. Winter crab was the best.

Knowing Logan and Olivia would be here any minute, and that Jean wouldn't tell her much in front of Wade's defense team, Sam asked for a quick update—anything she could tell her. Why was Wade in jail? What evidence did the police have to arrest him? Was it evidence collected at the crime scene or something Jean had discovered from the body? Sam was still a reporter, after all, and wasn't afraid to butt in where she wasn't invited. If she threw a whole bunch of questions at her, maybe Jean would answer one of them. That strategy had worked for Sam before.

Jean stalled for a while, then leaned forward.

"This has to be off the record, Sam," she said.

Sam nodded. She knew that when and if there was something her future sister-in-law could officially share with the press, she'd give the story to Sam first. She could wait.

"I think Wade's getting railroaded," Jean said. "From what I know of the two families, I'd vouch for an Ellis over a Collins any day. But without proof, there's nothing I can do to keep Kazinski from staying focused on the suspect he already has locked up.

"He could put him away for life. Wade had opportunity, and according to Monson, motive. As for means, unfortunately, I have forensic evidence they can use. It's not definitive, but it's strong enough for them to keep him in jail until they get more."

Sam leaned in, her eyes dancing with excitement, but she kept her voice calm, "What motive? What evidence? And what's all the rest?"

Jean shook her head.

"You know I can't give you specifics, and I don't want to talk about it when your friends get here—they're his defense team—but whatever they're doing, they'd better do it quick. Right now, I have clear, forensic evidence that someone drowned that poor girl—forcibly—this was not an accident."

"What evidence?" Sam insisted. "What did you find?"

Just then, Logan and Olivia arrived at the table. Sloughing off jackets, they both pulled out chairs and sat down.

"You found something?" Logan asked, taking the seat next to Jean, leaving the one near the fire for Olivia who held her hands out to warm them and nodded her thanks. "Are we talking about who I think we're talking about?"

"*We're* not talking about anything," Jean said, sitting back.

After the server arrived and took their order, Logan took a different tack. She decided to share what she and Olivia had discovered. Normally, they wouldn't divulge any information to someone who may be on the side of the prosecution, but

Logan had a good feeling about Jean. She seemed more interested in finding the truth than on supporting any particular side. Give a little, get a little—she hoped.

So, for the next half hour, they took turns telling Sam and Jean about Irene's journals and the tangled family histories. How Frank Collins raped Irene, his best friend's wife, just days after Jacob mysteriously disappeared. How Irene, when the baby girl was born, lied and put Jacob as the father on the birth certificate instead of Frankie. Her actions may have been difficult for the three modern women sitting around the table to understand, but seen in the milieu of her times, they made sense.

She didn't have easy access to a safe abortion even if she felt comfortable with that option. She felt her daughter, Mara, deserved a legitimate last name. Ellis. That was important back then. And finally, she reasoned that if Jacob had ever did come home, he would accept Mara as his own since Irene had gotten pregnant just days after she last saw him. If anyone did the math, it would all add up.

Logan summed the stories up with the last revelation they'd uncovered in the journals about Frank's two children, Emerson Collins and Mara Ellis. Unaware they were half-siblings, they had a child, although they did not marry. That child was Wade's father, Archer Ellis.

"Okay, Emerson ditched Mara and married the southern belle, Charlotte Collins, the one who owns the hotel now, right?" Jean said, now totally engrossed in the story.

"Yes, Mrs. Collins is Charlie's grandmother. Emerson Collins, now deceased, was Charlie's grandfather," Logan said.

"Wait a minute, so Emerson Collins was both Charlie and Wade's biological grandfather? What did that make them? Half-second cousins twice removed or something?" Sam asked.

"I don't know," Olivia said.

"If they are closely related, it's understandable why Grandma wanted to keep them apart," Olivia said.

"Yes," Logan said, "and remember, Archer Ellis was diagnosed as a paranoid schizophrenic, probably as a result of his parents being half-siblings. Grandma was probably worried that might happen to any children Wade or Charlie might have."

"But what does that prove?" Sam asked. "If Grandma was that upset about Wade and Charlie marrying and would have children, would she go so far as to kill one of them to prevent it? And if she did, she'd kill Wade, not her own granddaughter, right?"

"Actually," Jean offered, "Charlie and Wade's children would have only had a very slightly higher risk of genetic issues than any other non-related couple. People don't realize it, but you have to be more closely related, like first cousins or closer, for it to be a real problem. Of course, not everyone knows that, so that could still be a motive."

Olivia sat back in her chair and sighed, "And even if she was nuts enough to want to kill her own granddaughter, Grandmother Charlotte wasn't anywhere near the hotel when Charlie drowned. She was hours away up in Portland, giving that speech to her gardening club."

No one spoke for a moment.

Logan didn't have any answers. She wasn't sure how or if any of this information would help Wade's case, but somehow it was connected. Once the whole truth was unearthed, maybe this one piece of the puzzle would help.

"The only way you're going to know for sure is through DNA," Jean said.

"Yep," Logan said. "We've got that covered."

She told them about the two 'his-and-her' baggies sitting on the floorboard of the car out front. She and Olivia had carefully assembled any items from Wade and Charlie's room at the Collins that might have DNA on them into two separate baggies, one for Wade, one for Charlie. They hadn't wanted to leave them at the house. Logan was planning on putting them in a box and shipping them to the genetic tracing company in the morning.

"But won't that take too long? Those tests can take weeks, right? I mean, Kazinski is fast tracking everything," Sam said.

"If you're okay with me handling it," Jean said. "I think I can get it done faster."

They didn't know if this would be official or not, but they were absolutely okay with that.

Jean still wouldn't reveal her specific findings that indicated Charlie's death was a homicide versus an accident, but she had warmed up considerably.

"So far," Sam said, "nobody had a reason to want to kill Charlie."

"I believe in empirical evidence," Jean said. "I leave motive to someone else. Too fuzzy for me. Follow the evidence and things eventually make sense.

She finished off the last of her beer and set it back down on the table. "I do know this. Unless you come up with someone else who had a reason to kill Charlie and the opportunity and means to do so, the police are going to go with who they've got. And as far as I know, who they've got is Wade," she said.

"But what reason could Wade possibly have for wanting to kill Charlie?" Sam said, pushing the bridge of her cat-eye glasses back up. Blessed—or cursed—with a button nose, her glasses were always sliding down. "He didn't benefit from her death in any way."

Jean hesitated, then said, "They have motive, remember. Remember their argument? Supposedly Charlie was going to leave him and he was furious."

"Well," Sam said. "That makes it a crime of passion, *if* he did it, at least it won't be premeditated."

"There must be someone else. What about the sister? Did she stand to inherit Charlie's half if she died?" Logan asked.

"Don't know," Sam said.

Logan's phone *brrrrd* on the table. She glanced at the screen. Curious, she took the call and walked outside for a minute so she could hear. When she got back to the table, they were divvying up the bill. Logan held her phone up and waggled it.

"Guess who wants to have a chat?" she said.

Three sets of questioning eyebrows went up.

40

Amanda carefully placed the portable phone extension back into the wall charger in the dining room. Leaving the lights off, she stayed where she was, listening as Grandmother Charlotte left her office and walked toward the elevator. She waited until the doors dinged opened, accepted their passenger and began chugging up to the second floor before quickly stepping down the hall to her own room. She carefully pulled the door shut behind her.

Fear clutched her chest. This certainly complicated things.

What could Grandmother Charlotte want to talk with that Logan woman about? If she'd said, Amanda must have missed it. She'd only been able to listen in on the last few minutes of the conversation. Whatever it was, it couldn't be good.

Grandmother had been acting strangely all week. And Amanda had a pretty good idea why. She hadn't confided in her, but then, she never did. She only ever talked to Charlie, her favorite.

Well, Charlie's gone, now, Grandmother. Easy come, easy go!

For a few minutes, she lay back on the bed and allowed herself the luxury of reliving those final, delicious last seconds of Charlie's life, ebbing away under her fingers. She almost wished she'd struggled more, but she'd been too weak. It had been too easy. Why hadn't she gotten rid of her before?

Long before that, she knew their mother had suspected her, although she had been too afraid to confront her. Instead, she shipped Charlie off to Grandmother Charlotte's to protect her from the increasingly frequent 'accidents' she kept suffering. Girl was definitely a klutz.

Once again, Charlie had landed on her feet and Amanda was stuck at home.

Grandmother Charlotte was rich! So, instead of continuing to suffer under the hands of her big sister, Charlie got to spend her teenage years living in a luxury hotel, being doted on by Grandmother, while she had to stay and live in that tiny cracker box of a house, eating meatloaf and spaghetti with dull Dorothy and Robert in boring, ugly suburbia.

Within days of her high school graduation, good old mom and dad went and got themselves killed in a car crash. As usual, she had to take care of herself. Grandmother offered to pay for tuition, but she still had to work on top of keeping up a full-time course load, just to live on noodle soup and soda crackers in a little shithole apartment. Grandmother still let her come and stay at the hotel like before, but she knew she would always be a visitor. Charlie was the chosen one.

As fun as this trip down memory lane was, Amanda knew she needed to concentrate. She carefully flipped through every conversation, everything she'd seen and observed since she called Grandmother up in Portland with the news.

That had been a fun call to make.

How had she sounded? Devastated, of course, that her precious Charlie had died, but there had been something else. Surprise? Yes, that was it, Grandmother Charlotte had sounded surprised, as if she'd been expecting news, just not *that* news.

The last few days, something else had changed. Just a subtle difference at first, but Amanda had noticed. She'd been encouraging Grandmother's grief—so she could be the one to assuage it. She'd also been working to keep Grandmother's anger stoked and directed at Wade, the convenient scapegoat.

But another emotion surfaced, like the answers on the Magic 8 Ball she'd had as a kid. It was as if all the anger toward Wade and the intense grief was loosening its grip and flowing away. The dull expression on Grandmother's face and in her body language exuded one emotion and one only. Resignation.

And then this meeting. Inviting a stranger into her greenhouse, her private sanctum. Something Grandmother Charlotte never did.

Squeezing her eyes shut, Amanda went back over everything again. She ticked off the days in her mind. Wednesday, Grandmother had been in shock—hadn't said much at all. She'd been given a sedative by the doctor and gone to bed early. Thursday, she'd put a hold on the renovation work and begun making funeral arrangements. Next, she'd started going through the hotel, getting rid of any trace of Wade. She couldn't bring herself to go into Charlie's room yet, so she had said yes when his lawyer asked to send someone down to go in there and collect his things. Then Logan McKenna showed up. She didn't think they spent any time together talking. Grandmother was in her office while the McKenna woman cleared out Wade's things.

Grandmother even went through the kitchen, throwing out the pineapple juice he used for his shakes, and the canister of protein powder they all knew Charlie kept for him in the cupboard—anything he might have touched.

This whole week, she hadn't been able say Wade's name and grew rigid and angry when anyone mentioned him. But in the last day or so, she seemed to have lost her hatred of the man she thought killed her Charlie. Why? Unless she no longer thought he had.

The thought wasn't a reassuring one. Had Grandmother figured it out? But how could she know? Charlie had the flu and Grandmother Charlotte was over a hundred miles away when Amanda gripped the top of Charlie's head, pushed it underwater and held it there until she drowned.

Amanda shook the question free and made up her mind. Whatever Grandmother thought she knew—or guessed—she couldn't allow her to share it with anyone, let alone that nosy Logan woman. She'd probably bring in the cops and even though Amanda was pretty sure she'd covered her tracks, she wasn't taking chances. She never did.

No, this changed things, but she could handle it. Amanda had always taken pride in being able to adjust to conditions on the ground. The only difference this time was that she now had two problems to get rid of, not just one.

The more she thought about it, the brighter things looked. This might be even better than her original plan. With Grandmother gone, she wouldn't have to spend the next few years scraping and bowing to win her affection and a bigger piece of the pie, waiting for her to drop dead of old age. Being the only surviving relative, she would get Charlie's share, her own endowment, AND the hotel. With a good attorney and a little patience, she could probably cut out the garden club, too. She'd be set for life. Grandmother didn't know she'd seen her will, but Amanda made it her business to know every piece of paper in Charlotte Collins's files.

She couldn't help grinning as a solution began to take shape.

Yes! That might just work . . .

◦ ◦ ◦ ◦ ◦

LIES THAT BIND

Charlotte Collins stood at the window, hands clasped behind her back, waiting for her guest. Although it did not move her today, the view was as spectacular as ever. Pale blue sky stretched over a cerulean sea, dotted here and there with tiny fishing boats and the occasional light-gray puff indicating a spout from a migrating whale, far away near the horizon. A low bank of clouds, lit rosy by the rising sun, was quickly dissipating.

The muffled soundtrack of waves crashing on the rocks below always calmed her.

Perched as it was on the top of the cliff behind the hotel, the greenhouse commanded an even better view than the hotel dining room. And it was solid. Built, as Frank used to say, 'like a brick outhouse,' the greenhouse—*her* greenhouse—had been one of Emerson's more expensive apology gifts.

This one came on the heels of his dalliance with the Ellis girl, the unfortunate maid, Mara. She remembered the mother coming to her for money. Would things have been different if she hadn't refused? She saw it as blackmail then. So distasteful. She'd offered to pay for an abortion, but Irene said the girl was determined to keep the child. If she'd insisted, maybe none of this would have happened.

Or, she could have just given her the money and had her sent away. Mara's damaged child, Archer, would have been born in some other town, some other state, and Wade and Charlie would never have met. But how was she to know? Later, when Rowena was dying, she'd told her what Frank had done. If she had only known that Mara and Emerson were related . . . she couldn't believe it when Rowena whispered this last secret in her ear. At least Rowena was spared knowing her son got his half-sister pregnant.

Sighing, she turned and sat down in one of the two high-back, straw chairs. Known as peacock chairs, she'd always loved them. Angled toward each other, but still facing outward, they took full advantage of the view. She had spent many an hour right here, hiding out from the twisted family she'd married into.

A tea tray sat on the small table at the foot of the chairs. She reached down and felt the side of the pot. Satisfied it was still hot, she settled back to wait.

She and Charlie had often taken lunch out here. The memory brought her no joy.

The Logan woman would be here any minute. She'd called her last night and arranged for an eight o'clock meeting. She hadn't told her what it was for, just that she had something she wanted to discuss.

Amanda would show her back. Since all this happened, Amanda had been even more Gollum-like than usual. At least she made some tea. The woman was good for something.

Charlotte let her mind wander. Her unfocused gaze settled on a puddle of pale, yellow light pooled on the flagstone floor.

The last three days had been torture. But eventually she'd accepted the inevitable. Charlie was dead and she'd killed her. There was just no way around this horrible fact. It didn't matter that it was an accident. She'd planned to kill someone—even if that someone was Wade—so she wasn't innocent.

She'd already ruined young Wade's life. The young man shouldn't have to go to jail for the rest of it when he was only guilty of loving Charlie. The hate that had consumed her when she'd learned of Charlie's death was gone. Just like that.

It wasn't Wade's fault. He had no idea he was related to Charlie. But she knew Emerson was grandfather to both of them. Common sense told you that wasn't good. All you had to do was look at Wade's father, Archer.

Archer was the polluted result of two half-siblings, Mara

and Emerson mating and Archer was a full-blown schizo-phrenic. Who knows what issues Wade and Charlie's children, her grandchildren, would have had?

When she married into the Collins family, she took a vow. They were her family—their secrets to keep were her secrets to keep. But now she wondered how she could have followed them all so blindly for so many years. To protect what?

Charlotte Abbott Collins sat up straighter in her regal chair. Abbott blood ran in her veins, not tainted Collins blood. It was time to make this right.

41

She didn't mind the spiders. Amanda felt at home in dank, dark places and the crawl space beneath the greenhouse certainly qualified. She'd discovered it during one of her first two-week visits after Charlie was sent to live with Grandmother. You couldn't stand upright, but she'd long ago discovered it had its advantages. Like being able to come and go without being observed and listening in on conversations.

Whenever Grandmother and Charlie retreated to the greenhouse—excluding her as always from their private little world—all she had to do was crawl down here and press her ear against the main duct. She could hear every word—loud and clear. They never talked about anything very important. She heard all about Charlie's first kiss—which was beyond boring—her high SAT scores—did Charlie ever get any other kind?—and Grandma's plans for which colleges she should apply to.

As usual, Amanda hadn't been invited to today's party, either. But she doubted Grandmother wanted to discuss the pros and cons of attending OSU versus her alma mater back east with Logan McKenna. No, she had something very different in mind.

She'd thought everything through last night. Then she'd set her alarm early this morning to make a few last-minute preparations for Logan's visit. She was ready.

Amanda couldn't help giggling silently to herself. She listened carefully. Hearing movement above her and Grandmother's docent speech about the greenhouse, she relaxed. Whatever Grandma was going to talk to Logan about, she'd better make it quick. They didn't have much time.

Another giggle rose in her chest, but she kept it down. Excitement filling her, she leaned forward, holding her body very still, straining to hear. With her right hand, she reached up and adjusted the respirator mask on her face to make sure she had a tight fit, It made her look like Darth Vader, but was a necessary precaution. The groundskeeper always kept one in the shed. Being more than two times heavier than air, CO_2 sinks. Without the mask, she'd be affected before anyone in the greenhouse.

She didn't plan on wearing it long. She'd have it back on the shelf before anyone missed it.

❀ ❀ ❀ ❀ ❀

Mrs. Collins offered Logan a croissant from the plate Amanda had left, but didn't take one herself. In the pregnant silence, Logan looked out to sea, nibbling on the pastry periodically, giving this grieving grandmother space to get to the reason she'd invited her here.

Finally, without preamble, Mrs. Collins spoke.

"I want someone to know," she said, simply. ". . . all of it."

Logan put down her plate and sat back in her chair, giving her her full attention.

"I was rude to you the other day," she added. "I'm sorry for that. You were just doing what you were supposed to do, getting Wade's things. It is a relief to have them gone. Thank you."

She took a deep breath.

"When we are done here, you can call whoever you need to call. You're working with Wade's lawyer—your sister, I believe?"

"Half-sister, but yes, she is," Logan said.

"Ahh . . . another family with history," Mrs. Collins said. "But I'll bet not half as interesting as ours."

When Logan didn't respond, she continued, "Well, call her. She'll know what to do."

"Of course," Logan said.

It was obvious this woman was used to calling the shots.

"It was an accident," Mrs. Collins said, "a horrible accident. But I'd like to explain. Let me start over, so all this makes sense.

"Charlie never wanted to run the hotel. I see that now. She and Wade were filled with so much hope and optimistic energy. They were going to save the world, one village at a time. But I thought it was Wade keeping Charlie from me, from her destiny here—all Wade's fault.

"He couldn't help his ancestry, though, and that was the real reason I was against their marriage from the start. This all started long before either of them was born."

She looked into Logan's eyes, beseeching her forgiveness—anyone's forgiveness.

Before Logan could say anything, she said, "Hear me out. I need to explain some things."

For the next few minutes, Logan listened as Charlotte Collins lay bare the family secrets, beginning with Rowena's revelation that Frank raped Irene, on through the tragic events that followed. Frank marrying Rowena and having Emerson, the spoiled man-child who seduced Mara, his half-sister, then married Charlotte.

Everything Mrs. Collins said verified what Irene alluded to in her journals. But Logan still didn't see how this applied to Wade's defense. It sounded like a confession, but so far, Mrs. Collins had only confessed to other people's sins . . . grievous as they were.

Her face must have betrayed her confusion because Mrs. Collins tried again to get to the point.

"I know about plants. As you can see," she said, gesturing at the neat rows of roses, azaleas, and orchids behind her. "I've always had a green thumb. I can make just about anything grow."

The next words came harder, but she pushed them out.

"Well, I also know about wild plants. Mushrooms in particular. Many varieties grow in this climate. Not many people know this, but mushrooms actually benefit the forest. We don't think of them that way, but mushrooms are the fruit of something called the mycelium network, which is like an underground internet. Mycelium connects the trees in such a way they tell each other what they need, then transfer water and nutrients to each other. They help each other.

"Like families are supposed to," she added.

"Every year, I gather chanterelles, boletes, all kinds of edibles grow around here. Whatever we don't use fresh in soups, risotto, omelets, I dry. They're particularly abundant in the fall. Last fall, I made a special trip to collect one particular species, *amanita ocreata.*"

She looked at her one-member audience and felt further clarification was needed.

". . . otherwise known as the *destroying angel.*"

The greenhouse was silent as Logan let this bombshell sink

in, but it still didn't make sense. Was Mrs. Collins saying she poisoned Charlie? Was that why Charlie had been sick? Was it mushroom poisoning, not the flu? But Mrs. Collins couldn't have poisoned anyone—she wasn't even here.

"I know what you're thinking, but I haven't told you about a special feature of the amanitas. When *amanita ocreata* is ingested, the first symptoms are very similar to the flu. It doesn't last long, so the person thinks they're better and does not seek medical help."

Mrs. Collins could barely continue.

"But, over the next two or three days, the amanita is busy, silently attacking the internal organs. When the 'flu' returns, severe cramps, violent vomiting, and diarrhea often bring death."

If she heard her correctly, the kindly grandmother sitting in front of her had just confessed to killing Charlie.

Logan couldn't help it, the question just popped out, "Why? Why would you want to do that to your own granddaughter?"

42

M rs. Collins mouth twisted and a low moan escaped her lips. "I *didn't*," she shouted, tears streaming down her face. "I didn't mean to . . . I meant to kill Wade."

"Why?" Logan said. "And how could you have killed anyone? You were in Portland, giving a speech, right?"

"I wasn't supposed to know Wade stayed over when I was out of town, but of course I knew. I know everything that happens at The Collins. His habit was to make a protein shake every morning. He kept a canister of the awful stuff tucked behind the mixer in one of the bottom cupboards. There was only a small amount left in this one, so it was easy to mix the dried amanita powder into it and know he would get enough. Then I would throw it away when I returned."

Logan was curious in spite of herself. "Wouldn't he taste it?" she asked.

"The protein powder has a very strong flavor itself, and he usually mixed it with pineapple juice. No, he wouldn't have tasted anything," she said.

"How could you be sure Wade would drink it and not Charlie or Amanda?" Logan asked.

"Charlie *never* drank it! None of us would touch the stuff— it smelled awful," she said. "Of course, if I'd had *any* idea she would drink any of it . . ."

"So how did Charlie get it if no one else liked it and he was the only one who drank it?" Logan asked.

Mrs. Collins doubled over, sobbing, holding her head in her hands. Logan wanted to comfort her, but was rooted to her seat. How should you comfort a killer? Should you?

Her host regained enough control to continue, "I couldn't understand that either. Then when the detective was interviewing us, asking us to go over the last few days, I told him what I did from the time I arrived in Portland until I got Amanda's phone call.

"Then Amanda filled him in on everything that happened here. That's when it all started making horrible sense.

"She said Charlie had been tired the morning I left. Wade told her she needed to start building her immune system up before their trip to India. He was always raving about all the vitamins and minerals in his protein powder. Amanda said Wade gave up his morning protein shake for Charlie—insisted she take the last of it, that he would pick up some more later."

Logan couldn't imagine how horrible this grandmother must feel. But then again, it wasn't an innocent mistake. This woman was far from innocent. What a mess. What a tragedy.

Then Mrs. Collins supplied the last, cruel detail.

"She said Charlie laughed about how awful it smelled, then held her nose and drank the whole thing down."

"Does Amanda know?" Logan asked.

Under their feet, Charlie's other killer exulted.

She does now!

This was better than anything she could have planned! What poetic justice! Grandmother killed her precious Charlie. She,

Amanda, had just come along and finished the job.

She listened for the telltale slur in either of their voices. Should be any time now . . .

"No," Mrs. Collins said, "Amanda couldn't have known."

Mrs. Collins didn't look good. The confession must have taken its toll.

"If you don't mind, I'm going to go back to my room and lie down for a while," she said, ending the meeting. "I know you have a phone call to make. I'll walk you out. Don't worry, I will be here when the police arrive, I have nowhere to go."

With great effort, Mrs. Collins pushed herself up from her chair. Immediately, her face drained of color. Wavering slightly, she tried to take a step, but her knees buckled and she collapsed in a heap. Her head made a sickening thud as she landed, but Logan jumped up and managed to break her fall enough to prevent her skull from actually cracking on the flagstone floor.

"Mrs. Collins!" Logan said, holding her, patting her cheeks to try to revive her.

Mrs. Collins' eyes fluttered, but didn't open all the way. "Leave . . . get out! Must be the CO_2 . . . get outside now . . . !"

"Not without you," she said.

Logan reached under Mrs. Collins armpits and started to drag her toward the door—she'd only seen one door to get in or out of the greenhouse. Something must have happened to the CO_2 tanks—one of them must have leaked. Her dad had always warned them about venting the garage when they used the space heater. Carbon dioxide was colorless and odorless he told them—a silent, deadly killer. If they could just get outside, they'd be okay.

Redoubling her efforts, Logan used all her strength to pull

harder, but she only made it a few feet when a wave of nausea hit and her vision began to blur. They didn't have time to reach the exit. Fighting a rising feeling of panic, she realized she was probably only minutes or seconds behind Mrs. Collins in succumbing to the gas.

Logan ran back to the window, looking for anything at all that might work. The straw chairs were useless, but the little table might work. Sweeping everything off with her forearm, sending the tea things scattering and breaking across the floor, she plucked up the small, wrought iron table and swung it with all her might at the window.

It hit with a thud, but with a sinking heart, Logan watched as it bounced off and crashed into a tub of geraniums. She desperately looked around for something else that might work, but knew it would be a waste of time. Mrs. Collins had said something about this place being built to withstand tsunamis. No wonder it stood up to a little tea table.

Knowing their survival depended on it, Logan wasted no more time. Leaving Mrs. Collins where she was, she ran back to the entrance. Maybe if she could run out and drink in a few lungfuls of clean air, she could hold her breath and come back in for Mrs. Collins.

When she reached the door, it was shut. Several desperate yanks didn't budge it. All hope that this was an accident left her. Someone had locked them in. She didn't know anything about the mechanics of the tank, and there wasn't time anyway. The only other option was to get help to come to them. She started back for her phone.

Mrs. Collins lay on the floor where she left her, still breathing, but barely.

Grabbing her cell from her bag, she went through her recent call list and hit the number for the hotel. Pressing the phone to her ear, it took a while to ring. When it did, she breathed a sigh of relief. Cell reception was intermittent on the coast. Thank god the call had gone through.

Come on, come on, pick up, Amanda! I know you're there.

It rang six times before the answering machine came on.

Damn!

The room started swimming and a wave of nausea hit. Logan disconnected the call and tried to dial 911, but the numbers on the tiny keys were blurry. She blinked her eyes several times, finally forcing them to focus, and made the call.

"911, what is your emergency?"

Logan managed to mumble something, hoping she was more coherent to the person on the other end of the line than she was to herself.

". . . yes, The Collins . . . we're in the greenhouse . . . don't know . . . Depoe Bay . . . yes, yes, I'll be here . . ."

This last answer struck her as funny. Yes, she would be there. Where else could she be?

Whatever else the emergency dispatcher said was lost to Logan. As if from a great distance, she heard her cell phone clatter to the ground. It didn't have far to fall, though, because Logan was already there. Sometime during the call, she'd slipped off the chair. She lay on the greenhouse floor, staring through the damned window that wouldn't break, at some seagulls circling lazily overhead.

43

With the paper put to bed for the week, Sam was holding down a table at Pirate's, waiting for Logan. She was looking forward to their weekly morning coffee chat. She had news. If Olivia came along, all the better.

She'd picked up this bombshell from Jean during dinner last night. Plying her with fresh crab cakes and a good bottle of Pinot Noir, her goal had been to wrangle the details of her observations out of her, but Jean wound up volunteering it. She said her report would come out soon enough in discovery anyway, so she didn't feel too guilty about letting Sam in on the salient points a day or so early, as long as she didn't read about it in tomorrow's news blog.

Sam promised she wouldn't. It wasn't information that would help Wade directly—in fact, just the opposite—but at least Olivia and Logan would know what they were up against so they could start preparing his defense.

Logan wasn't here yet, so Sam got back to work. She plugged in her earbuds so she could monitor the police scanner in the background. She had a special app that worked great. She'd already returned some emails and made an appointment for a follow up story she'd been working on. A year ago, the building which housed the Lincoln County Animal Shelter was condemned and completely demolished. They needed a new home. Where that home should be was a topic of much heated discussion. They were trying for a space near the airport, but in the meantime, they were operating out of some portables and what animals they couldn't transfer to other shelters had been placed in local foster homes. She was scheduled to go interview one of the families who'd taken in five dogs and three cats. Saints, for sure. Sam, who kept very irregular hours, couldn't imagine being responsible for anything more than a goldfish.

She was just starting to work on her list of story ideas for next week when her phone rang. Pushing her glasses up her nose and taking one earbud out, she answered.

"Hello?"

"Hi Sam, this is Olivia. Have you seen Logan today? Is she there with you?"

"No," Sam said. "But I expect her any minute. I'm at Pirate's. Why? Do you want me to have her call you when she gets here?"

"Yes, if you could, I'd appreciate it," Olivia said. "She's not answering her phone. I really need to get ahold of her."

"Sure," Sam said. "She probably just hit a dead spot. Reception's spotty with all the trees around her house. Are you coming? I've got news for you guys."

"I can't right now, I'm tied up here," Olivia said.

Sam's reporter radar went off.

"What's going on?" she said, sitting up straighter.

"You won't believe this, but . . ."

"Wait, hold on a minute, Olivia," Sam said, pushing her remaining earbud further into her other ear so she could hear what was coming over the scanner better.

"Gotta go!" she yelled. "Call you later!"

For the second time in a week, Sam was out the door—in her own car this time—racing toward The Collins Hotel.

◊ ◊ ◊ ◊ ◊

Ambulance and fire department vehicles were clustered near the entrance when Monson arrived. He started toward the greenhouse, but stepped aside quickly on the narrow path to let the EMTs rush past. He barely recognized the woman on the gurney as the one he interviewed last week, but it was Mrs. Collins, the matriarch of the family and owner of the hotel. Pale and still, she was wrapped tight, securely strapped on, at least one IV bag dripping life-saving liquids into her. The EMTs didn't stop to chat. From the looks of things and the woman's age, it would be a miracle of she survived the ride to the hospital.

He continued up the path to what was left of the door to the greenhouse, which the fire fighters had hacked open with a hatchet. One of them saw him coming and stepped outside.

"What have you got?" Monson asked.

Len Fryxell—Fri*zell*—accent on the second syllable, a big man in his early forties, was a familiar face. Monson knew him from his first years with the department. He'd watched him grow from a skinny, hesitant kid to confident, knowledgeable professional firefighter. His belly had kept pace. A regular customer of Rogue Brewery, Len always looked six or seven months pregnant.

"Well," he said, pointing to a side room inside the greenhouse, "From what I can tell, the tank didn't leak, but the level was set to over 200,000 ppm."

"Is that normal?" Monson asked.

"Hell, no! Normal is more like around 2,000 parts per million. A lot of growers around here use these things. Anything over 100,000 can cause disorientation, dizziness, and eventually, brain damage."

"Can it kill you?"

"Oh yeah," he said. "Over 200,000 ppm, death is almost certain."

He pointed to the greenhouse as a whole.

"It had nowhere to go. Look at this place—it's built like a tank! Those windows? The ceiling? *Lexan*—polycarbonate— my brother has it on his boat. Windshield never cracks."

"So, it was airtight?"

"Yep," he said. "Of course, you want to be able to allow fresh air in now and then. Gotta have ventilation. You have to have vents, but those were all shut tight. They're open now."

"Okay, thanks," Monson said, letting the man get back to work. He trusted them to not disturb the scene any more than necessary. He didn't ask him to speculate on whether he thought this was an accident or done on purpose. He'd read his report later.

As they continued their work, airing out the greenhouse, checking for any other hazardous materials besides the CO_2, Monson went back to the hotel.

Dispatch said there were two victims. The second one wasn't as bad off. Monson spotted her on the front porch steps, wrapped in a silver Mylar blanket, on her phone. When he saw who it was he sighed. Logan McKenna. What was she doing here? How did that woman manage to keep getting in the middle of every act of violence that happened in Lincoln County?

When he got there, Logan disconnected her call and shivered, wrapping the blanket more tightly around her.

"You okay?" Monson said. "I hear you had quite a morning."

"You could say that," Logan said. "I'm all right, though. Did they say anything about Mrs. Collins? Is she going to be okay? Did they get her out in time?"

"I don't know," he said.

It had never been his style to give false hope.

"We can talk more later, but if you feel up to it, I just need to ask you a couple of questions, now," he said.

Like he was giving her an option.

The first question was obvious. Why was she there that morning? It seemed unlikely she had just dropped by. He heard she'd been sent to collect Wade's things the other day. They were working on getting a search warrant for those. Maybe she forgot something and had come back for it. But Logan said she'd been invited to come over for a tour of the greenhouse this morning, after expressing interest in flowers on her last visit.

Monson doubted Mrs. Collins was giving tours of any kind, but would come back around to this issue later. It was obvious Logan wasn't telling him everything.

They established Logan had arrived around 8:00 a.m. and was in the greenhouse with Mrs. Collins when the place began filling up with CO_2. She had also been affected, but not right away. Probably because she was younger and more fit. Logan explained how she tried to bust out of the place, but the door was locked and she couldn't break any of the windows. Finally, she managed to call 911 before she, too, succumbed to the gas.

Logan refused to go to the hospital. Said she was okay now, just a little dizzy. He left it at that. He knew where she lived.

44

After directing the responding officer where to place the police tape to secure the scene, he started up the steps to the hotel entrance. Before he got there, Amanda Daspitt came running out, jangling a set of keys at him.

"Here! Here are the keys to the hotel! I have to go to the hospital!" she said in a high-pitched voice, shoving them toward him. Waving her hand back at the greenhouse, she added, "I gave the officer the keys, but the firemen already broke down the door. I'll deal with all of that when I get back!"

Stopping her in mid-flight, he gently, but firmly directed her back inside.

"I know you are anxious to go to the hospital," Monson said, "but your grandmother will be in with the doctors when she first arrives. I'd like to talk to you for just a minute. Are you sure you are okay to drive? I can have one of the officers take you."

"No, no, I'm fine," Amanda said.

She went back in, but only perched on the arm of the nearest chair inside the lobby, clutching her purse to her chest.

"What do you need to know?" she said.

It was obvious he would have to make this short, she wasn't sticking around long.

"Thank you. We need to know how long your grandmother was exposed to the CO_2. What time did Mrs. Collins go into the greenhouse?"

"I'm not sure," Amanda said, furrowing her brow as if she was trying hard to remember. "She's an early riser. She often goes to work in her greenhouse in the morning."

"Did you accompany her?" Monson asked.

"No, that was Grandma's special place," she said. "She usually didn't let anyone in there but Charlie."

No harm in being honest now, she thought.

"So, no one else but Mrs. Collins was there this morning?"

"Other than Ms. McKenna, no," she said.

"Explain to me again how the CO_2 tank works," he said.

"I don't know the details, but it kind of beefs up the air in there for the plants," she said. "Plants need CO_2 like humans need oxygen."

"CO_2 is dangerous to humans, though. Did she have any kind of safety feature? Did you hear any kind of alarm go off this morning?"

"No, nothing," Amanda said. "The greenhouse is pretty soundproof, but I think there is one. Grandmother told me once there were levels. She must have forgotten to turn the safety feature on or set the levels correctly. I wish I could tell you more, but I don't know how it works."

Monson asked a few more questions, then walked her out. He couldn't resist asking her one more question as she got into her car.

"Has the CO_2 tank ever leaked or been set too high?"

"No, never," Amanda said, rolling down her window and backing out at the same time. "Grandmother's been so distracted this week, ever since Charlie's death. She must have set the wrong level or something or forgot to set the alarm. I don't know!"

Thoughtful, Monson watched her drive away.

What Amanda said made sense. Grieving people weren't themselves. They were often distracted, ran red lights, left burners on, forgot what day it was. It *could* just be a tragic accident. But two accidents in one week—with the first one turning into a homicide? That would be a huge coincidence. And Monson didn't believe in those.

If someone was picking off Collins family members one by one, he wanted to know why. Until this morning, he thought he had the who, but Wade couldn't have done this. Wade Ellis was miles away, cooling his heels in the Lincoln County jail.

Spitting gravel as she sped out, Amanda's sedan nearly side-swiped a dented green truck as it pulled into the vacant spot. A short, young woman with glossy black hair and pink, rhine-stone studded, cat eye glasses jumped out, notebook in hand.

Monson grimaced. The press. Specifically, a particularly tenacious, local reporter named Samantha Badger. He went down the steps to face the little terrier head on. Working with the sheriff's department all these years, he disliked the press almost as much as the perpetrators of whatever crime they were reporting on. Sometimes it was hard to separate the two. At least Ms. Badger seemed to be a good member of her profession. Her reporting so far had been as fair and balanced as the media got these days.

After verifying the information she already had from the police scanner, Monson ended the conversation with several "No comments . . . ongoing accident investigation . . . ," and started back toward the greenhouse. On the way, he stopped to check on Logan. She looked okay.

She was already standing, slipping off her space blanket, and gathering her bag. She and Samantha seemed to know each other.

Of course, they did.

Ignoring Sam, he gave Logan his card and said he'd be in touch. If she thought of anything else in the meantime, he asked her to give him a call. She said she would.

◊ ◊ ◊ ◊ ◊

"OMG, Logan! What are you doing? Why aren't you on your way to the hospital?" Sam said.

"I'm fine, really," Logan said. "There really wasn't room in the ambulance. And I don't need to go to the hospital. After they got me outside, they gave me some oxygen and had me walk a straight line and touch my nose a few times, shone a really bright light in my eyes. Asked me who the president was . . ."

Logan rolled her eyes and made a face, dispersing the tension.

"Now, I'm all ready for my next DUI," Logan said.

"Well, you still need to go get checked out," Sam said. "We can pick up your car later—don't argue with me—you're going to the hospital. On the way, you can tell me why Mrs. Collins called this little breakfast meeting—I've been dying to know."

"Oh, and Olivia's been trying to get ahold of you. If your phone's dead you can use mine. I don't know if she knows about the carbon dioxide, but she's probably worried sick. Do you have her number?"

They got inside Sam's car and buckled in.

"Thanks, but my phone's fine," Logan said, digging it out of her bag. "I'll fill you in in just a minute. Let me call Olivia back first, let her know I'm okay."

While she waited for Olivia to pick up, she turned to Sam and said, "You won't believe this, but Mrs. Collins . . ."

Just then Olivia answered.

Sam sped toward the hospital, rolled up the windows, turned off the heater and the police scanner, so she could hear every word of this conversation.

Olivia and Logan both started talking at once.

Finally, Olivia said, "What accident? What happened?"

Logan downplayed the incident, but Sam—butting in over the speaker phone—filled Olivia in about Logan being trapped in the greenhouse and almost dying from carbon dioxide poisoning, and Grandmother Charlotte being rushed to the hospital.

The next time Olivia spoke, it was with her take-charge lawyer voice.

"Sam, you there?"

"Right here, Olivia," Sam said, "Don't worry, I'm taking her to the hospital right now to get checked out, but she's good. She looks good."

Logan interrupted, "Olivia, I'm fine. Forget about that, now. I need to tell you what Mrs. Collins said . . . she confessed."

"She what?" Olivia and Sam said simultaneously.

"She confessed," Logan said, "She killed Charlie . . . not on purpose, but . . ."

Logan spent the next few minutes giving them the Reader's Digest version of how this Shakespearean tragedy unfolded. When she was done, she sat back, exhausted from the telling.

"Wow," was all Sam could say.

Olivia was silent on the other end of the line.

"Olivia?" Logan said. "I probably should have told Monson what she said, but I was still a little disoriented, and Mrs.

Collins was very clear I should tell you first. I suppose there are legal things you need to file or something, but you can get Wade out of jail now, right? I mean, there's no way they can hold him after this."

"That's why I was trying to reach you," Olivia said. "When I got here this morning, Wade was gone. Someone posted bail and he was released late last night. I've been trying to find him, but he seems to have dropped off the planet."

What? Didn't they deny bail?

45

Logan felt fine, but the emergency room doctor insisted she be kept overnight for observation. Sam promised to run out for an emergency order of fish and chips and curly fries, and Olivia was on her way, so she finally relented and agreed to stay—like a good girl.

She'd called Ben and let him know she was fine and no, he didn't need to drop everything and fly up, which was his first reaction. She mollified him with her room number, the number of the hospital, and the name of her doctor. Said she'd call him in the morning.

Olivia and dinner arrived at the same time. The wonderful, salty, vinegary smells emanating from the humongous, grease-soaked bag almost overwhelmed her. Logan started to shake. She realized she hadn't eaten since Mrs. Collins's tea and cookies. So, the shakes were either from low blood sugar or the doctor was right and she'd been deprived of oxygen in the greenhouse longer than she thought. Either way, she was starving and food couldn't hurt.

Luckily, Logan didn't have a roommate yet, so Sam pulled a chair over from the other side of the room for Olivia and they all dug in. They caught up between bites.

Olivia went first. Wade was out on bail, but MIA.

"I thought the judge refused to give bail—said he was a flight risk because of the airline tickets to India, through Vietnam where they don't have extradition," Logan said.

"Yes," Olivia said, "but Mrs. Collins pulled some strings. Apparently, she knows everyone in this town and has a lot of influence. She's been friends with Judge Pritchard for years. She gave him a call sometime yesterday. Not sure what she said to convince him Wade wasn't a flight risk, maybe she told him his trip really was for doing field work—that it was legitimate. But he set it and she paid it."

"Okay, I don't get it. If Mrs. Collins wanted to free Wade, why didn't she just confess—tell the DA she did it?" Sam said. "Then they would have just released him, right? Why jump through all the hoops?"

"I don't think she cared about the money at that point," Logan said, "I also think Mrs. Collins is used to getting her way, doing things in her own time. She felt bad about Wade being in jail, so she found a way to get him out without going to jail herself right then.

"Guess she wanted to tell her story in her own time and way. That's why she made the appointment with me to come over this morning. If she'd told the judge she poisoned Charlie yesterday, the police would have arrested her last night."

Olivia cleared the takeout containers and napkins off the bed while Sam refilled the water pitcher and topped off their plastic cups. Logan would have preferred a Sauvignon Blanc, but beggars couldn't be choosers. She also doubted alcohol was on the menu for recently asphyxiated women.

"Have room for one more?" a voice said from the hallway.

Logan looked up and saw a doctor walking in, complete with white coat and a stethoscope around her neck. For a second, she didn't recognize her, but as she came into the room, her distinctive white, racing stripe running back into a French twist identified her as Sam's soon-to-be-sister-in-law, Jean, the Lincoln County ME. Today's shoes were sleek, deep burgundy flats with gold flecks.

"Hope I'm not breaking up the party," she smiled. "I was in the neighborhood and thought I'd drop by."

It turned out she'd been visiting one of her patients and saw Logan's name at the nurse's station. Olivia offered her a seat, but she said she could only stay a minute.

Jean plucked her chart off the end of the bed and gave it a once over.

"You're lucky you're alive, Logan" she said. "Hypercapnia can be a silent killer."

Taking a little flashlight out of her breast pocket, she leaned over and lifted up Logan's eyelids one at a time, shining a bright light briefly in each one.

Satisfied, she clicked it off and popped it back into her pocket.

"Have you seen Mrs. Collins?" Logan asked. "Do you know how she is?"

Jean put her hands in her pockets and shook her head.

"I was here when they brought her in. I'm sorry, but Mrs. Collins didn't make it," she said. "The EMTs did a great job. They tried to save her. Nothing they could do."

A slew of emotions hit Logan hard. She wasn't surprised. Mrs. Collins was in her eighties. But she'd just been talking with her. It felt so strange. She wasn't sure what to feel. On the one hand, the woman was a confessed murderer, but she was also a victim—of her own making, but still. She'd lost her granddaughter, a young woman she loved very much and who, in her mind, she had only been trying to protect. Maybe it was a blessing she hadn't had to live with the guilt and pain of knowing she had killed Charlie. What would have happened to her if she'd lived?

Whether physically put in jail or not, she would always be imprisoned, convicted by her own conscience, never at peace.

Then another thought entered her mind. Now that Mrs. Collins was gone, there was no one to corroborate Logan's memory of their conversation—Mrs. Collins' confession. The police wouldn't believe Logan, she was part of Wade's defense team. They'd think she just made it up to help their client go free.

Olivia, thinking like a lawyer, was the one who pointed out the other sobering significance of this news.

"In the past week, two members of the Collins' family have died. Charlie's death," she said, nodding toward Jean, who she knew had forensic evidence that determined this, "was ruled a homicide. Wade was arrested for Charlie's death and charged with murder. Then he's released from jail and another Collins dies."

They all thought about that.

"The police are going to go after him for this," she said.

Silence filled the room, then Logan spoke.

"But what would his motive be?"

"Doesn't matter. They think he's killed once. He has the technical background and plenty of opportunity to mess with the CO_2 tanks in the greenhouse," she said. "And he knew his way around the hotel. He visited Charlie there all the time. They'll figure out motive later. Maybe he was mad at Mrs. Collins for keeping him and Charlie apart."

Then Jean spoke up.

"Sorry to have to share more bad news," she said, hands stuffed into her pockets. "I didn't tell you because I wasn't sure yet, but I suspected Charlie was a victim of some kind of poisoning. In addition to the bruising on her skull, I noticed a slight yellow jaundice to her skin. With the water damage, I couldn't be sure.

"I was going to take tissue samples and have some toxicology tests run to verify my suspicions, but when I got back into the morgue, the body had already been transferred to a facility for cremation. Mrs. Collins had requested it and the technician hadn't been informed she was a homicide, not an accident victim. We'd scheduled her to be sent up to Portland for autopsy, but he hadn't seen the paperwork.

"I can testify for you, I will testify for you," she said. "But I have no physical proof."

"What about the DNA tests?" Olivia asked.

"Oh, yes," Jean said. "I almost forgot about those. I was going to collect additional tissue samples from Charlie's body so the DNA lab would have plenty of biological material to work with, but with no body, that is no longer an option. I sent off what you gave me—the combs, toothbrushes, etc., to my friend for testing. He says there's enough to get Wade's DNA, but not sure he has enough of Charlie's to work with.

"Not that it matters much now, but it may give the DA's office a reason to believe your story about Mrs. Collins trying to poison Wade."

None of the women in the room thought this a remote possibility, but Logan clung to the silken thread of hope. Now that she knew for certain Wade was innocent, she was more determined than ever to clear his name and keep him out of jail.

But first, they had to find him.

46

Sam said she had some connections down at the docks. Tim knew Wade's friend, Pete, the one he'd been staying with after the sale of the house and until he and Charlie left for India. He was probably the one he called to pick him up at the jail when he was released. This whole coast used to be used by smugglers during Prohibition. Pete had a boat. Maybe he was hiding him out somewhere.

Sam cut her teeth on investigative reporting, so this was right up her alley. As she hurried out the door, keys in hand, she looked like a hunting dog who'd just picked up the scent.

Jean said she'd check on her tomorrow, but Logan said that with any luck, she'd be gone by then. She didn't let on that her headache had returned in full force. During dinner and visiting, she'd been sitting up, but now all she wanted to do was dim the lights, press the little button to lower the automatic bed, pull the thin blanket up under her chin and close her eyes. Hopefully, she'd feel better in the morning.

Jean tore off part of the takeout bag and scribbled something on it. She handed it to Logan.

"That's my cell," she said. "Call if you need me."

Wow. A doctor giving out her cell number? That never happened. Logan was impressed.

After refilling the water pitcher, straightening the covers, and making sure Logan had everything she needed, Olivia left. Since there was nothing more she could do until either Sam found Wade or he decided to contact her, the plan was for her to go home and get some sleep. They'd regroup tomorrow.

Lying flat helped. Logan could barely keep her eyes open. Even though she'd fought the doctor's orders to stay overnight, she was glad he had insisted. Right now, this generic hospital bed felt like a pillow-top mattress at a luxury hotel. The nurse had given her something—for pain or sleep she wasn't sure which—but it was working. Her limbs felt deliciously fuzzy. She'd have to get some more of this before she went home . . .

EARLIER THAT MORNING

The first body fell. Such a satisfying thud. Amanda smiled. They'd be *dead* bodies soon.

She'd set the CO_2 level pretty high. Grandmother must have fallen first, because she heard someone's frantic attempts at breaking out of the greenhouse, but failing. That must have been the younger, stronger woman—Logan. But she, too, would soon succumb to the carbon dioxide as it slowly choked the oxygen out of her body.

So sad.

Moving purposefully, but without haste, Amanda prowled through the crawl space, removing her mask and any trace of her presence. Not that anyone would look here—there'd be no reason. But still, better safe than sorry. The police weren't always as stupid as they looked on TV.

Within fifteen minutes, Amanda had showered, changed back to her normal work clothes, and opened up the lobby.

She had it all planned out. She even scheduled some emails to go out during the last hour so it looked like she was at the front desk working all morning.

When enough time had gone by—an hour or so—she would do what anyone would do if their grandmother and her guest had gone to the greenhouse for a visit, but hadn't returned. She'd go check to see if they were okay. With a slight twist.

She'd walk to the greenhouse, but then, she'd remove the long-handled hoe she'd shoved against the door to block it, reach around and lock the door to the greenhouse from the inside, then close it, making sure it was shut tight. No reason to suspect anyone locked them in—no, the door was locked from the inside. Grandma must be losing it. Locked herself in accidentally.

Beside herself with worry, she would then rush back to the hotel and call 911!

Poor Grandmother! Poor Logan!

Everything went according to plan until the part about dialing 911. Just as she reached for the phone, Amanda heard the sirens. 911 had already been called.

Without missing a beat, she ran through the possible explanations. All hotel staff had been given time off until after the funeral. There was only one other explanation. After her repeated attempts to break out of the greenhouse and get help, Logan had dialed 911.

Damn.

Instead of panicking, Amanda put on her concerned granddaughter, normal person armor. With a blank, questioning face of concern, she opened the door to greet her unexpected guests. She could still control the situation.

She didn't have to change her story. All Logan had done was move up the timeline. Grandma had been absentminded lately, must have set the CO_2 levels too high, forgot to set the safety alarm. She'd been so distracted ever since Charlie died . . . yada, yada, yada.

What she wasn't expecting, what she hadn't planned for, was for anyone to survive. How Logan stayed conscious enough to call 911 was a mystery. The damned woman had ruined everything. If she'd just died like she was supposed to, this would be over.

Why couldn't they just die?! But no, there was Logan, sitting there on her front porch—very much alive—knowing what she knew. All the lies. All the secrets. If she told the police, she could ruin everything. It was best if this case remained closed, with Wade blamed and in jail. No sense giving the police any reason to take a closer look at Charlie's body.

Interestingly, she hadn't heard Logan say anything to the Detective, Monson, about what Grandmother had told her. Maybe she was in shock.

Amanda wanted to stay there, to hear what the police and firemen knew, found, and theorized. She needed to make sure this was recorded as an accident. Period. But she had to play the part of the hysterical, dutiful granddaughter one more time. She had to rush to the hospital to be at Grandmother's side.

Bitch.

If they'd have let her ride in the ambulance, she could have taken care of the old biddy easily—finished the job—she didn't want her waking up and confessing to anyone else.

47

The darkened hallways bleeped and blipped in a soothing soundtrack. Nurse Agapito Reyes ate the last of his chicken adobo, then absentmindedly began emptying a bowl of peanut M&Ms one at a time while he tried to remember his password. Night shift messed with his sleep patterns, but Agapito didn't mind working graveyard. Especially when it was slow like this. Only three patients on the entire floor and all of them asleep. He'd caught up on paperwork, finished his bed checks, and still had a few hours to go before the morning shift came in. Hoping he wouldn't get locked out, he tried one more time. 'Sparkles5', the name of his daughter's favorite toy, a stuffed unicorn, and her age.

Within a few minutes, he was lost in his own private cyberworld, taking down insurgents, earning additional weapons and armor with each kill—winning the war. Against whom it didn't matter.

The cleaning cart rattled by. He nodded in greeting, but didn't look up or stop playing. Normally, he'd stop to chat, but he was almost at the ninth level. Sounded like the cart stopped outside the corner room at the far end of the floor. Mopping and emptying trash cans, the night custodian would work his way back. He'd catch him on this end.

◦ ◦ ◦ ◦ ◦

With great pleasure, Logan kicked through the warm, tropical water, amazed at the abundance and variety of marine life on the reef. Jewel-toned parrot and damsel fish, yellow tangs, and angel fish brushed by. Brightly striped clown fish darted in and out of colorful sea anemones. Gentle giants of the sea, blue whales, cruised by—a mama and calf. A dolphin invited her to play. It was everything she'd dreamed of—pure joy!

Then the ocean darkened. Instead of swimming through sunlit schools of colorful fish, she found herself surrounded by a towering stand of muddy green, undulating kelp. She tried to push through—find the sun again, but thick, broad fronds enveloped her, wrapped around her ankles. What? Where had that come from? There shouldn't be any kelp on a coral reef.

Several strands pulled tighter across her face, her mouth, her neck . . . she couldn't breathe!

Struggling to make sense of the signals her body was giving her, Logan struggled awake to find herself staring into the crazed, gloating eyes of Amanda Daspitt—only inches from her face.

Right forearm pressed against her neck, Amanda straddled her, holding her down. Her other hand was clamped tightly over Logan's mouth.

Logan tried to remain calm while she took stock of her situation. She hoped it was all part of some horrible dream and she'd wake up soon. Maybe those drugs weren't worth it after all.

"Good morning, Sunshine!" Amanda whisper hissed.

Nope. Not a dream . . . no, this was a living nightmare.

"Did you have a nice chat with Grandmother this morning?" Amanda asked.

Logan couldn't respond and was afraid to even nod her head. Who knew what would set this woman off? She was even afraid to break eye contact to look around the room for a likely weapon or any means of escape. Instead, she desperately tried to remember what her brother, Rick, a cop, had taught her about self-defense. 'Stay still, don't fight. Run when you can.' She wasn't sure if any of that advice would work in this situation.

Amanda deftly whipped a rag out of her back pocket. Releasing her grip for a split second, she stuffed it into Logan's mouth and quickly secured it with a strip of duct tape she'd had the forethought to cut and leave at the ready hanging off the bed railing. Like an elementary school teacher. Prepared. Efficient.

Next, Logan heard a sharp metallic click. Amanda smiled down at her, a seven-inch switchblade in her hand. The light from the hallway glinted off the blade, inches away from Logan's throat.

"Now don't you move, Sleeping Beauty," Amanda said softly.

Straining to fully emerge from the fog of whatever the nurse had given her, this was not a difficult command for Logan to obey.

Silently, Amanda slipped off the bed and stood beside her. Gone were the frumpy clothes and groveling nature. This was a different Amanda. One that was in a lot better shape.

"I could have killed you just now, you know," she said. "But what fun would that be? No, you're not going to get to slip away peacefully in your sleep. You've been a very bad girl.

"Actually, you're supposed to be dead already, but I wanted to have this little chat first," she said. "I didn't get to see old Grandmother die. Didn't get to spit on her body. Didn't have that luxury. You took that from me. Everything was fine until you came along."

Without taking her eyes off Logan, Amanda thumbed the blade, testing its sharpness.

"Sometimes circumstances require a change of plans," she said.

Barely controlled rage radiated off of her taut, still body. Glancing at the door, she listened. Apparently satisfied, she turned back to Logan.

"We don't have much time," she said, "but we're going to make every second count, you and I. You've ruined everything else. No inheritance, no home base. No nothing. I'll have to start all over. But at least I'll have the satisfaction of watching the light leave your eyes before I disappear. And they won't recognize you when I'm done."

Leaping back onto the bed like a jungle cat, Amanda straddled Logan and pinned her arms down with her knees. Logan felt the cold flat of the blade caress her face, then a sharp pain as Amanda turned it slightly and began slowly slicing across her forehead.

Not waiting to see what Amanda had in mind, Logan bucked and twisted, attempting to scream through her gag or knock something over—anything to make as much noise possible, hoping someone outside would hear and come to the rescue. But she only succeeded in knocking Amanda off center before she gripped her body more tightly with her knees, preventing any further attempts at escape.

With blood running in her eyes from the cut, knowing death was coming if she didn't break free, something deep in Logan's animal brain triggered an ancient response, one her cave women ancestors developed to survive. Electric signals flew from the amygdala to the hypothalamus, setting the sympathetic nervous system on fire, alerting all her senses, pumping adrenaline into her body. With a roar that would have been heard all the way down the hall if it hadn't been muffled by duct tape, Logan shoved her attacker off her chest and scrambled out of bed.

Amanda hit the floor and Logan heard the knife clatter to the ground.

Unsteady on her feet, still mentally foggy, and partially blinded from the blood streaming down her face, she went on the attack. Rounding the end of the bed, she came face to face with her predator, who had unfortunately regained her footing—and her knife.

Taking a West Side Story rumble stance, Amanda was crouched, grinning, tense and ready to fight. Logan half-expected her to start tossing the knife back and forth from hand to hand.

While keeping her eye on her attacker, Logan ripped the tape off her mouth and started screaming for help. She was brave, but she wasn't stupid. She couldn't take down Amanda herself, not in this condition, and without a weapon. All she had to do was stay out of the reach of that knife and someone would come.

Just then, Amanda lunged. Before Logan could block the attack with her arm, she felt a punch on her side. Looking down, she saw blood spurting out. Just as she realized she'd been stabbed, her knees started to buckle. She grabbed at the safety railing on the side of the bed, but missed.

Shit.

The night nurse rounded the corner, skidding to a halt at the doorway.

"What's going on, here?" he shouted.

Before everything went black, Logan saw Amanda sprint from the room, pushing past the nurse.

"Die, bitch!" she yelled.

48

"I'm okay, hon—really. Ben's on his way up and Olivia's taking really good care of me. They only kept me a day. It's just a few stitches—nothing serious. . . ."

Logan rolled her eyes at Olivia, who'd just come into the room with a tall glass of ice water for her patient. Making an exasperated face, she pretended to tear her hair out, then made the universal jabber talking motion with her hand aimed at the phone to indicate her daughter, Amy's inability to get off the phone.

Olivia smiled.

"Yes, Mom," Logan said, "I promise to take all my medicine and eat all my vegetables."

Amy must have laughed on the other end of the line, because Logan did, too.

"Call you tomorrow, hon," she said. "Give Ian and Liam hugs. Tell Ian Grandma will see him soon."

Laying her phone on the covers, she accepted the proffered water from Olivia and took a long drink.

"Thank you," she said.

The last of the day's golden light slanted in the window,

creating long shadows across the gleaming hardwood floor. Maybe when Ben got here, they could go online and look at furniture. It was just after five now. Ben said he was taking a red eye after work and if the stars aligned would get here sometime tomorrow morning.

Olivia pulled up a chair. Before she and Sam brought Logan home from the hospital, Olivia put extra layer of blankets under the sleeping bag on Logan's cot, making quite a cozy little recovery bed for her big sister.

The hospital treated Logan's stab wound, which, although super painful, had not hit any major organs. No surgery required. They would have kept her longer, but since she had someone at home, they released her this afternoon. The main thing was watching out for infection. That's what usually got people, the nurse said, handing her a packet of instructions, alcohol wipes, and bandages to hold her over until she could get more supplies at the drug store.

The only good thing about Amanda attacking her was that the police were finally open to at least listening to what Logan had to tell them. Yesterday, after getting stitched up and declared stable, Sheriff's Deputy Monson and Detective Grant from the Newport police department flanked her hospital bed and took her full statement. Monson deeply frowned when she told him she'd withheld this information previously, but said he'd hear her out.

She told him about what she and Olivia had discovered in Irene's journals. Then about Mrs. Collins sharing more family history, explaining why she was so vehemently against Wade and Charlie marrying. Logan didn't tell them about Jean sending the samples away for DNA testing. She didn't want to get her in trouble. Hopefully, the journals would be enough to back up Mrs. Collins's confession and show her motives.

Then, while Logan took a water break and Monson pulled out a fresh notebook, she went on to tell them about Mrs. Collins's confession. Her attempted murder of Wade, how that went horribly wrong, and how she wound up taking her beloved Charlie's life instead.

True to form, Monson didn't take her at her word, but promised to follow up and verify everything she'd just told them. He'd send someone to collect the journals. Then, and only then, if everything panned out, they would recommend the DA drop the charges against Wade. They were still looking for him.

Logan just hoped that happened quickly, before Wade became a permanent fugitive thinking he had to run or spend the rest of his life in jail. Sam called and said she had a lead, but hadn't found Wade yet. Logan wanted to get up and help look for him. He must be so scared. But she knew that didn't make sense. She wasn't from this area and knew almost no one here. She wouldn't know where to start. She was stuck in this hospital bed. She'd just have to let other people take care of things for a while. Not her nature.

"They still out there?" Logan asked.

Olivia went to the window.

"Yep," she said. "Parked in the driveway."

Ben had called the police department and raised all holy hell about getting someone to protect Logan. Monson had calmly informed him that an officer had already been posted outside her hospital room and would remain there until she was released—they'd transferred her to a new room and changed her name on it, just in case. He also assured Ben that until Amanda was apprehended, he would put a squad car on Logan's house when she was released from the hospital.

They still hadn't heard from Sam, but knew she'd call as soon as she heard anything. She'd gone home to finish writing up her story while waiting for her contact down at the docks to call and hopefully put her in touch with Wade or at least tell her where he was. Her editor was ecstatic with what she had submitted so far. He was holding the front page. This was going to turn into multiple stories. Sam's initial blog post already had the phone ringing off the hook. She was coming back over in the morning to meet Ben and promised to call if she heard anything before then.

Olivia lit the fire in the fireplace and turned on the one lamp in the room, an upright faux Tiffany find from the local Habitat for Humanity store. Multicolored glass splashed warm yellows and reds across the floor and walls. Making sure Logan was okay, she went to change out of her lawyer suit. She'd spent most of the day at the courthouse filing paperwork to get Wade officially released. She returned in yoga pants and a sweatshirt she borrowed from Logan.

"Too cold for PJs," she said.

"No fashion judgment from me," Logan said, indicating her own fleece sweatshirt, a stretched out, gray one, sporting her alma mater's unusual mascot, the anteater. Founded in the '60s, University of California at Irvine (UCI) students wanted to make a point that they were not the typical rah-rah party school. So, no football, no alcohol-soaked fraternities or sororities. And definitely no fierce mascots like tigers, Trojans, sharks, or cougars. Even though they had since acquired a football and other college sports teams, the ridiculous anteater mascot remained—a pacifist symbol of the university's sixties roots. Love and Peace. Logan loved it.

"Did your doctor say anything about wine?" Olivia asked, walking into the room with a bottle of Pinot Noir and two glasses. "Are you allowed a nightcap?"

"I didn't ask, but since I'm not taking any more of those pain pills, or sleeping pills, or whatever it was they gave me in the hospital," Logan said, "I'm declaring myself wine-approved."

49

Adrenaline depleted, Olivia and Logan sat—and in Logan's case, lay—comfortably in front of the fire. After debriefing each other on their respective days and checking for messages from Sam, there was nothing else they needed to do. Nothing else they could do. Sam would call when she heard anything.

Lengthening shadows spread, filling the room with a surprising comfort. Night's blanket tucked around them.

Logan was too tired to be afraid or worried. Amanda had done her worst and was probably miles away by now. Wade would be found. Mrs. Collins was dead. Charlie was dead. It was tragic, it was exhausting, but it was over.

Everything was out in the open—all the lies untangled and the secrets revealed. Nothing left but the cleanup. Yes, she'd been stabbed, but not mortally. With time, she'd heal. It was all going to be okay.

"How's your side?" Olivia asked.

Logan shifted in her bed, then winced.

"Thanks for reminding me," she said.

Lifting her sweatshirt up, she took a look at the bandaged wound and gave her report.

"Looks okay—not leaking through," she said.

Olivia got up and stretched.

"Good. I'm going to go brush my teeth," she said. "Might as well get some sleep. Need anything?"

"Nah, if I have any more wine, I'll just have to get up to pee," Logan said.

Nodding her head in the direction of the driveway out front, she said, "We should check on them. Make sure they don't need some food or blankets or to use the bathroom or anything. Do you mind?"

Logan wasn't sure what the protocol was for guarding a house, but if she were stuck in a car in someone's driveway in the middle of winter, she'd want to be comfortable at least. Officers Dietrich and Lisson, a middle-aged officer and a rookie, both with the Oregon State Police, introduced themselves briefly when they arrived to let them know they were out there and on duty until 7:00 a.m. At that time, their relief shift would take over.

She wondered if they took turns sleeping or just stayed awake all night. Cops on T.V. never seemed to need any sleep.

Olivia assembled a bag of cookies and a couple of bottles of water and took them out to their two protectors. When she returned, she locked the front door behind her.

"They said thanks and for us to go ahead and go to bed, they were okay for the night. Had everything covered," Olivia said.

Logan hoped that didn't include pooping in her yard at 2:00 a.m. She wondered how they took care of those necessities. Inquiring minds want to know . . . but, for tonight, it would have to remain a mystery. It was way down the list of things to worry about.

Logan thought the whole protection detail unnecessary. Hopefully, after an uneventful night, Monson would call off the next shift. Ben would be here by then anyway, or soon after. Clay was coming over to install deadbolts tomorrow afternoon. Another call Ben had made. He'd been a busy boy. Having taken care of herself for so long, it kind of irritated Logan to have someone be so protective, but she knew it was a sincere expression of love for her—he was just concerned. And given the trouble she kept getting herself into, his concern was not misplaced.

Olivia put her earbuds in to watch a video on her phone. Logan tried to play solitaire on hers, but couldn't focus. She finally gave up, pushed it under her cot so it wouldn't keep her awake, and closed her eyes.

The fire was burning down, but she was warm and snug under the sleeping bag.

The wind had picked up. A storm must be blowing in from the ocean. She smelled rain, heard the trees creak, the windows rattle, and raindrops pelt the roof. She was glad Clay had tightened up the old place. It was a good house. She felt snug and warm. Safe. Nature's violence she could handle. It was the manmade kind that scared her.

Uneasy dreams laced Logan's sleep. Amanda's face hovering over hers. The brutal force of the knife stabbing into her side. Amanda's creepy voice . . . whispering . . .

"So, you've got a babysitter this time, eh?" Amanda said.

This was no memory.

Not wanting to, Logan slowly opened her eyes. Amanda was standing at the side of her bed. At first, she wasn't sure it was her. She'd hacked off her hair and given herself a bad dye job. A few bright yellow-orange spikes stuck out of a black watch cap, but it was her. Amanda put her finger up to her lips making the universal 'Shhhh' signal.

"We wouldn't want to wake your babysitter, would we?" she

whispered, nodding in Olivia's direction, but not taking her eyes off Logan.

A scream froze in Logan's throat. She didn't dare move or make a sound. Amanda was holding a gun. Like she knew how. And it was pointed right at her.

How in the hell did she get past the cops? Or in the house?

"Very helpful of you to leave me a gun," Amanda said, ". . . with bullets, even. You made me lose my knife. That was one of my favorites, you know. Very responsible of you, by the way, to store the gun on a high shelf in the closet and the bullets in a box."

Gun? What gun?

Then Logan's heart sank. Of course. Ben. He must have gone ahead and bought a damn gun, thinking he'd talk her into keeping it later. Boy, was he going to be disappointed in how that whole 'protect Logan' thing worked out. If she lived through this, she'd have to kill him.

Keeping the gun trained on Logan, Amanda stepped softly around the foot of the cot. Just an arm's reach away, Olivia continued snoring softly, ear buds still in place, tinny music drifting out into the room, completely unaware of their visitor.

"Good thing I got here early. I see you've got company out front, now," Amanda continued, "You really should get better locks on your back door. With five seconds and a paper clip, anyone could jimmy their way in."

She waved the gun in her hand back and forth a bit, "This is just a little girl gun. Not as nice as mine, but mine's back in Iowa. A Glock will do in a pinch."

Logan could barely hear her, she whispered so quietly. She doubted Amanda was concerned about her security.

"Love what you've done with the place," she said. "It never looked this nice when those Ellises lived here. Made a great place for me to hide for a while, too. At least until you got home and I could finish what we started."

She'd finished her slithering journey around the cot and come to a stop between Logan and Olivia. The windows were dark. Clouds covered whatever moonlight there may have been. The only light in the room came from the fire.

Amanda's deep, colorless eyes glowed with such a fierce hate, Logan felt it like a physical blow. Then Amanda's demeanor abruptly changed. A smile crawled onto her face.

"No time to dawdle . . . places to go, people to see . . . !" she confided brightly. "But first . . ."

Amanda slowly rotated left, turning her attention—and the gun barrel—toward Olivia.

50

Absolute fury surged through Logan's body. She'd had enough! There was no way she was going to let this crazy woman hurt Olivia, or anyone else. She needed to be stopped—now! The only weapon at hand was the iron poker Olivia had been using to stoke the fire, but it was just out of reach. With no other options, Logan used the only other weapon she had within her control—her body.

She threw off the sleeping bag, put one foot onto the floor for traction. Searing pain shot down her left side. Pushing through the pain, Logan launched herself off the cot, aiming her left shoulder for Amanda's torso, like some high school football player. She knew she didn't have much force, but if she could just knock her off balance, maybe she could wrestle the gun out of her hand, or at least throw off her aim.

Logan thudded into Amanda and the gun went off. It was so loud. Pain stabbed deep into her ears and she was momentarily stunned. She heard the gun skitter across the floor, but Amanda was already scrabbling for it.

"Run! Go!" Logan yelled.

Not exactly a plan, but it was all that came out. Her voice

sounded very far away. She only hoped Olivia could get away before Amanda got the gun.

Jerked awake, Olivia yanked her earbuds out and rolled off her bed onto the floor, landing on the other side. Logan couldn't see her face, but she assumed she was regrouping, trying to figure out what was happening.

Logan lunged, grabbing one of Amanda's ankles to bring her back down. A fresh wave of pain spasmed through her. She almost lost consciousness. Her fingers grazed the heel of Amanda's shoe, but she easily shook Logan off.

"Not this time, Sunshine!" Amanda growled. No need to whisper now.

In that few seconds, Logan saw Olivia crawl to the fireplace, where she grabbed her own weapon—the fireplace poker. Medieval in comparison to Amanda's gun. Not exactly evenly matched.

With no one to stop her, Amanda grabbed the Glock. Not bothering to stand up, she rolled onto her butt, leaned back, braced her feet on the floor. Gripping the gun in both hands, she aimed straight between her knees, straight at Olivia.

Logan watched helplessly as Olivia rose up—a mighty young warrior, arm raised, iron lance in hand, rushing forward into battle . . . right into Amanda's sights.

Olivia, her brave little sister, the one who'd only been in her life for a couple short weeks, was going to die. Sounds from the storm outside—a splintering tree and something like shouting—registered on the periphery of Logan's overloaded senses.

Olivia was just inches away now. Logan watched, breathless, as Olivia swung her weapon around at her attacker. She was going to make it! Primal feelings welled up inside her. At that moment, she fiercely wanted to see Amanda die. She lusted for it. If Olivia made contact, there was no way Amanda would withstand the force of that blow!

Then Amanda pulled the trigger. The loud shot exploded, reverberating off the walls. Olivia stopped dead. Her waterfall of long, shiny hair, lit golden by the firelight, wavered. Just before she passed out, Logan hit the floor. Then all went black.

❖ ❖ ❖ ❖ ❖

"Whoever invented smelling salts should be shot," Logan said.

"Technically, they're called ammonia inhalants," said Officer Dietrich. "And officially, we're not supposed to use them. It's nasty stuff, but my dad always kept some on hand. He was a trainer for the Edmonton Oilers back in the day—hockey team up in Canada. Best way to get his players back on their feet after a hit. Or so he said. They were always getting knocked out."

Officer Dietrich—Barry—they were on a first name basis now, had administered first aid, staunching the bleeding and expertly rewrapped her wound where some of the stitches had pulled out. They were waiting on the front porch for the ambulance to arrive. This time, Logan offered no resistance. She knew when she needed help.

Satisfied his handiwork would hold until the ambulance got there, Dietrich went to help his rookie put up the crime scene tape and make sure no one disturbed the body inside. They'd radioed in the incident and Deputy Sheriff Monson and Detective Grant were on their way.

Earlier, they'd separated the two survivors and taken their initial statements. Monson and Grant would conduct more detailed interviews later. The rookie, Officer Lissom—Sarah—had taken the uninjured woman, Olivia, to the squad car.

She was now hurrying back. The rain was still coming down and she held a jacket he'd loaned her over her head. Olivia ran up onto the porch, took off the jacket and shook off the rain.

"Thanks," she said, holding it out to Officer Dietrich.

"Why don't you keep it for now? I can pick it up later," Dietrich said.

Looking past Logan into the open doorway, he added, "You'll need it. It's going to be a while before you can get back in and get your stuff."

Olivia put the jacket back on and thanked him. Logan forced herself to lift her body up with her hands, shift herself a quarter turn and look into her formerly peaceful living room. Olivia's gaze followed hers. The fire still crackled warmly. Except for the dead body on the floor, it looked very inviting.

The body looked so small, hardly took up any room. Almost like she was sleeping. More like a victim than a vicious killer. Except for the blood.

Logan shivered. The dead woman on the floor had almost killed her. Twice. But Amanda was no longer a danger to anyone.

How had she become a killer? And one who enjoyed it? How did anyone enjoy inflicting pain, taking life? Logan couldn't understand it. And hoped she never would. Then she remembered her own unvarnished, violent feelings. Ones she didn't know she could ever have. When she wanted Amanda dead. Not the same, but still . . .

Officer Lissom walked up onto the porch. "They're almost here. ETA five minutes."

"Thank you for everything—both of you," Logan said, looking mainly at Sarah. "I don't know how to thank you for what you did."

Olivia agreed.

The second gunshot, the one that had all but deafened Logan for real this time, had been from Sarah's gun. Dietrich explained the bare bones of what happened.

As senior officer, Dietrich had driven to their assignment and Sarah was in the right seat. The patrol car was parked about ten feet down from the house, in the middle of the steep driveway, positioning Sarah closest to the front porch.

As Logan knew the two law-enforcement officers would have to repeat multiple times to multiple interrogators over the next days and weeks as part of the officer-involved shooting investigation, when they heard the shouting and banging from inside the house, they responded immediately, jumping from their car and sprinted through the rain toward the house.

The front door was locked, so Dietrich kicked down the door. Sarah—who was the better marksman—took the shot. Dietrich was fine with that. He qualified with his firearm every month, but just barely.

Logan was just grateful. She and Olivia were alive.

51

Being raised in a small, coastal town in California, Logan learned to never plan parties on a long holiday weekend. Too crowded with tourists. Since Ian's birthday was May 26th, they decided on the weekend *after* Memorial Day for their first official family BBQ in the new house up here in Oregon.

Clay had all of the major work done, but still stopped by now and then to do some finishing work. She and Ben had been burning the candle at both ends furnishing and stocking 354 Barber for everyone's arrival. It was going to be a full house.

They'd put Amy, Liam, and the birthday boy in the downstairs bedroom where there was plenty of room for them to spread out. Kids came with what was to Logan an incomprehensible array of carriers, toys, and other equipment deemed absolutely indispensable by Amy's generation. When she'd had Amy all they had was a car seat and a diaper bag.

Plus, they'd be near the kitchen and bathroom, which did make sense to Logan. Kids were born mess-makers, and Ian was always hungry, just like Amy had been at his age.

She and Ben staked out the upstairs bedroom. It was smaller, but it had a deck with the ocean view. No one else was staying over, but several friends were stopping by to help celebrate. Sam and Tim, and Jean and her husband—she forgot his name, and even Clay said he wouldn't say no to a hotdog or two. He wanted to see the landscaping Ben was doing along the side of the house.

The kids' flight was due in tomorrow. They'd get a rental car and should arrive by two or three.

"Did they have that Piper Heineken champagne?" Logan called, starting to unload the groceries into the fridge. She'd tried some at Sam and Tim's wedding last month and really liked it.

Ben smiled and hoisted the last bags onto the counter.

"Piper-*Heidsieck*, and yes, they even had those Greek olives you like," he said.

"Yeah!"

Those were her favorite and they didn't always have them. They were getting used to the fact that they had to plan ahead here on the coast. This wasn't southern California where they could just run out to five stores until they filled their every foodie desire. If they didn't have it at Fred Meyers or Safeway, they didn't have it. Unless you wanted to drive to Salem, which people only did every few months for a Costco run.

With Fractals running smoothly under Tilly's efficient and creative control, Logan had been spending more and more time up here. She found herself craving the quiet and the large chunks of uninterrupted time. The last couple of months, she'd experienced a surge of creative energy, composing several new pieces which she planned to record in the sound studio back in Jasper.

Tilly was temporarily housesitting for her until her divorce was final. Dimebox barely tolerated his new mistress, but Lola,

Logan's sapphire blue '58 Corvette, was enjoying being taken out for spins on Pacific Coast Highway. A graduation gift from her father, no matter how few miles to the gallon Lola got, she'd never sell her. There were signs Dimebox was warming up to Tilly, though. She told Logan she'd discovered a nice, fat field mouse on her doorstep last week. A true Dimebox present.

Ben was happy, she was happy. The kids were okay. Logan didn't know what the future held, but for now, things were right where they should be.

"You hear from Olivia yet?" Ben asked.

"Yes," Logan said. "She can't make it out this time, but is planning a trip this summer. She's up to her neck in criminal defense cases—she's decided to make that her niche at her firm and they're happy to let her work those."

After Olivia got all charges against Wade officially dropped, she flew back to her job and life in New York. But not before Sam, Wade, Jean, and Logan threw her a goodbye and thank you dinner at the Side Door Cafe. Olivia promised to come back soon.

Wade, it turned out, had no idea anyone was looking for him. He'd been shocked when Mrs. Collins bailed him out. He couldn't reach Olivia, but deciding not to wait for her, he called his friend to come pick him up. They'd gone directly to his friend's boat and headed out on a two-day tuna trip, just to get away from it all. He'd left a message for Olivia to let her know where he was, which the clerk forgot to give her. Through her connections at the dock, Sam tracked him down and radioed him with the good news that the real killer had been caught. It was over. He did have to come back in order to be officially released, but he was very okay with that.

With all of Charlie's immediate family members gone, Wade decided against a large, formal funeral and planned to simply scatter Charlie's ashes at sea and grieve her loss privately. Logan wondered what he would do now. Would he stay here or go to India as he and Charlie had planned?

When Logan met Wade to give him the rest of the storage boxes, including Irene's journals, she'd debated about whether to tell him what they'd discovered in those journals about the rape that started it all, the half-sibling great-grandparents, the whole sordid mess. She figured knowing his and Charlie's tangled family history would go a long way toward helping him understand why Mrs. Collins had been so opposed to them marrying, and why she did it all. On the other hand, with everyone gone, what did it matter now?

In the end, Logan went with her gut. If it were her, she'd want to know the truth. And it would probably be in the official case report anyway. She'd given him a bare-bones summary of what the journals contained, then let him read them for himself. She also told him how much she had grown to respect and admire the strong women in his family. Irene, Mara, and his mother, Pam. Surviving heartbreak, evil, and great loss, they'd raised and loved their children in often unimaginably difficult circumstances—with very little support. He could be very proud of them.

They'd all but forgotten about the sibling DNA test Jean sent in. When the results came back proving Charlie and Wade were related, this information caused an unexpected turn of events. With Mrs. Collins, Charlie, and Amanda all gone, Wade and his sister became the only blood relatives left. As such, they would eventually inherit the entire Collins fortune. The hotel, of course, but also the many investments Mrs. Collins had made over the years, which were substantial.

Probate might take up to a year, the lawyer said, but eventually, the two remaining members of the Ellis family would at least not have to worry about money. If Wade's sister was anything like him, Logan knew they would find ways to use their new-found fortune for good.

Wade was already talking about selling the hotel to the cook and his wife for next to nothing. He didn't understand all the details, but Olivia said a good tax attorney would work all that out. They worked long hours for little pay for Mrs. Collins with no hope of improving their lives. They'd lost everything when their country had been taken over by a corrupt dictator in bed with violent cartels. Life there had become untenable. They'd escaped with nothing but the clothes on their backs.

The young couple reminded him of his great-grandparents, Wade said. He'd read Irene's journals. It just seemed right, he said, to help this young couple achieve their dreams, even though Irene and Jacob had had theirs stolen.

Wade didn't know how apt his phrasing was.

No one knew Frankie had stolen Wade's great-grandfather's fortune, his future, his very life . . . and then gone home to rape his wife. No one knew of that fateful night in 1932 when a Canadian rum runner tossed that gold nugget to Jacob Ellis, intending that he use it to build a future for his family. But the ocean knew. And the ancient cedars. Like the ebb and flow of the tides, they knew evil may dominate for a time, but is always replaced by good—an infinite cycle.

For many years, and particularly at the end of his rather short, shallow life, Frankie suffered greatly from an unknown condition. What started as a rash in his younger days, subsided for some time, then came roaring back in the prime of his life, presenting as a collection of painful, often disgusting, frightening symptoms.

He avoided seeking medical help until it was too late. Whether from a sense that God's judgment had finally come upon him and payment for his sins was due, or from pure laziness, no one ever knew. When he finally saw Cramer, the good doctor promptly diagnosed him with an advanced case of syphilis. Within a year he was totally blind and had lost all control of his bowels.

Fortunately, his wife, Rowena, was spared. They hadn't shared a bed in years.

◊ ◊ ◊ ◊ ◊

A half hour later, fridge filled and wine poured, Logan followed Ben out onto the deck. They both put their feet up and settled into the sturdy teak chairs and thick, brightly-colored cushions—a housewarming gift from Rita and Jackie, her partner. Ben had already zapped and brought out what was left of the Tide Pool's Meat Lovers pizza they'd had last night, placing it on the low table between them.

Logan scooped up a slice and after sprinkling on some hot red-pepper flakes, bit into hot, cheesy heaven. As they ate, they watched the sun make its way toward the horizon. Sunset was still a few hours away, an hour later than she was used to back home. Winter had passed and even though they still had to contend with rain, the last few days had been spectacular. She hoped the weather held for the kids.

It was almost dark now.

A brisk wind ruffled the indigo waters in the bay. Bright white caps glowed through the dusky sky. The fog buoy bobbed and called in the distance. Logan spotted a whale spout and pointed it out to Ben. They both still got excited whenever they saw one. She hoped it never grew old. Earlier, an eagle swooped down from the rocks at the foot of Smuggler's Inn, snatched a fish in its talons and lazily flew out of sight to enjoy its dinner. The ocean and its denizens—living out their lives much as they had for millennia.

She reached across and took Ben's hand. Life was good.

Family Tree

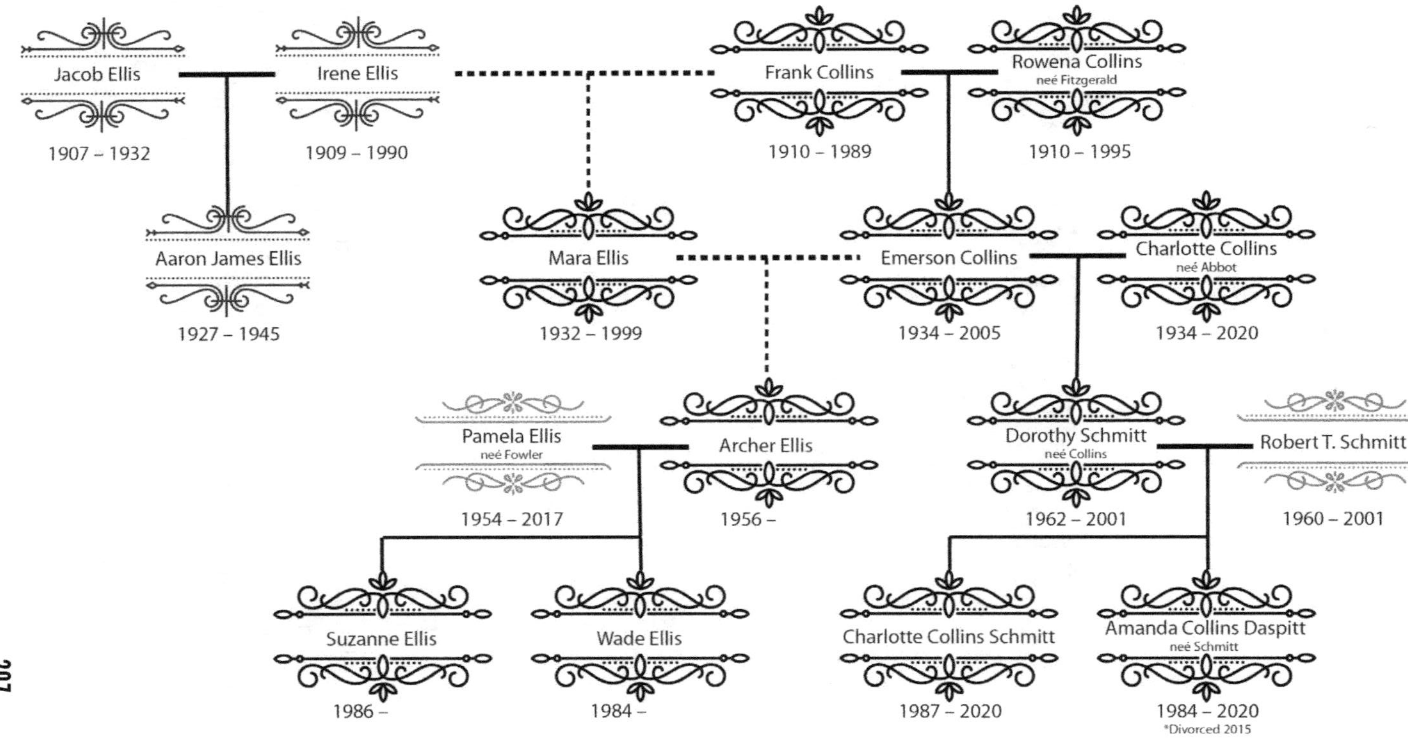

Jacob Ellis
1907 – 1932
Irene Ellis
1909 – 1990
Frank Collins
1910 – 1989
Rowena Collins
neé Fitzgerald
1910 – 1995
Aaron James Ellis
1927 – 1945
Mara Ellis
1932 – 1999
Emerson Collins
1934 – 2005
Charlotte Collins
neé Abbot
1934 – 2020
Pamela Ellis
neé Fowler
1954 – 2017
Archer Ellis
1956 –
Dorothy Schmitt
neé Collins
1962 – 2001
Robert T. Schmitt
1960 – 2001
Suzanne Ellis
1986 –
Wade Ellis
1984 –
Charlotte Collins Schmitt
1987 – 2020
Amanda Collins Daspitt
neé Schmitt
1984 – 2020
*Divorced 2015

ACKNOWLEDGMENTS

Lies That Bind, Logan's sixth adventure, is very much inspired by my new home here on the Oregon Coast. The seeds for the dual story lines have been swimming around in my head since 2017, when I stumbled across two things while out on one of my first walks in the forest where we live.

The first was an old, rusted-out, abandoned still left over from Prohibition. Many of the coves in and around Depoe Bay, I later learned, were smuggling havens for Canadian rum runners. This whole era in American history was a wild ride. People's fortunes were made and lost by the capricious laws passed and then repealed during that time. Criminals flourished, but every day, regular people got caught up in it, too. I wondered what would happen to one of them.

The second discovery was the plethora of marvelous mushrooms littering the forest floor. So many different weird shapes and colors just pop up overnight after a good rain each fall—I was hooked! I can still only identify two wild mushrooms well enough to collect and consume them, the lovely chanterelle and the beefy lobster, but in the book, as you know already, Charlotte Collins is much more knowledgeable than I.

I have many people to thank for helping me bring this story to you. Every city, county, and state have unique law enforcement organizations and procedures. Thanks to Ron Benson and Linda Snow, Cold Case Investigator and Investigator, respectively, of the Lincoln County District Attorney's Office for answering questions as they came up. Also, thanks go to Marilyn Fraser, MD and Lincoln County Medical Examiner. Dr. Fraser gave my fictional ME not only a name, but a signature style, including a fondness for bold and colorful designer shoes and the good taste to roast her own coffee beans. We hope to see more of her in future books.

Kevin G. Chapman, Associate General Counsel, Dow Jones & Company, provided not only helpful advice on legal procedures and norms, but went the extra mile and helped hone the first draft manuscript as well. An author himself, his observations were spot on and helped polish the story.

This story required a knowledge of local history I did not possess, so after digging around on the internet, I turned to the experts. Jeffrey Syrop, Director of the North Lincoln County Historical Museum, generously shared the resources of their local history files, including the article Rum Runners at Whale Cove in the Depoe Bay Beacon, January 24, 2007. This article sparked the 1932 story line involving the Canadian rum runner's boat that foundered in Whale Cove, half a mile from where I live. The story of the crash and their dramatic escape was sparked by this article, but the characters and attendant events that follow are all entirely fictional.

My knowledge of mushrooms is, as I said, still very rudimentary, but I enjoyed—and am still enjoying—learning about the fascinating 'Fungus Amongus' as the Lincoln County Mycological Society dubs the mycelium internet just under the forest floor. The mushrooms are only the tip of the iceberg, so to speak. Two books were recommended to me and it was while I was skimming through one of them that one of the murder weapons jumped out at me. All That the Rain Promises, and More, by David Arora and Mushrooms of the Pacific Northwest, by Steve Trudell and Joe Ammirati. Also, Harvard University Herbaria Botany Archives article on Amanita phalloides poisoning was enlightening.

The genetics of the children of related persons is a complicated one. As an anthropologist I knew that until recently, much of the world favored first cousin marriages. While those don't tend to be dramatically problematic, I was curious what would happen if more closely-related people had a child. The math was beyond me, so again, I turned to the experts. Research from the National Institute of Mental Health and geneticist Tiong Tan, among many sources, gave me an inkling of what those consequences could be.

As Logan gets more and more into her music, Angie, my violinist friend who works with the local Youth Symphony Orchestra, was very helpful in sharing with me what tools she uses for composing and practice, as well as what it feels like to play the violin. I, unfortunately, do not play anything but a few chords on the guitar I learned in college. That's one of the fun things about being a writer. You get to give your characters skills you wish you had!

Cheri Brubaker, News Reporter and columnist for the NewsTimes, Newport, Oregon provided insights into her job as I wrote the new character, Samantha Baker, news reporter, into this story. It's also helpful just to know how the media and law enforcement interact.

My thanks, as always, go to my editor and cover designer, Kim Peticolas. She's creative, patient, and talented. Appreciated also are my fellow author friends who share ideas, resources, and solutions to problems common among writers. Kudos and hugs to my beta readers, Kevin C. Chapman, Mary

Anne Wilmouth, and Diane Grubb Bays, for helping to catch continuity errors and polish the story.

My biggest debt of gratitude goes to my sister, Michelle Montclaire, who passed away in April of this year after surgery for colon cancer. Other than my husband, John, she was my best friend and is missed by many. She was also a champion of the Logan McKenna series and helped shape it from the beginning. I miss being able to pick up the phone and discuss a plot point or new character with her. Logan's fierce loyalty and independence were definitely inspired by Michelle. This book's for you, Sis!

ABOUT THE AUTHOR

A self-admitted book addict, Valerie Davisson was the kid with the flashlight under her pillow, reading long after lights out. After a life of travel, she now lives on the Oregon coast with her husband, John, and their new puppy, Finn. When not working on her latest book, she's probably in the kitchen, cooking up a storm for family and friends.

Enjoyed the Book?

If you enjoyed *Lies That Bind*, please consider leaving a review on Amazon or Goodreads. And be sure to check out the rest of the Logan McKenna series.

Shattered (Book 1)

Forest Park (Book 2)

Devil's Claw (Book 3)

Vanishing Day (Book 4)

Safe Harbor (Book 5)

Want to know more about Valerie Davisson or her next book? Make sure to visit www.valeriedavisson.com and sign up for her newsletter.

www.ingramcontent.com/pod-product-compliance
Lightning Source LLC
Chambersburg PA
CBHW061921130726
47908CB00016B/535